NICK'S AWAKENING

ROGER HYTTINEN

Rambling Wordsmith Press

Nick's Awakening

By Roger Hyttinen

ISBN-13: 978-1-943005-07-9 (Paperback edition)
ISBN-13: 978-0-9915186-3-0 (Ebook edition)

Roger wishes to thank you for reading his work. Please consider leaving a review wherever you purchased this book. Also consider telling your friends about it to help me spread the word about my book.

License Notes

Thank you so much for supporting my work!

Visit me at:
www.rogerhyttinen.com

Chapter One

A hulking blackness followed Nick around and he had no idea what it was or what was causing it. Lately, he'd been out of sorts, feeling like there was a cloud of darkness hanging over him, squeezing him and sucking the life out of him. He had turned inward as of recent, keeping more to himself. At least, that's what everyone kept telling him. Especially his parents. Nick had overheard his dad reassuring his mom that it was just a typical phase of adolescence. Nothing to worry about. But Nick wasn't so sure. This weird emotional state that would descend upon him was new and different; something he'd never before experienced in the past and over the last few months, it had increased not only in frequency but also in intensity. And then there was the wave after wave of stomach upset that seem to come out of nowhere. The GI tests that his family doctor ordered had shown nothing. He was fine. Fit as a fiddle. His nausea and stomach flutters were most likely due to nerves, a common occurrence in teens Nick's age. It'll pass.

Maybe they all were right. Maybe it was just being sixteen.

"Mr. Michelson? Are we still among the land of the living?"

Nick hadn't realized he'd been holding his breath until the teacher's voice jarred him from his thoughts. Once again, he'd had zoned out in class. What was going on with him?

"Yes, Mr. McNeil?" Nick said.

"Ah, he returns to a state of semi-awareness." The man pursed his lips. "Is someone having a case of the Mondays?" His voice was sing-songy which was almost always an indication that he was about to humiliate a student.

Several chuckles erupted in the class. Nick felt the hot creep up his face.

"Sorry," Nick said. "I spaced out for a sec."

Mr. McNeil cleared his throat. "I'm looking for victims — I mean volunteers — for the next oral book report. I don't believe that you've yet had a turn. Is that correct?"

"No. I mean yes, that's correct. I haven't done a report yet."

"Then you're up. Choose a book from the approved list. We will then expect you to grace us with your riveting account next Thursday."

"Will do," said Nick.

Okay McNeil, you can move on to someone else. You've had your fun.

Nick loathed being the center of attention and went out of his way to avoid it. Not that he wasn't a good student. He was, with English being one of his favorite subjects. He especially enjoyed this particular literature class — except for the teacher, who was a condescending jerk. McNeil had a way of getting on Nick's nerves in a way that nobody else could.

Nick was halfway through his next class when his phone buzzed in his pocket. Luckily, Mrs. Kircher didn't hear it. She had a 'no tolerance policy' for using phones in any manner in her class. Nick discretely slid the device out of his pocket, hid it behind his book and glanced at the screen. A text from his dad.

"Call home as soon as you can."

Now that was beyond weird. His dad never texted him at school. Nick debated whether to tell Kircher he had to leave but decided to wait until the next break between classes. His dad hadn't said it was an emergency and he didn't want to risk her figuring out that he was using his phone.

"Got your text," he told his Dad. "Something going on?"

"It's your grandmother. It's time."

His grandma had been in the hospital for the past several weeks, and it was common knowledge that she would not be coming home again. Stomach cancer. His aunt Carol was stricken with exactly the same type of cancer but lucky for her, they'd caught it super early. She'd had a mini-stroke a few years ago, and while she was in the hospital, the doctors discovered the stomach cancer. As the disease was still in the very early stages, the doctor was able to remove it with one surgery. With his grandma, things had not turned out so well. By the time she was diagnosed, it was too late. The cancer had spread everywhere.

"Should I come to the hospital?"

"There's nothing you can do here," said his dad matter-of-factly. "You saw her yesterday. She's in a coma now, and it's unlikely she'll come out of it before she passes. Your mother just called from the hospital and said that she probably won't last the hour. I just wanted to let you know what was going on in case there was nobody here when you got home."

"Did you tell Missy?" Nick asked. "Do you want me to find her?" Melissa, a.k.a. Missy, was his sister, two years younger than him. She wasn't as close to his grandma as he was.

"No need. She called a while ago and said she's going to Karen's after school. I imagine she'll stay there the night."

"What about Uncle Mitch?"

"He's in Chicago this week. Or at least I think that's what he said." He sighed into the phone. "Not that it'd make much of a difference if he were here."

Next to his grandma, Nick was the closest to his Uncle Mitch. When Nick and his sister were little, Uncle Mitch would pop by the house only on rare occasions but never without a gift for them. As Nick grew older, he and his uncle spent more and more time together, going on occasional camping trips, hunting trips, and fishing excursions together. Nick's parents had distanced themselves from Uncle Mitch, and they made it known to Nick that they didn't particularly relish the idea of Nick spending so much time with him; but they would never tell him why. Nick couldn't help but wonder if it was because the guy might be gay. Nick had never seen him with any women. But then again, he'd never seen Uncle Mitch with any men either. But being gay might make sense as Nick's parents were not the most open-minded of folks, even though they claimed to be liberals.

"Thanks, Dad." He was just about to hang up but stopped himself.

"Oh, Dad?"

"Yeah, Nick?"

"Tell Mom that I said I'm sorry." His grandma was his mom's mom, and she was taking it pretty hard. He'd hardly seen his mom at all during the past few weeks as she'd spent all her free time at the hospital.

On his way home, the strange feeling increased. There was a peculiar heaviness in the pit of his stomach, and his skin felt tingly and prickly, so much so that the mere rubbing of his shirt against his arm caused him to wince. He glanced across the street, and the eerie feeling increased. A rather overweight man and woman were walking down the street. The woman was about a foot behind him and was yammering away in his ear. The man ignored her and kept on walking. As they moved further away, the woman's voice grew louder until she was almost shouting. A shiver crept up his spine as he realized that he had seen this same scene a lot lately — a person talking to someone and the other person ignoring the talker. A few days ago, he was at Starbucks and across from him was a younger guy typing on a laptop. Next to him, a beautiful young woman who Nick guessed to be his girlfriend, talked to him continuously. But he completely ignored her, never looking up once as far as Nick could tell. It was as though the woman wasn't even there. This scene had caught his attention because he remembered thinking what an absolute ass the guy had seemed to be. What's with people?

THE HOUSE WAS QUIET WHEN HE GOT HOME. HE FELT A TUG in his chest when he thought about his grandma passing. He'd always been close to her, more so than even his parents were. Though he was well into his teens, his grandma still called him 'pup' — her pet name for him ever since he was a little kid. Nobody but her called him that, but he didn't mind. It was a special thing between him and his grandmother, a bond that nobody else in her family had with her, not even his mom. He knew some bad blood occurred between his mom and his grandma when his mom was younger, but he never learned the specifics. Nick had always assumed that it had something to do with his dad. His grandma had mentioned to Nick once that back then, she did not approve of his mother marrying his father. More specifically, she didn't approve of her marrying into his family. But all that was supposedly forgiven and forgotten long ago. Nick wondered how much his mother had actually forgiven his grandmother because whenever they were together, there was an obvious chill between them, a coldness that suggested that they merely tolerated each other. Maybe that's why his mother had been taking the impending death of his grandma so hard. Maybe she has regrets about being such a bitch to her own mother.

He checked his messages, but there was nothing. He felt particularly on edge now, knowing that his grandma was going to die at any minute. He regretted letting his father talk him into staying at school and now wished he had gone to the hospital. He should have been with her during her final moments, even though it had been against her wishes. He recalled their conversation from last night.

He had gone to visit her after school and had spent several hours at the hospital with her. She was wide-eyed and alert, and her gauntness seemed to disappear behind her wide, toothy smile. In fact, he'd wondered if she was getting better because this was the first time in a long time that Nick had seen her so full of life.

"Pup!" she said when she saw him at the door. She gestured him in. "I'm so glad you came. How was school today?"

Nick was about to sit down on the chair by the door when she gestured to the bed. "No, come sit down next to me. I want to chat with you, and you know my hearing isn't quite what it once was."

He sat next to her. She reached over and mussed up his hair, as much as one can muss up curly hair.

"So school was good?"

They chatted for awhile about school, and then her expression darkened. She seemed to grow somber.

"How old are you now pup?" Her voice betrayed her weariness, and it now sounded as though she struggled to speak.

"Sixteen, soon to be seventeen."

She raised her eyebrows. "Seventeen? So soon?" She

wrung her boney hands. "You know, your father was seventeen when he met your mother. My goodness, how taken she was with him. I liked him too. He was the quintessential gentleman."

"I thought you couldn't stand Dad. Wasn't he the reason why you and mom didn't talk for many years?"

She frowned and shook her head. "Not at all. It was only after meeting your Uncle Mitchell one Thanksgiving that I didn't want my daughter to have anything to do with that family."

"Uncle Mitch? Wow. What did he do or say to offend you? I can't imagine Uncle Mitch pissing off anyone."

"Pup," his grandmother said in a scolding tone. "Tongue."

Nick grimaced. "Sorry. So why were you so angry at Uncle Mitch?"

"Let's just say that he was more different than anyone that I'd ever met." She creased her brow. "What is he, four years older than your father?"

He shook his head. "I think three."

"So that would have made him twenty, the same age that I was when I met Dennis, your grandfather. I guessed Mitchell to be older because he wasn't like any typical twenty-year-old that I had ever met. He was so worldly and had this mysterious air about him like he was wise beyond his years."

"I know what you mean," he said. "He can be a pretty no-nonsense guy."

Grandma nodded. "Now you need to know that back then, I was a much different person than I am now. I'd just lost my Dennis the year before so I was still mourning his passing at the time when your father came into our lives. I was also a lot more rigid in my religious beliefs than I am now. Not that I've abandoned my faith, mind you. Not at all. I'm just a tad more open-minded these days. Age and wisdom have that effect on a person." She leaned back into her pillow and drew in several sharp breaths.

"Did Uncle Mitch say something against your religion?" Nick had always just assumed that Uncle Mitch was Christian, although he'd never said so explicitly. He never went to church with Nick and his family, but considering the tension between them, that wasn't surprising.

She shook her head. "Not specifically. It's not my place to tell you more than I have because that's his story to share. But let me just say that I made some harsh judgments about him and your family that night. I suppose I was afraid that your father might be like him and I didn't want my daughter anywhere near him. I never did find out whether your father shared Mitchell's proclivities. He never mentioned it, and I dared not ask."

Nick had no idea what his grandmother was talking about. Did she also suspect that Uncle Mitch might be gay? But why would she mention Nick's father? Surely he couldn't be gay; he's married to a woman.

"What proclivities?" he asked. His voice cracked as he spoke. "I'm not quite sure I know what you mean."

"Again, it's up to Mitchell to tell you, if or when he decides. But regardless, I said some things to your uncle that evening that I regret." She looked down and was silent a moment. " I know now that he was only trying to help." She met Nick's eyes. "Can you tell him that for me, pup? Tell him that I'm sorry?"

Nick nodded. "I'll tell him. But maybe I can get him to come down here to see you when he gets back. Dad said he's in Chicago."

"Oh honey, I think it will be too late for that."

"Don't say that Grandma."

"Pup, you have to accept the fact that I'm not going to be here much longer. Believe me, this is a lot harder for me than it is for you." She laughed and then broke out in a coughing spell. At that point, Nick knew it was nearly time to leave. He didn't want to tire her out.

Before he left, his grandma had again strongly hinted that this would likely be that last time they'd see each other and insisted on saying a proper goodbye. He'd dismissed it at the time, confident that she'd be around for awhile. She seemed to be so much better than the previous time he had visited her.

Nick heated some leftover lasagna for dinner and had just finished his homework when his skin once again got all tingly, and he felt that familiar hole in his stomach. He was just about to go and see if there was anything in the medicine cabinet that might help when his cell chimed. It was his mom, and he could tell from her voice that she was crying.

"She's gone, Nick."

He curled his fingers tightly around the phone. "Is there anything you want me to do? I can take the scooter and come down."

"No, just go to bed. We'll be home soon.

"Mom, it's only 7:00."

"Oh. Well, do whatever it is you usually do then. We shouldn't be too much longer here. You could call your uncle and let him know. It'd be nice if he could be here for the funeral."

"You scheduled the funeral already? Nick asked.

"Next Thursday," she said. "Time as of yet uncertain."

As hung up, the first thing he thought of was that now he wouldn't have to give his book report on Thursday. He chastised himself for thinking such a self-centered thought and then pulled out his phone to dial up his uncle.

Chapter Two

✿❀✿

The next few days flew by as his family prepared for the funeral. He tried not to think about how much he was going to miss his grandma and their visits together. He didn't want his parents to know that every time he thought about her, he felt a deep hole form in the pit of his stomach and didn't want to envision a future without her in it.

On the bright side, Uncle Mitch had been around more than usual and had even been in the same room as his mother although only briefly. On Tuesday, his uncle invited Nick over for a meal. Finally alone with his uncle, Nick passed along the message that his grandma had given him.

Mitch nodded. "I wish she had the opportunity to tell me in person. I always assumed that she was still angry with me."

"Because of what happened that night? That night at Thanksgiving?"

Mitch nodded and then raised his eyebrows. "How much did she tell you about that evening?"

"Not much," Nick said, hoping he could pry additional

information from him. "Just that you said something that offended her."

Mitch let go of a short chuckle. "*Offended?* That's putting it mildly. She would have torn my head off if given half the chance."

"What did you say to her that got her blood boiling so much?"

Mitch sighed. "It's a bit tricky to explain but I suppose I have to, given that it concerns you as well."

"Me? What have I got to do with it?"

"I'll get to that in a moment. I've been meaning to have this talk with you for awhile and now's as good a time as any." He wrung his hands. "But first, back to that night."

"Thanksgiving?"

"Right. We were all enjoying a nice uneventful dinner and getting to know each other. I was nervous because I didn't want to do anything to mess this up for your dad so I avoided talking too much. Your father let me know over and over again how important this dinner was to him and how much he needed to impress your grandmother. So everything was going fine until at one point during the dinner, I glanced up from my plate, and there he was — he was looking right at me. I must have gawked at him wide-eyed and unable to stop myself, I gasped. That gave me away because he knew right then and there that I could see him. I don't know who was more surprised, him or me. He begged and pleaded with me to tell your grandma that he was not having an affair, that the woman she saw him with was actually his daughter, whom he'd had with a woman he'd dated long before he met your mother."

Nick creased his forehead. "Who are you talking about and why couldn't the man just tell her himself? Why tell you?"

"The man was Dennis, her husband. Your mother's father and your grandfather."

"Wait a minute. Just the other day she told me that her husband had died the year before.

"He was dead," Mitch replied. "That's what she got so brassed off about."

"You're not making much sense, Uncle Mitch. How could Grandpa be at the dinner if he was dead?"

Mitchell fiddled with his napkin and then rested it on his plate. He finally met Nick's gaze. "I see ghosts, Nick. Ghosts that are stuck here. They come to me for help."

Nick was silent. Did he mishear what his uncle had just said? He didn't just say that he sees ghosts, did he? Nick tried to open his mouth to speak but found he had no words. How could he respond to that?

Mitch continued. "Like I said, the spirits I see are stuck on earth, unable to move forward until they resolve whatever issues are keeping them here. What I do, is help them resolve those issues."

Wow. So Nick hadn't misheard him. His uncle truly thinks he can see ghosts. Now Nick understood why his parents didn't want him spending too much time with his uncle. He met his uncle's gaze and swallowed.

"So you're telling me that you see dead people."

"If you must phrase it like that, yes, though I'm ashamed to admit that sometimes I pretend I don't see them — especially if I'm with other people or simply too busy to help. But that night, your grandfather heard me gasp so he knew darn well that I could see him."

Okay, I'll bite. "So what happened?" asked Nick, playing along. "Did grandma see him too?"

"No, nobody could see him but me. Dennis implored me to tell her the truth, to tell her that he loved her and would never cheat on her. He told me that he'd been trying to get her attention for over a year, but had been unable to get his message through. Until now. Until me."

Nick bit his bottom lip to stop himself from breaking out into a grin. "So what did you do?"

"When spirits ask me to do things, like pass on messages to their loved ones, I often hesitate to do so. And do you know why?"

Nick shook his head and stayed silent.

"Because people look at me like you're looking at me right now. They act like I'm crazy or as if I'm making it all up in an effort to scam them somehow. Some people scream at me and threaten me until I leave."

"Then why do you do it?"

His uncle narrowed his eyes. "If I don't help them, who will?" He gave Nick a weak smile. "But back to night at your grandma's house. So I passed on to her what the ghost was telling me, and she didn't react well at all. She screamed at me, accusing me of lying and making it all up. She claimed that I was being cruel to her out of spite."

"Yikes," said Nick. "I don't think I've ever seen grandma scream at anyone."

"Some people are so closed-minded, that they refuse to believe in anything that's not one hundred percent proven by science. Your grandmother was one of those people. If she couldn't see it with her own eyes, it didn't exist."

"Did you end up convincing her?"

"At the point when she began screaming at me, your grandfather told me to call her Molly because nobody ever called her that except for him. Supposedly, when they first met, she said 'Good golly, Miss Molly' and ever since then, that was his pet name for her. So I said, 'He told me to call you Molly and said that this was his own personal nickname for you.' I thought for sure that would do it."

"But I take it she didn't buy it."

Mitch shook his head. "After I told her what Dennis had said, she stiffened and shouted 'Liar! Liar!' over and over again. She threw me and your father out of the house, tells us to never darken her doorway again. She also forbade her daughter from ever seeing your dad again."

"I bet dad was pissed."

"Nick, I couldn't even begin to describe how angry your father was with me. We didn't speak for months. He blamed me for breaking them up."

"Apparently, they got back together somehow."

Mitch nodded. "Yup. They snuck around behind Rose's back until she finally relented. She did make it clear however, that I was not welcome around her, her daughter or in her home. That's why I've kept my distance.

"Wow," Nick said. He avoided meeting his uncle's eyes. Was he for real? "That's quite a story."

"I imagine that my ability to see spirits comes somewhat as a surprise to you then?"

"You could say that," Nick said. "I've seen the Ghost-busters movie but I've never met a real live ghostbuster."

Mitch laughed. "We're not actually called Ghostbusters but rather mediums. A more recent term is Ghost Whisperer but personally, I prefer medium. I never understood where the word Whisperer came from. I've never seen a ghost whis-pering — they're usually shouting at the top of their lungs to get somebody's attention."

"Medium," Nick repeated. His heart started pounding wildly in his chest, and he forced himself to remain calm. "So can you talk to the ghost of anyone who has died?"

Mitch shook his head. "I can only see spirits who haven't moved on. That is to say, those who have not crossed over yet."

"What do you mean by crossed over?" Nick asked.

"To the Other Side," Mitch said.

"The other side of what?"

"The other side of our reality, the place where spirits go for the next phase of their journey."

"You mean like Heaven?" Nick asked. "Do you know what it's like there?"

"Not a clue. When I cross over a ghost, I never hear from him or her again. Some mediums refer to the Other Side as heaven. Others call it The Summerlands or The Underworld. To be truthful, I don't know if any of them are correct and I have no idea what it's like over there. Even the folks who are able to talk to spirits on the Other Side aren't privy to that kind of information. It's something that's never divulged."

"So some people can talk to ghosts on the Other Side?"

"Yup. There are two types of mediums: those like me who can see spirits still stuck here on earth and those who can communicate with those who have crossed over. I've yet to meet a psychic who could do both."

"So a medium is a psychic?" Nick asked.

"All mediums are psychic, but not all psychics are mediums."

"Come again?" Nick's head was swimming as he tried to make sense out of what his uncle was telling him.

"By that, I mean that not all psychics can see spirits. Some have the ability to foresee the future. Others to communicate with spirits." Mitch paused and then locked eyes with Nick. "Are you with me so far?"

Nick nodded. "I've heard about some of this stuff before I've never paid all that much attention to it. I figured it was all fiction; that it was nothing more than made-up stories. I've certainly never met anyone who could see ghosts — not that I know of, anyway."

"It's not only me. My father was a medium too."

"Grandpa could see ghosts?"

Mitch nodded. "I'm guessing that his father could too but nobody knows for certain. Back in the old days, people didn't talk about those sorts of things."

Nick took a deep breath. "So you're saying it's hereditary?"

"It appears to be, at least in this case."

"What about my dad? Can he see ghosts too?"

"No. Or at least that's what he's always told me. After that Thanksgiving, he made it clear that this was a topic that he would no longer discuss with me. Ever. I tried to broach the subject a few times, but he shut me down quickly." Mitch sighed. "When we were younger, I used to talk about it all the time with him, but no more."

"You you think it's possible that he can see them too?"

Mitch considered this for a moment. "Possible, but unlikely. He never gave any indication. But if he ever did have the ability to see spirits, he no doubt turned it off ages ago."

Nick was quiet for a few moments. His thoughts snaked around in his head as he tried to make sense out of everything his uncle had just told him. He finally asked, "So you can shut this thing down if you want?"

"If you ignore them — if they don't know that you can see them — then they can't ask you for help. If your father did have the same ability, he probably wouldn't even notice a ghost anymore; he'd be so used to not acknowledging them. Or maybe he would. Who's to say? But whenever I've been with your father and have seen a spirit, he's never given any indication that he could see it too."

"What kind of help do they ask you for?" Nick asked. "Is it mainly passing messages?"

"Mostly," Mitch replied. "But oftentimes, they have something important they need to tell one of their loved ones left behind, like the location of legal documents, old letters or photos. Or they may need to express feelings that they didn't get a chance to — or chose not to — express when they were alive. You'd be surprised how many times they just need to tell their husband, wife, mother, father, boyfriend or girlfriend that they love them."

"That doesn't sound too difficult."

"Oh, but that's not all of it. Things aren't always that easy. Sometimes, what they need is a bit more complicated, especially in situations like murder or suicide. I've seen it all, believe me."

Nick shuddered at the mention of murder and suicide. "How old were you when you first started seeing them?"

"I think I was around sixteen or seventeen." He paused. "Around your age, I think." His uncle raised his eyebrows and then lowered his head as though he were looking over imaginary eyeglasses.

Nick took a deep breath. "Not me. I've never seen any ghosts."

"How do you know?" Mitch asked.

"I'm sure I'd know if I saw a ghost, wouldn't I? What do they look like?"

"That's the kicker," Mitch said. "They look just like normal people."

"You mean they appear solid, like you and me?"

Mitch nodded "It's hard to tell that they're ghosts until you see them disappear or walk through an object. Another giveaway is when you see them talking to someone who appears to be ignoring them."

Nick's head snapped to attention and then almost as fast, he turned his regard away from his uncle. His heart pounded even more quickly now.

"*So you have seen them*," his uncle said. Nick could hear the excitement in his voice. "You've seen exactly what I've described, haven't you?"

Nick shook his head. "No, I don't think so. I saw this jerk the other day ignoring his girlfriend. But she wasn't a spirit. I'm pretty sure of that."

"Let me ask you this Nick. When you saw this guy ignoring his girlfriend, did you feel funny? Like a tingling sensation? Maybe goosebumps? Perhaps an odd feeling in your stomach?"

Nick swallowed and thought of the many times he'd experienced those exact physical manifestations — and come to think of it, it was usually when he noticed someone who was ignoring someone else.

"I dunno," he said. "Maybe." He paused. "But even if I did, I'd never want those them to know that I could see them."

Mitch nodded. "I understand that. Believe me, I know what a difficult path this can be. I've been screamed at more times than I care to remember, both by the living and the dead." He pointed to his phone and smiled. "But there's always email."

"You can email ghosts?'

Mitch laughed. "What I'm saying, is that you don't always have to have a face-to-face confrontation with a ghost's family. Often, you can pass on messages through email. It's one of those things that makes this path a little bit easier for us."

Nick's thoughts whirled like a black vortex and he shuddered. The other kids at school thought he was weird enough now. What would they think if they knew he could see ghosts? If he really could see ghosts, that is. Sure, he'd experienced some of those strange skin sensations that his uncle mentioned. But that didn't mean he could see spirits. No, he was confident that it was nothing more than a coincidence. People get goosebumps all the time.

"I get the shivers all the time but I'm sure that it has nothing whatsoever to do with ghosts," Nick said finally. "There no way in hell that I —"

Nicholas," his uncle said. His voice was barely above a whisper. "Pretending you don't see them will not make this go away. My father called this ability a gift and once told me that he was given this gift for a reason — and that was to help."

Nick eyed him doubtfully. "Help how?"

Your grandfather would say that in this world, anything we can do to help is a good thing. He explained that mediums are offered the opportunity to assist others in ways that so-called normal people cannot."

"Because mediums can see them. I get that."

"But Nick, take a moment to imagine how frightening it would be to die, and then wake up only to realize that not one single person can see you. How would you feel if faced with the thought that you are going to wander around aimlessly on earth for eternity?"

Nick shuddered. "Kinda scared, I guess."

"And completely and utterly alone, with nothing to look forward to. You see Nick, this is where you and I come in. We can help these souls move onto the next phase of their journey, whatever or wherever that might be. I feel that the work that I do, helping these people to move on, is not only a gift. It's a duty. Some call it a sacred duty."

Nick's heart slipped into heavy punches against his ribcage as he considered his uncle's words. He felt the itch of tears. Helping dead people? *This was his calling?* Of all the things he could have done, working with freakin' ghosts was his destiny? Just the thought of it made him want to run away. Far, far away. And never return.

"You know I hate horror movies, right?" Nick said, barely recognizing the sound of his own voice.

Mitch gave Nick a warm smile. "They're not usually scary at all. They look just like me and you. There's no reason to fear them — they are just folks who are lost, perhaps needing to take care of unfinished business before they can move on. Even the scary ones are not really that scary — or at least, not for long."

"What do you mean by the scary ones?" Nick asked.

"The spirits you may see on the street and in buildings typically look like regular people. But sometimes, when they first materialize, their appearance can be rather...," he paused as if looking for the right word. "Disturbing."

"Disturbing?" Nick repeated. "I don't like the sound of that.?"

"If someone died in a fire for instance, their face and body might appear burnt. Or if someone passed away from a blow to the head, a part of their head might be missing or be blood-stained."

"The hell with that!" Nick exclaimed. "There's no way I'm talking to someone who has brains gushing out of their head."

His uncle looked disappointed. "They only appear like that when they're recently deceased and may not even yet realize that they're dead. Let me give you an example. A few years ago I worked with a young woman who had drowned. The first time I saw her, she scared the living crap out of me. Her skin was chapped and completely blue. Not only that, hunks of her torso were missing, as if she had been gnawed on by something. Fish, I would venture to guess."

Nick cringed in his chair and shivered. "Eeew! That's gross."

"It was. I was so terrified at first that it was difficult for me to even look at her. But when we spoke, I learned that she had no idea what had happened to her or where she was. The last thing she remembered was being out on the lake in her kayak. Once I explained to her what had befallen her, she slowly began to take on a more healthy humanlike appearance."

"She started looking like a regular, living person?"

Mitch nodded. "It didn't happen right away mind you. It took a few manifestations before she finally looked normal. But those spirits that have been here awhile tend to look just like anyone else. Chances are, you'd have a difficult time telling them apart from the living."

"So what kind of help did the lady want from you?" Nick asked.

"The kayaker? She had gone out alone for a paddle and inadvertently leaned over a little too far to retrieve her water bottle. Before she could stop it, her boat flipped over and she found herself in Lake Michigan's chilly water. The waves were so rough that she was unable to right the kayak. Given that the water was only about 40 degrees, it didn't take long before she died of hypothermia. Nobody knew that she had gone out boating by herself so naturally, her loved ones feared that she had been kidnapped or murdered. She needed to let her people know what happened to her."

"So what did you do?"

"I contacted the authorities anonymously and told them where to look for her kayak. They found her body and the boat shortly thereafter." Mitch's face grew serious. "Now Nick, in these types of situations, the ones where you need to get the police involved, you must learn to be as stealthy and discreet as possible. By that, I mean contacting them by public phone if possible or by anonymous email. This is especially true if the ghost was murdered. You never, ever want to implicate yourself in anything. Experience has also taught me that authorities will not believe you if you tell them that you received your information from a ghost. Always cover your tracks."

"You said Dad knows that you help ghosts. Does Mom?"

Mitch nodded. "I explained it all to your mother after that Thanksgiving night so she would understand why I told your grandmother what I did. I don't know if she believed me. I know she definitely didn't like me after that." He narrowed his eyes and rested his hand on Nick's shoulder. "It will be up to you to convince them of the truth of what you do. You'll need a strong support group Nick, people who you can talk to and who will understand your work. Something that I never had."

"Tell my parents," Nick stammered. "Yeah, I don't think that's a good idea at all. You know how they are. They don't even like it when I spend time with you."

"I know it'll be difficult, but telling those closest to you really does make things easier in the long run. Otherwise, you'll be lying to people constantly and Nick, that's no way to live your life. Promise me that you'll at least think about sitting them down and talking to them."

Nick looked down and wrung his hands. After a minute or so, his uncle broke the silence.

"Nick?"

Nick's eyes locked onto his uncle's gaze. He took a deep breath and braced himself. "I'm sorry Uncle, I can't do this."

"Your parents might not understand at first, but I'm sure they'll come around. You're their son and they love you."

Nick shook his head. "No, I'm not referring to telling my parents about my so-called abilities. What I mean, is that I can't do this." He gestured in the air with his hand. "Any of this. I'm enough of a freak as it is. There's no friggin' way I'm going to start talking to ghosts as well."

His uncle looked stricken. He stood up and crossed his arms. "Nick, this isn't something you can simply ignore. It's your calling to help them. It's what our family does. You can't just turn your back on them."

Nick pushed his plate away and jumped to his feet. The tears behind his eyes threatened to erupt at any moment. "If they need help so badly, then you help them. I don't want any part of this."

With that, he pulled open the door and dashed out of the house.

Chapter Three

"Your Uncle Mitchell called," his mother said to him after he entered the kitchen. "He sounded concerned about you." She raised her eyebrows. "Did you two have a disagreement?"

Nick shook his head and glanced at the kitchen clock. "He called already?"

She nodded. "I think he gets up even earlier than I do."

Nick swallowed. "Did he say what he wanted?"

"Not really. He asked for you and when I told him you were still sleeping, he said to have you call him first thing when you get up."

She sat at the kitchen table in her powder blue bathrobe, which was out of character for her as she was typically showered and dressed before anyone else in the house awoke. The spoon clinked against her cup as she stirred her coffee.

Nick looked around the kitchen. "No breakfast?"

"I overslept so you're on your own today," his mother said. "There's bread for toast or cereal in the cupboard."

"You're not going to work today?" Nick asked.

His mother shook her head. "I'm taking the week off,

with the funeral and all. I'm just not ready to face everyone yet. It's been a rough road with your grandmother."

Nick pulled out a chair and sat down. "Are you doing okay?"

His mother gave him a weak smile. "As well as can be expected. I've known she was going to die for months now and thought I was prepared for it, that I would be ready when the time came. But there's no true way to prepare yourself for the loss of a parent. I remember how tough it was for me when my father — your grandfather — passed away. I don't know why I thought it'd be any different this time."

"How old were you then? When grandpa died?"

"Fifteen. But I barely knew him. He was one of those dads whose entire life was his work so he was rarely around. And when he was at home, he was distant and self-absorbed. I was sad when he died but it was nothing like this. I've had a lifetime of memories with my mother. There's just no way to prepare yourself for this." She sighed. "How does one deal with losing one's mother?"

Nick could see the anguish on his mom's face and guessed that she felt guilty for all the years that her mother wasn't a part of their lives. He shifted forward in his chair and rested his hand on top of hers. "Mom, can I do anything to help?"

She wiped her eyes with her sleeve and looked at him soulfully. She shook her head. "Oh honey, I know that you were close to her too and will miss her. We all will."

"I'm sorry that I wasn't there when....you know."

"There was no need," his mother said. "I told your father to tell you and your sister to stay at school. The doctor said that she was done and it was unlikely that she'd regain consciousness. And she didn't." She paused and looked into Nick's eyes. "Did you have a nice visit with her? Did you get a chance to say goodbye properly?"

"She was chipper and alert, like she wasn't even sick,"

Nick said, emotion heavy in his voice. "She told me all about you growing up and dating Dad."

"How sweet," his mother said. "You were fortunate that she was so lucid when you saw her. We all were. The doctor said that this often happens right before someone goes. It's like they get one last burst of energy to say their goodbyes before they leave."

Nick swallowed. "She told me about the Thanksgiving when you were first dating Dad and what happened with Uncle Mitch."

His mother's face darkened and she pulled her hand away. "I wish she hadn't done that. It was an embarrassing evening for everyone involved. There are some things that are better left unsaid and stories better left untold." She narrowed her eyes. "Did she tell you what your uncle said to her?"

"You mean about what grandfather Dennis said to him?"

She sighed loudly and tensed up. "What that man was thinking, I have no idea. He had no right to say such things to her, so soon after her husband — my father — died. We were all beyond horrified." Her gaze met Nick's. "You didn't mention any of this to your uncle, did you? Is this why he called this morning?"

"I might have mentioned it to him."

"Oh honey, you shouldn't have. Mitchell has deep psychological problems. It's best not to get him riled up."

"Grandma asked me to apologize to him for her. To tell him that she was sorry about the things she said to him that night."

His mother eyes grew wide. "She did?"

Nick nodded. "She said that she knows now that he was only trying to help."

"I say bullshit," she said, waving her hand in front of her. "If he had wanted to help, he wouldn't have made up such awful stories and upset her so." Her eyes locked onto Nick's.

"It was because of him that your father and I almost didn't get married. Did you know that?"

"Grandma mentioned it when I was there."

"After that horrid dinner, my mother forbade me from having anything to do with him or his family. Did you know that she refused to step into our house for several years after we were married? I was beyond surprised when she showed up at our wedding — thought for sure she wouldn't come. She was so upset that I married your father, all because of your Uncle Mitch." She folded her hands and rested them on top of the table. "Well, she should have apologized. Your father had nothing to do with Mitchell's demented stories."

Nick's heart sunk at her words. He was silent for a moment. Does he dare ask her the question? But he had to know.

"Did you believe him?" Nick asked, finally. "Did you believe what Uncle Mitchell said to Grandma?"

Her face hardened then she blinked and looked away for a moment. It was obvious his words had startled her.

"Has Mitchell been telling you stories? I don't want you listening to anything that man has to say. In fact, your father and I would prefer that you not spend so much time with him. It's not healthy." She stood up, shuffled to the refrigerator and opened the door. "Do you have time for breakfast? I can fix you something. An omelet? French toast?"

"No, I'll just grab something quick on the way to school. It's getting late."

"Oh, right," she said, closing the refrigerator door. "Are you sure you don't want to stay home from school until after the funeral on Thursday? I know you must be upset. I'll write you a note if you need me too."

Nick shook his head. The last thing he wanted to do was hang around the house, especially if there was a possibility that Uncle Mitch would stop by and corner him again.

"I'll be home right after school," Nick said. He kissed his mom on the cheek and yelled for Missy that it was time to leave for school.

~

NICK LOOKED OVER AT MISSY WHO SAT IN THE PASSENGER'S seat, staring out the window. He'd been neglecting her recently, being so caught-up in everything that was going on. He had no idea how she was taking her grandmother's death.

"How are things at school? You still hanging out with Karen and the gang?" Nick asked.

Missy nodded. "Uh-huh."

"And school?"

She shrugged her shoulders. "Kay."

"You're awfully quiet today," Nick said. "It is because —"

"I'm mad at you," she said, cutting him off.

"What did I do now?"

"If you'd taken off from school today, then I could have too. I have a stupid math test today that I'm not ready for at all." She rolled her eyes. "I hate math."

Nick laughed. "You could have told mom you had a sore throat or felt the flu coming on."

"Nah, she wouldn't have bought it. I've pulled that one too many times and she's on to me now."

"Or you could have simply asked her. She probably would have let you stay at home. She seemed extra generous this morning."

"Tried that. She told me that if my brother can go to school, so can I."

"Oh," Nick said, trying not to grin. "Sorry about that. So you'll need a ride home from school?"

"No. I have soccer practice. It's Monday, remember?"

"Right. So you're getting a ride home from Karen's mom?"

She nodded and sat quietly, saying nothing more. Nick figured that she was in one of her pouty moods and decided to let her be. He supposed that she had her own issues to work through. He then wondered if she could see spirits too. The thought hadn't even occurred to him when he was at Uncle Mitch's yesterday. He hoped not. He wouldn't wish this on anyone, especially his little sister. The more he thought about it, the more he concluded that he wanted nothing whatsoever to do with ghosts or spirits or spooks. What he wanted was to be normal and to live a normal life. Was that too much to ask? As long as he pretended not to see them, he could pull it off.

Missy finally broke the silence. "I'm riding with Mom and Dad to the funeral on Thursday and we're picking up Auntie Laura, Uncle Mark, and Jimmy. That means you have to ride with Uncle Mitch."

"Crap," Nick grumbled.

Missy shifted her gaze over to him. "I thought you liked Uncle Mitch."

"He's okay," Nick replied. "I just don't want to ride with him, that's all."

"Weirdo," said Missy.

"Oh, you're just figuring that out now?"

She giggled. "You mad at Uncle Mitch?"

Nick took a deep breath but kept his eyes on the road. "Not really. His tendency to pry in my business irritates me sometimes."

"He doesn't do that with me. Heck, he hardly even talks to me. I always thought that he was kind of an ass."

Nick smiled in spite of himself. "He's just different, and you know that he does that with everyone. Some people just aren't the talkative type."

"Or some people are jerks."

They arrived at school and after Nick had parked the car,

he and Missy marched toward the building. He noticed Josh Gerard in front of him with an elderly woman walking at his side.

"What is it, bring your grandmother to school day?" he said.

"What do you mean?" Melissa said.

Nick gestured with his head to Josh and the woman. "Josh Gerard. He has an old lady with him, probably his grandma. I wonder what she's doing here?"

Missy punched him in the arm. "Ha-ha. Very funny Nicholas."

Nick hated when anyone called him Nicholas. "What's funny?"

"There's nobody with Josh, stupid. He's walking by himself."

Nick jerked his head to look in front of him and blinked his eyes. There was no doubt about it. Josh Gerard was heading towards the school with an old lady at his side. It was then he felt it. That tingly, prickly feeling. His stomach lurched and somersaulted. Shit. She wasn't really there, was she? It was a damned ghost. He snapped his head and turned his gaze to the sidewalk, ensuring that he didn't accidentally make eye contact with the old woman. He did not need to be accosted by a ghost while walking with his little sister.

He breathed a sigh of relief when he saw them disappear into the school. That was close. He was gonna have to be a lot more observant than he'd been in the past. Whenever he felt that weird stomach feeling, he needed to make sure that he didn't inadvertently make eye contact with anyone around him. This way, he could blend in and never catch any unneeded and unwelcome attention.

Ignoring ghosts just might be a lot more challenging than he had originally thought.

Chapter Four

✦❖✦

Because of his grandmother's funeral on Thursday, he was able to reschedule his oral report for the following Monday. Usually, Mr. McNeil was a complete wad about postponing anything, but when Nick explained that his grandma had passed away and her funeral was on Thursday, he was surprisingly understanding. It's a good thing too because Nick hadn't even begun reading the book. Still, the idea of having to stand in front of the class and talk filled him with dread. Just the thought of it made his hands all sweaty and caused his stomach to clench. He recalled the last time he had to give an oral report. His hands shook so badly that he could barely hold on to his index cards.

At the end of the day, he left school and was driving home when a strange scene caught his eye. A slender young woman was hunched over at her mailbox while a man towered over her. He wore a black three-piece suit which struck Nick as odd, being that it was the middle of the afternoon. Judging by the look on the man's face, he was furious. The man's eyes were opened wide, and his face was red with rage. Nick slowed down the car. He could hear the man's screams from inside the car, even with the windows rolled up. He stopped the car and lowered the window a crack so he could hear what was going on.

"You bitch!" the man screamed at the woman. The loudness his voice startled Nick. It sounded like he was shouting into a microphone. "You rotten, conniving bitch. You're going to pay for what you did. I'll figure out a way to make you regret it. You won't get away with it, I'll see to that!"

The woman recoiled and desperately flung her head back and forth, as if she were looking for help. Nick slowed down the car even further. Just as he did, he saw the man raise both of his fists, each one aimed for the side of the woman's head. Holy shit, he was going to hit her. A blow like that could kill her.

Without thinking, Nick slammed on the breaks and dashed out of the car.

"Hey Fuckface!" Nick shouted. "What in the hell do you think you're doing? Leave her alone."

The man's head snapped, and a look of complete surprise crossed over his face. Then the man's face contorted in anger. He pointed at Nick and then rushed at him. Instinctively, Nick backed against his car. Whoops. Maybe it wasn't such a wise move to confront a violent stranger. Perhaps he should have thought this through before getting out of the car.

He fumbled for the door handle hoping to make a hasty retreat before the scary dude reached him, but then he stopped, frozen in place. The man continued to move toward him but at an unnaturally fast pace, faster than any normal person could move. What was strange though was that he didn't really walk or run so much as jerked forward. It was then that Nick noticed the familiar physical sensation. Uh-oh. This could be trouble. There was now little doubt in Nick's mind that the man rushing toward him was a ghost — and an angry one at that.

Before he knew it, the man was right in his face. His skin was deathly pale, and his face was tensed tight over his jaw.

The man screamed at him. "You mind your own business twerp! This is no concern of yours. This is between my wife and me. I don't know who you are or how you can see me, but if I catch you near her again, you'll be sorry. So bugger off!"

With that, the man disappeared. He was there one moment and gone the next. Nick's heart slammed in his chest so hard that he was afraid of collapsing. He leaned heavily against his car and gasped, nearly hyperventilating as he attempted to regain control of himself. This was the first time in his entire life that he'd literally lost his breath. As he wheezed and choked, the woman approached.

"Are you okay?" she asked.

"I'll be fine."

Her hard gaze met his. She appeared visibly shaken. "I heard you. You saw something, didn't you? There was something there. Was it a man?"

Nick didn't know whether to answer her or jump in his car and make a hasty retreat. He reached again for the car door. "I saw nothing."

"No, don't go," she said. Her voice was soft, but it cracked as she spoke. She touched his sleeve. "Please don't leave. I need to know what you saw."

Nick stopped and met her gaze. "So you can't see them too? The way you were cowering I thought...". His voice trailed off, not quite sure how much he wanted to say to this strange woman.

"Them?" She shook her head. "No, I can't. But I can feel this heavy, dense cloud of blackness suffocate me whenever it's around. It's like I'm restrained or paralyzed, unable to move and all I can do is brace myself until it's gone. Today was the worst it's ever been." She paused and sighed. "I'm sure this all sounds strange to you, doesn't it? Hell, I couldn't blame you if you thought I was crazy. Maybe I am."

Nick shook his head. "You know lady, a couple of days ago I wouldn't have believed it. A lot has changed since then."

She took a step back, and her eyes opened wide. "So you did see it then?"

Nick nodded. "Who in the hell was he?"

"He?" She asked.

Nick nodded. "It was a man."

Her jaw tightened, and she took a sharp breath. "A man," she repeated, and locked eyes with him. "What did he look like?"

He was tall, well over six feet with dark brown hair, pale face and piercing green eyes." Nick shuddered at the thought of the man's eyes. When he had looked at Nick, the man's eyes chilled him, causing him to feel as though he were trapped in a deep freeze. He won't forget that look for a long time. "He was dressed in a formal black suit and a vest. It looked like he was going to the opera."

"James," she whispered. "So it was him. But why?"

"Who's James?" Nick asked.

"My husband. Or as you figured out, my deceased husband." She shook herself as if attempting to regain her composure. She held out her hand. "I'm sorry I haven't even introduced myself. I get so rattled everytime this happens. My name is Janet Pearce."

"Nick Michelson." Nick shook her hand. "So you can't see him but you can feel when he's around?"

She looked thoughtful and nodded. "I feel this dark despair whenever he's near. That's the best way to describe it.

When it happens, all I want to do is crumple up into a ball and hide."

"If you can't see him, what made you suspect that it was your husband?"

"It starting happening shortly after his death, nearly eight months ago. All of a sudden, I began experiencing these black moods accompanied by temporary body paralysis. I felt depressed, confused and frightened. It grew worse and worse. I went to various doctors but they diagnosed me with grief-related depression. Nobody would believe me. I finally went to a psychic."

Without thinking, Nick snickered and said, "You believe in that stuff?"

She creased her brow. A bewildered look crossed her face. "Didn't you just tell me that you can see ghosts?"

"Right. Never mind. So what did the psychic say?"

"She said that there was an entity causing the feelings I was experiencing and she had little doubt it was my husband. She also felt that this entity wanted to cause me harm."

Nick nodded. "Yeah, that's definitely the impression that I got. It looked like he was about to punch you in the head." Janet's eyes widened, and she brought her hands to her throat. He probably shouldn't have told her that.

"I don't think he can hurt me physically," she said, a tremor to her voice. "At least he hasn't thus far. The psychic said that most spirits couldn't affect the physical world. But he doesn't have to. Just being around him is damage enough. It's like the darkest, deepest feeling of hopelessness that I've ever experienced. I don't know how much more of it I can take."

"Can the psychic lady help you?" Nick asked.

She shook her head. "She told me that she's a psychic, not a medium. She can sense spirits but cannot see them or communicate with them. Only a medium can do that."

Nick recalled the conversation with his uncle during which he told Nick that all mediums are psychic, but not all psychic are mediums.

"So she didn't give you any advice at all?"

She nodded. "Only that I needed to find a medium — someone who can speak with spirits. She said such a person could find out what he wants and help him to cross over to where he needs to be." She narrowed her eyes and then pointed at Nick. "But you can see him! You're a medium, aren't you?"

"Not really," Nick replied.

"What do you mean not really?" she said, with a sudden nervous insistence. "You saw him. You described him to me."

"Lady, I only found out about this the other day myself. About seeing ghosts, I mean. I wouldn't know where to begin. Until today, I've never spoken to a ghost, much less helped one."

What Nick didn't tell her, was that the ghost of her husband terrified the bejesus out of him. He didn't want to go anywhere near it again.

She grabbed hold of his shirt. "Please Nick. Oh please. You are the only one who can help me. The only one who can make this stop."

"What do you want me to do?" Nick asked. "He threatened to hurt me if I come anywhere near you again."

"He did?"

Nick nodded. He pursed his lips. "But there might be someone who can help."

"Who?" Janet asked. "Do you know someone else like you, another medium?"

"My Uncle Mitch. He's the one who told me about my ability. I know that he's helped with ghost intrusions in the past, so he's experienced at doing this kind of stuff. I can ask him to step in."

Tears ran down her cheeks. "Would you? You have no idea how much it means to me that someone is willing to help. I had no idea where to turn to next." She sighed. "Do you have a cell? Can we exchange phone numbers?"

"Sure." He reached into his pocket, pulled out his phone, opened the contacts application and held out the phone to her. When she had finished typing in her name and number, she handed Nick her phone. It was the same brand of phone as his. Made things easy.

"I don't mean to push you but do you have any idea when you'll be able to talk to him?"

Nick shrugged. "Dunno. Maybe today. Probably tomorrow. It's kind of rough right now because my grandma just died and everyone is kinda busy with the funeral-related things."

"My condolences," she said. "I'm sure this is a difficult time for all of you. It wasn't all that long ago when my husband passed." She narrowed her eyes. "But you do understand how serious this is, right? I don't know if he can hurt me and I don't want to find out."

"I'll talk to Uncle Mitch this evening and let you know," Nick said.

Nick stumbled. A ball of white exploded in his brain, and without warning, a flash of images poured into his thoughts. He saw the ghost of Janet's husband clearly, but this time the images were in his head and not in front of him.

The man wore the same suit that he was wearing earlier. He sat at an enormous wooden desk, flipping through a pile of papers. In front of him on the desk stood a glass of brown liquid in one of those glasses his mother referred to as a highball glass. It reminded Nick of the foul tasting brandy that he and a few friends shared last year. The man tensed and grabbed his throat. It looked like he attempted to get up, but his body slammed back down. He grasped his stomach like he had excruciating pain and cried out. His body convulsed a couple of

times then he slumped over, his head hitting the top of the desk. The
cocktail glass next to the man's head jumped out at Nick.

Then, just as quickly as they started, the images disappeared. Nick snapped back to awareness. He found himself being held up by Janet.

"Nick! Are you okay? Do you want me to call 911?"

Once he realized where he was, he pulled back. A hot flush rose up in his face, and he was sure his face was glowing red. "No, I'm fine."

"What happened?" she asked. "I was afraid you were going to faint."

"I dunno. It was freaking weird. I was talking to you one moment, and then the next thing I knew, I saw your husband." Nick's head throbbed so much that it was difficult for him to speak.

Janet jerked her head to the left and then to the right. "James? He's here again?"

Nick shook his head and noticed that his hands were shaking. He felt wobbly. "No, it was only in my head this time. I think I saw his death." He locked eyes with Janet. "How did he die?"

"Coronary Thrombosis," she said. "Massive heart attack."

"That doesn't make sense."

"How so?"

"What I just saw didn't look like any heart attack. He never once grabbed at his chest."

"What did you see?"

Nick described the images that he saw as well as he could. He noticed that Janet's face had turned white. Maybe he shouldn't have gone into so much detail. This was her husband after all.

"The doctor seemed confident that it was a heart attack. It made sense because James did have heart disease for which he was seeing his cardiologist. They were so certain of the cause of death that they saw no need for an autopsy. I vaguely remember them asking me if I wanted one done and I must have said no. Nobody saw the need."

"I don't know if what I saw really occurred," Nick said. "Maybe it's just my mind playing tricks on me. This is the first time that this kind of thing has happened to me. Seeing strange scenes in my head, I mean. It could be the result of all the crap that's gone on in the past few days, including me finding out that I can talk to dead people."

"Maybe," she said. She tapped her chin several times with her index finger. "But what if he did die of something else? What if the doctors were wrong?"

Nick opened his words to reply, but no words came out. He didn't want to ask her the next question, but he had to if he was going to figure out what in the hell was going on here.

"Janet, why is your husband so angry with you?"

She threaded her fingers through her hair. "That is what's so strange. James and I got along reasonably well. Oh sure, we had our disagreements from time to time like any married couple but for the most part, we were happy, especially the past few months before he died. But I can't figure out why he would be haunting me. And you're positive that it looked like he was angry?"

"Absolutely. He was really, really pissed off," Nick said. "He was screaming at you and calling your awful names."

She flinched at his words. "It doesn't make any sense. Can you ask him next time?"

Nick considered this briefly. *Lady, there isn't going to be a next time.*

"Sure," he said. He pulled his phone out of his pocket to check the time. "But now, I need to get going home. I'll call you once I find out what my uncle says."

"I don't know how to thank you," she said.

"Don't thank me yet. I haven't done anything."

"But I know you will," she said. And with that, she turned and rushed up the sidewalk toward her house.

Chapter Five

While he waited for his uncle's response, Nick tipped his chair up on its two back legs and then rocked it back down. He repeated the motion.

"Would you stop that Nick?" Mitch said. "You're going to end up flipping over. And it's driving me nuts."

"Sorry," Nick said and brought the chair back down. "So will you help?

"No."

His uncle's response was unexpected. "What do you mean no? I thought that this is what you do. Didn't you tell me that it's our responsibility to help people?"

"I did tell you that, and it was true. But what I didn't share with you is that I've had to give up the work on the advice of my physician."

Nick creased his brow. He recalled his father once saying something about Uncle Mitch's health but unfortunately, he hadn't been paying attention at the time.

"But you're not all that old."

Mitch smiled. "Old enough. But it's not about age. I have

an unfortunate condition, and because of it, I need to avoid stress and excitement." Mitch tapped his chest.

"You have a bad ticker?" Nick asked. Thoughts of James, Janet's deceased husband, popped into his mind.

"Something like that. Nick, the work I did was taxing and exhausting. The last time I was on a job, it affected me more than usual. I had no energy for several weeks afterward and nearly landed in the hospital. Figured that I had best heed my doc's advice and lay low from now on."

"But weren't you just in Chicago on a job?"

Mitch laughed. "No, it was actually in New York and it was for a Tarot conference."

"Tarot? Like in fortune telling?"

Mitch nodded. "In a way. Remember I told you that all mediums were psychic?"

Nick nodded.

"Tarot cards can help you to focus your abilities and often, the images trigger visions like the one you experienced earlier."

"So that was a vision that I had?" Nick asked. "Wow. It seemed so real at the time. I didn't even know it was happening."

"Many psychics receive visions, although perhaps not to the extent that you experienced. Apparently, your psychic abilities are a lot stronger than I had thought. Tarot cards can be a valuable tool in your work."

"So you have visions as well?" Nick asked.

"Not like the one you described. I see only quick flashes of images, never an entire scene." He studied Nick's face for a moment. "It appears as though all your abilities came to fruition at once. It takes some psychics years of focused work and dedication before they have visions like the one you just experienced. Some never do."

"It was like I was watching a movie or play," Nick said.

Without saying anything, his uncle left the room. Nick could hear shuffling and then the slamming of a drawer. A moment later, Mitch returned carrying a small brown wooden box. He handed it to Nick.

"These are for you," Mitch said.

"What is it?"

"Your first Tarot deck."

On the cover of the box was a strange symbol that Nick didn't recognize. He picked it up and studied it more closely. Judging by how faded the markings were, Nick guessed that it was old, probably older than him. Maybe even older than his uncle. Nick brought the box up to his nose and inhaled. A musty but pleasant odor of pine drifted into his nostrils. The lid of the box was attached by two faded golden hinges, one of them loose. He carefully opened it. The cards were wrapped in a fuzzy black cloth.

"Can I look at them?" Nick asked.

Mitch laughed. "Of course. They're yours now."

"But why are you giving them to me?"

"I have more decks. But this one was my main working deck for many years. It was the one with which I connected the best."

Nick unwrapped the pack and studied the picture on the first card. It was a man who looked like he was about to walk off a cliff. A little white dog snapped at his ankles. "What do you mean by working deck?"

"Though many Tarot readers have several decks, if not hundreds, there is usually one or two decks with which the reader resonates most strongly. This is called the working deck — that is to say, the deck that they typically use for doing readings. I call it my workhorse."

Nick flipped the deck over. Each card had a blue, black and white plaid pattern on the back. "So what kind of deck is this?"

"It is called the Rider-Waite-Smith deck named after the company that printed it, Rider and Sons, the author of the deck, Arthur E. Waite, and the artist, Pamela Coleman-Smith."

Nick creased his brow. "Do I need to know all of that information?"

His uncle chuckled. "No. You can read with a deck without knowing its history or origins. But a Tarot reader should at least know the author and artist of his or her deck."

"What's the difference between author and artist? A deck only consists of pictures. How can there be an author?"

"The author comes up with the concept for the deck and has an idea of what the pictures should look it. The artist has the talent to turn that concept into reality."

"So there are other kinds of decks besides this one?"

Mitch nodded. "There are many different styles of decks out there that you can purchase with all manner of themes." Mitch tapped on the deck in Nick's hand twice with his index finger. "But this is the best deck to start out with. If you learn to read with this one, you can read with most any deck." He paused. "Well, maybe except the Thoth — that one requires a bit of study. Oh, and The Tarot de Marseilles has a bit of a learning curve as well."

Nick slowly flipped through the cards. He paused at some of the stranger images and then continued sifting through the deck.

"I don't know what any of this means," Nick said.

"You will. That'll be the first step in your training. Learning Tarot." Mitch gave Nick a nod. "Go ahead. Shuffle the deck and then pick a card."

"How do I shuffle?"

"Just as you would with a standard deck of playing cards."

Nick turned his attention to the cards. He clumsily shuffled the deck and then drew the first card off of the top.

Upon seeing the card, Nick felt an odd heaviness in his chest and an unexplained burst of fear. The afternoon's encounter with the woman and the ghost of her husband came to his mind. He studied the card. The image depicted a woman, sitting up in bed, her head in her hands as though she were crying. Above her were several swords floating in the air.

"What's this card?" Nick asked. "She looks paranoid or scared. It reminds me of the lady I told you about, the one whose husband is haunting her."

His uncle smiled. "You're already getting the hang of this. This one is the Nine of Swords, often referred to as the nightmare card. It symbolizes pain, suffering, anxiety, abuse or torment. This card makes perfect sense from what you've told me. If you look at the woman on the card, she is apparently in mental agony."

"Just like Janet," said Nick.

"Exactly. She is being tormented by her husband's ghost and is experiencing all of the emotions of the woman in this card. It certainly fits her situation well and reinforces the need to help her."

Nick was silent. "Okay, I see how these work now. But how do you learn all the meanings?"

"By studying, listening to your intuition and most importantly working with the cards. As you flip through them, look at their pictures and try to determine what the image is trying to tell you. Most of the time, you'll be right on the mark."

Nick felt overwhelmed. "Isn't there something like a master list of meanings I can memorize?"

"Yes and no. There are no set meanings — card meanings depend on the situation or question and the person reading the cards. That is to say, you and I can interpret the same card in different ways." He rubbed his chin. "I'll give my master binder which contains Tarot card meanings that I've learned or have come up with on my own over the years. This might be a good starting place. But remember, these are only *my* meanings. Try starting a Tarot journal yourself and write down your own interpretations of the cards."

Mitch rose again, walked to a shelf and retrieved a well-worn black binder. He handed it to Nick.

"You can study this on your own," Mitch said. "Now let's get back to your friend's situation."

"She's not my friend," Nick said. "Just some lady that I came across today. I know you said that you no longer deal with ghosts. But isn't there anything you can do to help her? I promised her that I'd talk to you."

"And you are talking to me," Mitch replied.

"But I promised her that I'd get you to help."

Mitch raised his eyebrows. "Without asking me first?"

Nick hung his head. "I know, I was wrong. But she was so insistent once she found out I could see her husband. I guess I said anything to get her to stop bugging me. Her husband is way too scary for me to get involved. Plus he threatened me."

Mitch sighed. "I know what you're going through. I remember when I first started seeing spirits, they seemed pretty scary. Most of them aren't, I promise you. Most of them are as scared as you are."

"So they can't hurt me, no matter how scary they act?" Nick asked.

Mitch took a deep breath. "I'd like to tell you that was true but to be honest, I'd be lying. You see, once ghosts have been around for awhile, some of them can become powerful enough to move objects around. You've heard of haunted houses, right?"

Nick nodded. "You mean like flying dishes and ghosts flicking light switches? I always thought it was all made up."

"People's imaginations can get the best of them. But sometimes, these happenings are real and are caused by angry ghosts who have built up enough energy to move things. I've only heard of this happening in a couple of instances and have never personally encountered a spirit who could manipulate the physical world. I'm thinking that this woman's husband may simply be confused about where he is."

"I don't know if I can agree with you on that. This guy — or whatever he or it was — seemed pretty sure about whom he was talking to and where he was — and he was not a happy camper." Nick ran his fingers through his hair. "Do you think that his wife might have murdered him?"

"Murder? Didn't you tell me that he died of a heart attack?" Mitch asked.

"That's what she said. That's not what I saw in the vision."

"Right. Now Nick, you need to be careful not to jump to conclusions. Having a heart attack can produce a variety of different symptoms, and I imagine that it would be extremely difficult to breathe while in the midst of a cardiac arrest. That may have been the reason you saw him grab his throat."

"He also grabbed his stomach," Nick said. "A couple of times. What I saw did not look like a heart attack to me."

"Perhaps, perhaps not. While it's important to follow and listen to your intuition, you shouldn't make any determinations until you know for sure what happened."

Nick wanted to tell his uncle to go screw himself but thought better of it. He didn't want any of this. He certainly never asked to be able to see ghosts. Damn it. Why did he stop the car when he saw the man attacking the woman? Why didn't he keep on driving? He should have paid attention to his physical sensations and known right from the start that it was a ghost and not a real person. Janet hadn't been in any real danger at all.

After several moments, Nick finally broke the silence. "Uncle Mitch, I hope you understand but I just do not want to get involved with her. With this." He reached into his pocket and took out a piece of paper upon which he had written down Janet's cell number earlier to give to his uncle. He placed the paper on the table between them. He pushed it toward his uncle. "Here's her number in case you change your mind about helping her."

Mitch pushed the paper back toward Nick. "I told you my situation, Nick. I can't. I'm not physically capable."

"You look okay to me," Nick said. But in actuality, his uncle did not look okay. Nick hadn't noticed at first but Mitch had lost a lot of weight, and his clothes hung loosely from his thin, frail-looking frame. He had dark purplish circles underneath his sunken eyes, and his unusually pale skin sagged, all of which made him look haggard and tired. Maybe his uncle really was sick.

"Regardless of my health status, it's time for you to learn how to use your gift. It was you who had the vision, not me. This tells me that you're the one who is supposed to help Janet. Even the Tarot turned up the right card for you." His uncle sucked in a deep breath. "Nick, I'm sorry, but I'm done with this kind of work, at least for now. It's up to you to take over."

"I don't want to take over," Nick said matter-of-factly. "I can choose whether or not I want to do this. You said so the first time we talked about this." He crossed his arms in front of his chest. "I apologize if you're disappointed in me, Uncle Mitch. But this is not what I want to do with my life. I'm a freakazoid enough as it is."

"What do you mean by that?"

Nick stayed silent.

"Is there something else you want to tell me? Something else you want to talk about?" His uncle's voice was almost a whisper.

Nick locked eyes with Mitch for a moment and then looked away. He wondered what his uncle's reaction would be if he told him the real truth, the truth that he had been hiding from everyone, including himself, for a long time, the truth that would ruin his life if it ever came out. He forced himself to still his thoughts.

"No, not right now," Nick said. The tone of his voice came out sharper than he had intended. "I don't want to talk about anything, especially this ghost stuff."

Mitch stared at Nick expressionlessly. "Nick, I'm not forcing you to do anything. I didn't mean to come across that way. Your father's right about one thing — I can be a bit overbearing at times. I only wanted to help you understand the strange things that were happening to you and to guide you along this path, which can be a challenging one. But ultimately, the choice is yours. What you do with your abilities is entirely up to you."

"Then I choose to ignore them and be a normal person."

"You do know that you need to call this Janet person and tell her that you can't help her, right?"

"You mean, tell her that *you* won't help her," Nick said.

"Now Nick, I already told you —"

"Never mind. I'll call her." He rose from his chair and stared at his uncle. "But I don't want to talk about the ghost crap anymore."

"At least take the Tarot deck," Mitch said. "Look it over. You might find that it'll come in handy for many things. Not just helping spirits."

Nick paused and then scooped up the deck, box, and the binder, He walked toward the door.

"Don't forget you're riding with me tomorrow," Mitch said. "I'm leaving at 10:00 a.m. sharp."

Nick stopped. "Tomorrow?"

"Your grandmother's funeral."

"Oh, of course. The funeral." He turned to face his uncle.

"Is she around? Grandma I mean? I haven't seen her since she died."

Mitch shook his head. "You and I can only see spirits that haven't crossed. Your grandmother must not have had any unfinished business here. Once they cross over, they're gone. That's how things go with life. We're supposed to say everything we need to say to our loved ones before they go, not afterward."

"See you tomorrow," Nick said and shut the door.

Chapter Six

Nick slipped his over-the-ear noise canceling headphones and cranked up the volume. He bobbed his head up and down in time to the music. He wanted to forget his chat with Uncle Mitch, forget all of the events of the past few days. When he had arrived home from Mitch's, his brain was in turmoil. The thoughts of that desperate woman and her scary husband tugged at his chest. His subconscious screamed at him, trying to make him listen to his heart. But he'd made his decision. She was on her own. All he wanted to do now was listen to his music and be left alone.

With almost a Herculean effort, he finally cleared his thoughts. He was just about to doze off when his phone buzzed in his pocket. Damn. He should have put it on his dresser.

Sup.

He smiled when he saw the text. It was his friend Gabe, whom he'd hardly seen at all as of late. It wasn't as if Nick been deliberately ignoring him. He liked Gabe and loved spending time with him more than anything.

But how do you tell your best friend that you can see ghosts? Especially someone as down to earth and practical-minded as Gabe? On second thought, maybe Nick *had* been ignoring him.

What's going on?

He waited for a response.

Wanna go to the Ren Faire on Sat? Missed it last year.

He stared at the text for a moment. He and Gabe had planned on going with a few of their other friends last July. Unfortunately, they'd waited until the last weekend to go. Pounding rain had put a stop to their plans.

Who's all going?

He waited. If anyone else besides Gabe were coming, he'd decline. He didn't want to risk being with a group of his friends until he learned how to figure out this ghost thing. The last thing he needed was a spirit noticing him and then latching on to him while he was kids from school. His phone chimed.

You & me thus far. Thinking of asking Sam. So?

It might be fun to get away and do something different, something exciting. His life has been way too serious lately with his grandmother's death and the bombshell his uncle had just dropped on him. Fun would be a good thing, right about now.

He kicked off his shoes and sat cross-legged on the bed. He leaned against the headboard and thumbed out his reply.

Sounds good. You driving?

I'll pick you about at 9:30. CU

He was going to type out one more message to let Gabe know that he wouldn't be at school tomorrow but changed his mind. He'd try to connect with him on Friday and tell him all about it. He briefly considered revealing the other thing to Gabe but quickly changed his mind. No need to do that now.

If he stuck with his self-promise and ignored the ghosts when they appeared, there would never be a reason to tell anyone. Ever. It'd be his secret. Well, his and Uncle Mitch's.

He felt a sharp ping of regret for the way he had talked to his uncle earlier. He shouldn't have been such a dick to Uncle Mitch. Nick knew that his uncle was only trying to help. Yet he didn't like it that Mitch pushing him into something that he didn't want — and this ghost business was definitely something of which he wanted no part. He'd hoped that his uncle would have helped out Janet and that would've been the end of it. How come things are always so bloody complicated?

He took off the headphones and glanced over at his dresser. The box containing the Tarot deck sat next to his alarm clock. He'd forgotten about the cards. He made a mental note to hide the deck in a safe place. He didn't want his mom to accidentally stumble across it when she came into his room to clean. He picked up the deck and began shuffling. As he shuffled, another vision grabbed him.

This time, he saw his Uncle Mitch. He was sitting at a small table upon which were several Tarot cards, all of them face down. Across from him sat a middle-aged woman, her face streaked with tears. Mitch was talking, no doubt explaining the meaning of the cards to her. As he spoke, he made wide sweeping gestures with both hands. All at once, the woman jumped up, ran to his uncle and hugged him tightly. When she pulled away, Nick saw that she was now smiling.

The vision faded with a pop in his brain. His bedroom came back into view. Nick shook himself and took a deep breath. How real it had seemed. It was as though he were there in person, watching Mitch and the lady from a corner of the room. Apparently, his uncle read cards for other people. Nick made another mental note to ask him about it next time they were together. Tarot might be kind of fun after all.

Nick stuffed a couple of pillows between his back and the headboard. He continued shuffling and then closed his eyes, trying to ignore the newly-formed headache that stubbornly pounded his temples. After a few more shuffles, he opened his eyes and turned over the card on top of the deck. The image depicted a young man with a foul look on his face sitting against a yellow tree, his arms crossed. The first thing that Nick thought of was that the guy was acting like a brat, being all pouty. A puff of golden clouds floated in the air out of which extended a hand that was holding something that looked like an elaborate cup of some sort. The hand seemed to be offering the chalice to the young man, but he pretended the hand wasn't even there. On the ground were three more chalices.

Nick got up and retrieved his uncle's binder from his bottom desk drawer, remembering that it included pictures of all the cards. He thumbed through the pages until he found his card. It was the Four of Cups (so it was a cup). His uncle had written, "The Brat Card" underneath it. Nick smiled. He was dead on. He might be getting the hang of this after all. He continued reading:

Self-absorbed. Apathy. Self-pity. Lack of interest or commitment. Making little effort. Lack of motivation. Unwilling to accept help. Refusing to see or acknowledge the gifts that are offered to you.

Nick stared at the card for a few seconds. Was this him? Was the card trying to tell him that he was being a brat? If so, it was wrong. He wasn't *unwilling* to accept help — he just wanted to make his own decisions about his future. Was that so wrong?

His thoughts drifted back to the encounter with Janet and her dead husband. Try as he might, he couldn't stop thinking about it. When the image of the terrifying ghost popped into his mind, he shuddered. What was his name? James, yeah, that was it, James and Janet. Nick had never seen anyone so angry, so full of rage — and it was all directed at his wife. Yikes. What could Janet have done that could have pissed him off so much? He did call her a whore, which made Nick suspect that she'd cheated on him. Why else would he call her that? But the real question was: what was his unfinished business?

Unless Janet had killed her husband.

If the vision he'd experienced earlier was telling him that the ghost didn't die from a heart attack, then it's possible that James was murdered by his wife. That'd certainly explain why he was so enraged with her. But did would she kill him? She didn't seem like the murdering type but who knows? Nick's dad once said to him that people are capable of doing anything, to anyone, at any time, for any reason. When Nick had met Janet she was obviously frightened; there was no faking that. But then again, who wouldn't be frightened if the person they had killed was haunting them?

Even though he wasn't going to get involved, his curiosity nagged at him. He looked down at the cards. Could they tell him whether or not Janet killed her husband? He remembered reading in the binder that to use the Tarot correctly, you had to think about your question, shuffle the cards and then turn the cards over.

Nick said out loud, "Did Janet murder James?"

He closed his eyes and shuffled. He wondered how many times he should shuffle. Seven seemed like a good number. When he finished, he turned the card over.

The Lovers.

What was this telling him? That someone James loved murdered him? Nick didn't get that impression from the card. This seemed more like a card of love or romance. He flipped through his uncle's binder until he found the definition.

Love, marriage, harmony, a spiritual union. A harmonious situation or a life-affirming choice.

No mention of murder. On the contrary, this card seemed to be saying that James and Janet had a good relationship, confirming what she'd told him when they met, although she admitted that they did fight occasionally. But still, this card could be suggesting that someone he loved played a part in his death.

Damn. He wished the message was a little clearer. He needed more information. He closed his eyes and tried to formulate the next question in his mind. He now needed to ask whether somebody killed James or if he did in fact, simply die from a heart attack.

He closed his eyes and asked his question.

"Was James murdered?"

He turned over the card. No need to look up this one. Its message was perfectly clear. The image portrayed a figure (he couldn't tell if was a man or a woman) lying on the ground with a bunch of swords stuck into his or her back. The Roman numeral *X* was printed in the top center of the card so Nick guessed there were ten swords in the person's back. A river of blood flowed from the body. He or she appeared really, really dead. He looked up the card in his uncle's book just to verify his impression.

Pain, defeat, ultimate ruin. An irrevocable ending. You have lost the battle.

So if this card were true, then James was murdered, possibly by his wife. This reinforced Nick's decision that he wanted nothing to do with this situation. If Janet was the murderer, then he didn't want to be anywhere near her. What if she discovered that Nick suspected her? He could end up in the same situation as James. Dead. And even if she didn't kill her husband — which for some unexplainable reason, Nick felt that she didn't — that meant that there was someone else out there who did.

Nope, he wasn't going to go anywhere near this. He'd leave the ghost hunting and crime solving to other people who knew what in the hell they were doing.

He then remembered that he hadn't yet called Janet. He didn't want to talk to her in person, afraid that she might try to push him into helping. He'd just send her a text instead.

He reached for his phone and then realized that he couldn't remember her last name. He opened his contacts app and searched for *Janet*. The only matching entry was Janet Pearce. He selected the entry and typed out his message.

"Uncle ill, unable to help u w/husband situation. Sorry. Good luck. - Nick

He tapped the Send button. He waited. No response.

Just as he was about to put the phone on the dresser, it buzzed. Damn.

How about u? Will u help?

Nick took a deep breath. This was why he hadn't wanted to talk to her in person. He typed in his reply.

Death in the family. Must stick close to home. Sorry.

He hit Send. He wasn't lying. There were family problems — his grandma's funeral and his relationship with Uncle Mitch. He mentally chastised himself for not having the balls to help her but his mind was made up. Didn't his uncle say that in all the time he'd been doing this, he'd encountered only one or two ghosts who were murdered? Nick supposed that if you dealt with ghosts, you'd eventually meet at least one who had been murdered. Why did it have to be his first one?

He glanced again at his phone. Nothing. Good.

He tossed the phone on the bed next to the Tarot deck. He picked up the cards and shuffled them a few times. These were actually pretty cool. Even though he decided that he didn't want to get involved with ghost busting, he could at the very least learn the cards. They might come in handy for other things.

He put the deck down next to him and stretched out on the bed. He reached over for the binder and rested it upright on his chest. He flipped it open to the first page and began to read.

Chapter Seven

Nick preened in the mirror attached to his dresser and adjusted the tight-fitting black suit. His freshly trimmed curly brown hair no longer touched his shoulders, and his bright green eyes stood out against the dark suit. Now that he was almost seventeen, he'd finally begun filling out. His mother recently joked that he was losing his boy body and was morphing into his man body. She was kinda right. During the past year, he'd sprouted chest muscles and arm muscles, and had gone from being a lanky pimply-faced boy to a more mature looking teen. At least that's what people told him. His workout equipment, last year's birthday present, had helped him with that. He still didn't yet have six-pack abs, but he was working on it. Unfortunately, he hadn't worked out at all the past week, with all that was going on. Maybe after the funeral, things would settle down enough so that he could get back to his normal routine.

Normal sounded good right about now.

He took one last look in the mirror and then headed downstairs. His uncle had already arrived and was sitting at the kitchen table sipping a cup of coffee with his mother. Now that was something you didn't see every day. They both looked equally nervous around the other. Nick tried hard not to chuckle, thinking it inappropriate for funeral day.

"You just about ready?" his uncle asked.

Nick nodded. "You look nice."

He couldn't recall ever seeing his uncle Mitch all dressed up, and Nick was amazed at how handsome he was. He also noticed that the dark blue suit he wore was much too big for him. He looked like a little boy wearing grown-up clothes.

His uncle smiled. "I clean up pretty well when I want to. Although I'm sorry I didn't try on this suit earlier. It's a tad baggy."

A tad? Did you look in the mirror after you got dressed?

"You've lost quite a bit of weight," his mother said. There was a slight tremble to her voice.

"Too much apparently," Mitch said. He pulled at the suit jacket. "Maybe you can have it, Nick. Another year and it'll fit you perfectly.

"There'll be plenty of food after the service," said Nick's mother. "The local ladies are all bringing a dish so make sure you eat your fill."

"I certainly will take advantage of everyone's delicious cooking, Liz," he said. He turned his regard to Nick and gestured toward the door. "Our chariot awaits us."

Nick rose and kissed his mom on the cheek. "See you at the service."

"Make sure you sit in the front row with all of us," she said. "We're all sitting together for this." She turned to look at Mitch. "And that means you too, Mitchell. Family sits together."

"I appreciate that Liz."

She dismissed him with a gesture of her hand. "Get a move on. You don't want to be late."

"But the service doesn't start for more than an hour."

"It's good for family to arrive early," she said. "People like to offer their condolences. So off with the both of you." She began gathering up the coffee cups from the table.

"But I didn't get any breakfast," Nick said. "Can I at least have a quick piece of toast?"

"We're eating immediately after the service. I'm sure your stomach will survive."

"How about a cookie?"

"Get!"

In the car, Mitch and Nick sat in silence for several minutes. Nick stole occasional side glances at his uncle who didn't acknowledge him. Nick figured that he was still pissed. At least he didn't have to talk about ghosts with him.

His uncle finally broke the silence. "Did you look at all at the cards that I gave to you?"

"They're kind of cool," Nick said. "I've been reading the book as well."

"Any interesting impressions while using the cards?"

"Impressions?"

"I mean did anything pop into your mind like the last time?"

"If you mean have I had any more visions, the answer is no."

His uncle nodded but kept staring straight ahead. "I'm glad you're working with them."

"Wait. One strange thing did happen when I first picked up the deck. I saw you sitting at a table with some lady. There were cards spread out in front of you, and you were talking. I couldn't hear what you were telling her. She got up, walked over to you and hugged you."

Mitch's eyes grew wide. "That's amazing Nick. I mean you're amazing. What you saw actually occurred. I was doing a reading awhile back for this woman whose husband had passed. I was using Tarot cards but they were just for show. Her husband was there right next to her telling me everything I needed to know."

"What did you say to her that made her hug you like that?" Nick asked.

Mitch creased his brow. "So here's your first lesson of doing readings. What happens and what is said during a session is private, between you and a client. The client has placed their trust in you and an ethical reader respects that trust. The short and sweet of it is: I would never divulge to anyone — not even to you — what is said during a reading. And you mustn't either."

Nick nodded. "Maybe that's why I couldn't hear what you were saying."

"Very likely. It might be the Universe's way of telling you to mind your own business."

Nick chuckled. "What if I used the cards to find out? That way, you wouldn't have to tell me."

Mitch turned and wagged his finger at Nick. "That's also a no-no. It's called psychic snooping." He turned his gaze back to the road. "Okay, lesson number two. You never do a reading to pry into someone's personal life. That's giving you an unfair advantage. Plus people have a right to their privacy. You wouldn't want me snooping through your private thoughts, now would you?"

"You can read minds?" Nick asked. He desperately tried to clear his mind of all potentially incriminating thoughts. "You can find out what I"m thinking?"

Mitch laughed. "No, although I don't doubt that it'd come in handy. I'm talking about doing readings for snooping purposes. Remember to always respect the privacy of others. For instance, imagine that a client comes to you and asks, 'Is my boyfriend cheating on me?' Performing a reading on such a question would be considered unethical because you're prying into her boyfriend's life without his permission."

"Wow, I never thought about it like that. So you'd tell the client that it's none of her business?" Nick asked.

"Not quite. You'd want to guide her or him to rephrase the question in such a way that it's within ethical boundaries. For instance, you might ask instead 'Why do I not trust my boyfriend?' or 'Why am I having trust issues in the relationship?' These types of questions put you on a more ethical plane."

"Got it. So basically, you wouldn't answer the question."

Mitch shook his head. "It's a gray area. Some readers would; others wouldn't. It depends on how strictly you define what's ethical and what is not. For example, I might rephrase the questions to be, 'What do I need to know about my relationship with my boyfriend?'. In this way, the question is about the client, not about the boyfriend's behavior. Now if a card like the Seven of Swords should pop up, I'd most likely tell her, 'Honey, dat man is cheatin' on you!'."

Nick laughed. "Sounds complicated, all of it. I just pulled one of those swords cards the other day. I'm learning about the different suits and the Majors."

"Which card did you pull?"

Nick swallowed. He hadn't wanted to discuss the Janet and James situation. He wanted to forget about it. So much for that idea.

"I was thinking about the ghost and the vision that I experienced. Remember I told you that it seemed like James didn't die from a heart attack at all?"

Mitch nodded.

Nick brushed his hands through his hair. "So I asked the cards if he was murdered."

"Murdered? What card did you pull?"

"The Ten of Swords."

A dark look crossed his uncle's face. "Did you get any visions or impressions when you saw the card?"

Nick shook his head. "The only vision I've had was the one I told you about; the one I had when I first met Janet and her creepy husband. Although, I did have this odd, nagging feeling in my gut that something was not quite right with the ghost — with how he died."

"I've often suspected that the spirits themselves send us these flashes. My theory is that once they pick up on our abilities, they pass information to us through visions. It could be easier for them to communicate that way. The vision and hunches that you received could have been James's way of showing you what happened to him."

"And letting me know why he was so angry with his wife."

Mitch took a deep breath. "Now Nick, remember what I told you about jumping to conclusions. You can't accuse people without knowing all the information."

"But what about the vision?" Nick asked. "And the Tarot card?"

"Did you see Janet kill him in your vision?

"Um...no."

"Exactly. Until you have all the facts — and I do mean all of them — you need to be careful about hinting that someone is a murderer."

"But he was screaming at Janet in a furious rage. I'm guessing that he wouldn't have been doing that if he hadn't known that Janet had killed him."

"Here's another thing to keep in mind about the dead — just because they've passed away, doesn't make them all-wise and all-knowing. They're the same as they were when they were alive, only without a body. They aren't privy to any special knowledge or information now that they're gone. What I'm saying, is they make the same mistakes and assumptions that we do. It's easy to misinterpret a situation, and I've seen this time and time again with spirits. What they think happened to them and what did happen to them are often two very different things."

Nick thought about this. Maybe he was jumping to conclusions. Not that it mattered now. He hoped that he'd never see Janet again regardless of whether or not she had murdered her husband.

"We're here," his uncle said.

They pulled into the driveway of the funeral home, and Nick felt a shiver run up his back. It had been many years since he'd last attended a funeral. Or at least a funeral where there was a body. A classmate of his had been killed in a car accident last year, but there was neither a wake nor a viewing. The service was held at a hall several months after he'd died. The only time Nick had attended a real funeral was when his cousin Anne died. She was only four years old and had died of an odd infection. He didn't remember much about the funeral as he was much younger. But he did remember the intense sadness that hung over and swallowed up the room. He had avoided going to funerals since then. Until now. This is one that he didn't even try to get out of.

"The parking lot is almost empty," said Nick. "Where is everyone?"

"The service isn't for an hour. Most people arrive at the last minute."

"How come we're here so early?" Nick asked.

"So we can pay our proper respects," his uncle said. Whatever that meant, Nick had no idea. But by the look on his uncle's face, he felt it best to leave it alone.

A bell above the door chimed when they entered. Nick crinkled his nose at the sweet powdery smell that hit him when they walked in. It wasn't an offensive odor really, just odd. It reminded him of his cousin's funeral and made his stomach a bit queasy.

A moment later, a lanky older man wearing Harry Potter glasses and sporting a bad comb-over appeared and apologized for not having greeted them properly at the door. He looked like an owl wearing a cheap toupee. His uncle dismissed him with a wave of his hand.

"It's fine," Mitch said. "We didn't expect to be greeted. We just wanted a bit of quiet time with her before the other guests arrive."

"I understand perfectly, gentlemen." The man's voice was almost a whisper. Nick thought it creepy the way the man spoke in such an odd, faux-formal manner, slowly enunciating every syllable. And why was he whispering? What did he think he was going to do, wake the dead?

The man gestured to a room on the right. Nick could see the rows of chairs already set up with a couple of people scattered throughout the room. As he moved closer, he caught a glimpse of the edge of the casket. Immediately upon seeing it, his body tensed and grew heavy, like a heap of wet clothes. He started shaking uncontrollably and a lump formed in his throat. He wished that he didn't have to go into that room. He didn't want to see his grandma like that, see her all lifeless in the coffin. No, coming here was a bad idea. He should have tried to get out attending the funeral somehow. Why didn't he?

"You okay?" Mitch asked. "Do you want to wait a bit before we go in?"

Nick wanted to say that he would just wait in the car, that he couldn't do this. Instead, he nodded.

His uncle put his arm around Nick's shoulders and gently edged him closer to the room. "I know how difficult this is for you, especially considering how close you were to her. I only regret that I didn't have the opportunity to get to know her better."

Nick kept his head bowed and looked at the floor. He

didn't want to see the figure in the coffin. He didn't want to see his grandma's dead body.

All at once, Mitch stopped at a row of chairs. "I'm going to go up first alone. Why don't you sit here next to this lady for a moment?"

Nick took a deep breath and nodded. He could feel his entire body trembling. His skin had goosebumps, and his stomach flip-flopped. He hoped he wasn't going to get sick.

He took the chair at the end of the aisle, head still glued to the floor. How was he going to get through this? He was aware of the lady next to him but didn't look at her. He didn't want to talk to anyone. He was sick of everyone saying 'my condolences' or "my deepest sympathy' to him.

A familiar voice interrupted his thoughts. "Hello, Pup."

He recoiled, and his head jerked to the right. Sitting one chair over from him was his grandmother. The same grandmother who was supposed to be in the coffin up front. His breath came quick and sharp, almost like he'd been running a marathon.

"Grandma!" he said, his voice cracking as he spoke. "How are you here? What's going on?"

Her eyes flickered, and she smiled. "I needed to see you one more time before I go for good." She got up out of her chair and moved to the one right next to him.

He felt his face flush. Then, his heart sunk. She was a ghost. Of course. For a moment, he had forgotten about his new ability. For just a moment, he thought that she might be alive, that it was all a mistake. But of course. He should have noticed immediately how radiant she was. Moreover, she looked twenty years younger — maybe more — and almost glowed with health. He couldn't remember ever seeing her look so good.

He heaved a sigh. "For a moment I thought —"

She nodded. "I know. This is all new for you, huh Pup?"

He nodded. "I think it's been happening for awhile, but I only learned what it was last week. Uncle Mitch told me all about it. I don't think I ever would have figured it out by myself."

She appeared in deep thought, as though she were revisiting an ancient memory. She then looked to the front of the room and nodded. "Ah, your Uncle Mitchell was there to help you. I'm so glad. Funny. The thought never occurred to me that you would end up like him. Being able to see them, I mean. Us." She chuckled. "Lucky for me you can."

He let go a nervous laugh. "I'm going to miss you so much, Grandma."

She reached over and put her hand over his. He couldn't feel her touch at all. "I'll always be around; you remember that. And pup, I want you to know how proud I am of you."

"Proud of me? For what?"

She nodded and gave him a warm smile. "Mitchell tried to explain to me once how he uses his gift to help people, to heal people. Unfortunately, at the time I was too pigheaded to listen to him. But the moment I gained awareness after passing away, I had a strong feeling about you — a feeling that you were in good hands with your uncle and that you would be okay. But not only that. I know deep down that you're going to end up helping a lot of people in the years to come."

He felt his face redden, knowing that he had no intention of getting involved with ghosts. However, he felt that there was no need to discuss that with her now.

"Now that you're here, do I still have to go up there and look at your body?"

His grandmother laughed. "Oh, honey. That's not me up there. Not anymore. That was only a shell for my spirit, the real me. You can see that I'm right here, next to you. So there's no need to be afraid of going up there. No need at all. Think of it as a box of candy. The outside carton is only a place to store them. All the goodies are inside." She chuckled again.

"I guess it wouldn't hurt then," he said. All at once he became aware of a presence next to him.

"Mitchell, how nice to see you again," his grandmother said. "How long has it been now?"

His uncle was standing next to him.

"Ma'am," Mitch said and bowed his head. The falter in his eyes was fleeting, but Nick caught it. Apparently, Grandma had too.

"Now Mitchell, there's no need for you to be nervous around me." She turned her attention to Nick. "Pup, would you be a dear and give your uncle and me a minute to chat?"

"Sure," Nick said. He didn't want to leave his grandmother's side, but he was sure that she had private matters she wanted to talk over with Mitch.

Nick rose and shuffled toward the front of the room. *It's only a shell*, he kept telling himself. *It's not really her. It's only a shell*.

After several moments, he took a deep breath and then looked up. The woman in the casket didn't at all resemble the grandmother he knew. For one thing, her lips were painted bright red, the same color as a fire truck. He'd never known his grandmother to wear any sort of makeup. Her face had a waxy, plastic look to it, making her appear more like a mannequin than a real person. He wanted to reach out and touch her, to see if she would feel like plastic but restrained himself.

He glanced over at his grandmother and uncle. They were both still deep in conversation. Nick thought about how it would look if anyone else arrived and saw his uncle talking away to an empty chair. The two other people that were there stared straight ahead, oblivious to what was going on in the back of the room.

He then wondered how many other people like him were out there. He'd love to meet someone his own age, someone whom he could talk to about this stuff. Someone normal, like himself and not some crazy gypsy-looking lady with dangly bracelets, a fake accent and wearing a turban, like the ones on those late-night television psychic commercials. But how would he go about finding others? Are there psychic medium Internet forums? Groups?

He then heard his grandma call his name.

He looked over, and she was gesturing him over with her hand, a radiant smile on her face. She and his uncle were both standing now.

As he got closer, he noticed that his uncle was smiling as well, which looked kind of strange given that his face was wet with tears. He put his hand on Nick's shoulders, nodded his head a couple of times and then turned to walk up front. Nick turned to his grandmother.

"Did your talk with Uncle Mitch go okay?" Nick asked.

"It most certainly did," she said. "I am so fortunate that I got the opportunity to make amends with him before I left. To think about all those wasted years that passed with me being angry at him. That anger also kept me estranged from your mother and father for a long time. I don't think either of them ever quite forgave me for trying to keep them apart."

"It's a shame that you couldn't tell them that in person."

"That's why your uncle reminded me how fortunate I am to have you."

"Me?"

"I need you to pass on a couple of messages to them from me."

He drew a short breath, about to protest but then thought better of it. "What you do want me to tell them?"

"I want you to tell your mother that the afternoon we were

in her room — the day I tore up all those letters that I found from your father — that I was wrong; wrong about him, wrong about your uncle. Tell her that she needs to be supportive of both you and Mitchell. Can you remember that Pup?"

"I think so," he said.

She offered him an easy smile. "I also want you to apologize to your father for me, for meddling. Tell him that I regret the way I acted and that I understand now."

"You know I'm going to have to tell them that I talked to your ghost, right?"

She gave him a surprised look. "They don't know about your abilities?"

He shook his head. "I didn't know until last week. I don't think they'd be too crazy about the idea."

"You're their son, honey. I'm sure they'll love you and accept you as they always have."

"You didn't accept Uncle Mitch when you found out about him."

She closed her eyes. "You're right. I didn't. But I'm from a different era. Things were different back then. You're fortunate to be growing up in these modern times. I have little doubt that your parents will love you and accept you as you are."

"You don't know them as I do," Nick said.

"I've been around for a long time Pup, and have known all types of people. Now, I may not know your parents as well as you do, but I know people. Family supports their own, no matter what. Look at me. I came around. Although I admit, it took me awhile." She lowered her voice. "So can I count on you to tell them?"

He felt his apprehension rising but nodded. "I promise." Then a thought struck him. "Grandma, Uncle Mitch said that I could only see spirits who are stuck here because they have unfinished business. Why can I see you then? Why are you still here?"

Instead of answering him, she looked up and gasped. She pointed at the wall. "I don't think I'll be here very much longer. You see that hon? I'm guessing that's for me. Right?"

"He can't see it, Rose," said Mitch. "Only you can. It's your light. Your path to the Other Side."

Nick looked at his grandmother who now brought her hand up to her mouth.

"Oh my god, it's Dennis! He came to meet me. He looks just like he did when we were married."

It was Nick's turn to gasp. His grandmother had transformed into a young woman. She was beautiful, with flowing blond hair and rosy cheeks. Her glacial blue eyes sparkled.

She turned to Nick. "It's time for me to go. Thank you. Thank you both. And remember Pup, I'll always be watching over you."

Nick hadn't realized that tears were streaming down his cheeks. He reached out for his grandmother, but she was walking toward the wall. Then in an instant, she was gone.

The sudden quiet seemed deafening, and Nick knew — could feel — that she was now truly gone. She had crossed over.

A moment later his parents and sister came through the front door. Nick looked up at them, held up his hand in a brief wave and then walked up toward the front row.

He heard his mother behind him. "Who would have guessed that he would take it so hard?"

Chapter Eight

Nick glanced at the clock on the classroom wall. Only fifteen more minutes and he was free for the weekend. Friday certainly took its sweet time in getting here. He shuffled in his seat, trying to pay attention to what was going on in front of the class but his thoughts drifted. He was excited about to going to the Renaissance Faire with Gabe, and his heart skipped a couple of beats just thinking about spending time with his friend. After everything that has gone on this past week, he was ready to have some fun. Getting to spend time with Gabe was a major plus.

When 3:30 finally arrived, he dashed out of school, jumped in his mom's car and headed toward home. He still had not passed on his grandmother's messages to his parents. His grandmother was right, of course, This was something that he couldn't hide from his parents forever, and he'd have to tell them eventually. His grandmother's request only sped up the process.

Over the past couple of days, he'd practiced over and over in his head what he was going to say to them but still hadn't found the right words. Every rendition of the speech in his head seemed weak, stupid or lame — never coming together quite right. He should have asked Uncle Mitch to be there with him. But maybe it was better if he did this himself. His uncle has been estranged from his parents for too long, and he didn't want them thinking his uncle put him up to any of this.

Instead of going right home, he drove past Janet's house. With its enormous front yard and protruding porch, the immense white house stood out from the rest of the more modest sized houses on the block. Seeing nobody out in the yard as he drove by, he breathed a sigh of relief. However, guilt descended on him as he thought about leaving that poor woman to the whims of a nasty spirit. But there was no way in hell he was going anywhere near that James creep again. In spite of his resolve not to get involved, he slowed down the car to see if he could catch sight of Janet, to make sure she was okay but saw no one. All at once, Nick felt the familiar stomach flip, and he noticed James standing on the porch in front of the door, arms crossed. The ghost appeared as though he were glaring right at Nick. Nick shivered. The blatant contempt in the spirit's eyes sent an icy chill down Nick's spine.

Nick shuddered once more and stepped on the gas. He was not going to mess with that ghost today, or ever again for that matter. He watched the house disappear in his rearview mirror and as the image of it grew smaller, the shaking in his hands lessened. He hoped Janet was still okay. Maybe he should have manned up and confronted the ghost, to find out what James was so pissed off about and discover whether or not he was murdered. But too late now. Janet's house had already faded from his rear-view mirror.

He pulled the car into the driveway and shut it off. He sat and waited, trying to muster up the courage he so desperately needed. He looked in the mirror and ran his fingers through his hair. His heart pounded wildly in his chest. He scowled at his reflection.

Wus.

He shook himself and got out of the car. He opened the front door and listened, but could hear nothing. Maybe he was in luck, and they weren't at home. His heart sunk when he heard the rustling of pots in the kitchen. No more stalling. It was time to come clean.

His mother was in the kitchen stirring what appeared to be cookie batter in a huge bowl. The sweet odor of vanilla and chocolate floated in the air.

"Oh, you're home," his mother said. "Good. Maybe you could help me eat some cookies in a few minutes." She flashed a broad smile. "I figured we all could use a little cheering up."

He hadn't spoken very much to either of his parents since his uncle had dropped him off at home after the service. His mother had been unusually quiet the past couple of days, and his dad had pretty much stayed in his basement office. He wondered how long it would take his parents to get back to normal. Might take them even longer once he drops his bombshell on them.

"Sounds yummy," Nick stammered. He sucked in a deep breath. "And I'm glad you're home. I have something that I need to talk to you about."

His mother raised her eyebrows. "Oh?"

"Both of you, actually," Nick said. "Is Dad around?"

"I imagine he's where he usually is, in his office. I think he's working on his paper."

"What paper?"

"Don't you remember? He's presenting a paper in Cleveland in a couple of weeks. So don't expect to see too much of him until then."

Nick's dad was a science professor at Gallowspine Mountains University, and it was Nick's father who got Nick first interested in science, to such an extent that at one point Nick had considered becoming a scientist himself. He'd won the science fair twice at school and always got good grades in his science classes. He thought about trying to reconcile his new abilities with science. How can science explain that?

Recently however, he had begun reading some of his father's old Psychology Today magazines and changed his mind about where he wanted to go in his future. Psychology or psychiatry would be his new career path, though he wasn't sure which. He also enjoyed creative writing, so that was another possibility. It seemed he changed his mind about what he wanted to do with his life on a weekly basis. It was so hard to decide. Many of the other juniors at school knew exactly what they were going to study at college. The last time he mentioned all of this to his father, his father laughed and assured him that he didn't have to make any decisions now. He told him that in all likelihood, he'd change majors a couple of times. Everyone did.

"Nick?" his mother said.

"Yeah?"

"Is it something serious?" his mother asked. The concern was evident in her expression. "Are you in trouble of some kind?"

Nick could understand his mother's concern. He never instigated serious chats with his parents. Truth be told, he never talked to them about much of anything except the most mundane of matters. Nick simply wasn't an 'open your heart and bare your feelings' type of guy.

Nick shook his head. "Nothing like that. Just something I need to talk to the both of you about."

His mother creased her brow, her face dark with concern. "Do you need to speak with us right this minute?"

"It's not that urgent," said Nick. "It can wait until the

cookies are done." Nick's stomach grumbled at the thought of warm, gooey cookies, fresh from the oven.

"I'll call you when they're ready," his mother said.

Without answering, he left the kitchen and bounded up the stairs towards his room. He spent a few minutes scooping dirty clothes up off the floor and tossing them in the hamper. He bent over and picked up his three fluffy pillows which were lying next to his nightstand and tossed them on the bed. He thought briefly about making his bed but decided against it. Too much trouble. He reached for the wrinkled t-shirt on his nightstand, and as he did, the stack of paperbacks that were piled next to the bed tumbled loudly to the floor, almost knocking over the long black lamp that was clipped to the nightstand. He pushed the lamp out of the way. No matter how hard he tried to keep his room in order, he was never quite able to succeed at it.

After he'd piled the fallen books on the bookshelf above his bed, he sat at his desk, pulled out his phone and typed a text to Gabe.

We still on for the faire?

He waited a moment and then his phone chimed. His hands trembled as he fiddled with the phone.

Yup. Can't wait.

Anyone else coming?

Nope. Just us.

U R driving, right?

Yup. 9:30. Or do u wanna go for breakfast first?

Nick hesitated before replying. Going out to breakfast would be fun, but that would mean getting up an hour earlier. Why rob himself of an extra hour of sleep? That'd be too much of a pain, especially given that he hadn't been sleeping all that well recently. Nick replied.

Nah, I'll eat breakfast at home.

Okay. c u.

He tossed the phone onto the desk, got up and opened the door to his closet. He dropped to his hands and knees and pushed a pile of shoes out of the way to get to the small box he'd hidden there. He retrieved it and pulled out the deck of Tarot cards. He'd stored them way in the back of his closet to ensure that his mother didn't accidentally stumble upon them. Once he came clean to his parents, he could leave his cards out in the open. Or maybe not. It all depended on how receptive they'll be to what he has to say.

He pulled the cards out of their box, sat at his desk and shuffled. He closed his eyes and thought of his question.

"How is my conversation with Mom and Dad going to go?"

His uncle had talked about spreads in his binder and how pulling more than one card can provide extra insight into a situation. So this time, Nick drew three cards and laid them face down on the desk.

He turned over the first card. It depicted what looked to be an angel floating in the sky and blowing a horn. Below the angel, people appeared to be rising out of coffins, their arms raised toward the heavens. Kinda creepy. On the bottom of the card, was one word.

Judgement.

Not at all surprising. Yeah, there'll no doubt be some major judgments going on once his parents find out that their son can see spooks. He studied the card. The people coming out of the coffins — were they ghosts? Was the card telling him that there'll be judgments against him because he can see ghosts? Possibly.

He looked up the card in his uncle's binder. Other keywords for the card were:

Rebirth, hearing a call, momentous choice and reinventing yourself.

Yeah, that made sense. He certainly was going to be reinventing himself in the eyes of his parents as possibly some sort of freak. He noticed that there were words written in the left margin on the page. He turned the binder sideways and read the text in the margin.

The end of one cycle and the beginning of a new one. Revelations.

He put the book down. That was an understatement, as this was going to be one hell of major revelation to his mom and dad. He didn't much care for the idea of changing cycles, however. He did not want to reinvent himself. He didn't want to start a new life cycle. He wanted his life to stay as was. He wanted to stay as he was — to be a regular person, and nothing more.

The aromatic smell of chocolate chip cookies wafted up the stairs, causing his mouth to water. He turned over the next card. This image depicted a person (a guy?) carrying a bundle of sticks which he now knew were actually called wands. The figure was looking downward, his face buried in the middle of the sticks as he trudged onward. On the very top of the card was an X. So seeing that sticks signified wands, this card would be the 10 of Wands. Nick looked it up in the book.

Carrying a heavy load, a struggle. Heavy responsibilities, but you can do it. Don't let your path become obscured by your burdens.

Nick then glanced back at the card on the table. Burdens. He could see that — this whole damn ghost business was turning into one gigantic, burning ass pain. And yeah, it was certainly a struggle. A struggle to figure out how to tell his family. He thought about that last sentence again, about letting your path get obscured by his burdens. He'd have to think on that one.

He turned over the last card. This one depicted a blind-folded black-haired woman wearing a red dress or robe standing outside, her hands bound behind her. Surrounding her were a bunch of swords stuck in the ground. On top of the card was the Roman numeral VIII. Nick assumed that this meant that this card was the 8 of Swords. Nick flipped through the book until he found the card.

Fear of change, feeling restricted, anxiety, confusion, denial of the truth.

Okay, so there was no difficulty at all applying these cards to his situation. He knew that he'd been fighting and struggling with this ghost thing ever since he found out about it from his uncle and yeah, he was confused and maybe anxious. But he didn't agree with the phrase that said he was denying the truth. He accepted the truth — he could see spooks. He just didn't want anything to do with them.

He swept up the three cards and stuffed them back into the deck. He was amazed at their accuracy, how they perfectly reflected his present situation. He now understood why Uncle Mitch had been so adamant that he learn Tarot.

He thought back to the Judgement card, with the angel blowing the horn and it hit him what scene this card was depicting. It represented Judgement Day and the angel in the card was the Angel Gabriel. It made him think of Gabe and couldn't help but wonder how his friend would react if he found out. Not that this was gonna happen anytime soon. He had no intentions of telling Gabe. Ever.

Nick shuffled the cards and closed his eyes. What question to ask now. Then it struck him. He asked about the faire.

"What will tomorrow be like with Gabe?"

He turned over the card. As he looked at the image and then read the words on the bottom of the card, he felt his skin flush and his mouth go dry.

The words on the card said, "THE LOVERS".

"Stupid deck," he said aloud. "That makes no sense at all." Just then, his mom called for him to come down for cookies. He crammed the cards in the middle of the deck and tossed it, along with his uncle's binder, in the top drawer of his desk.

HE SAT ACROSS FROM HIS MOTHER AT THE DINING ROOM table. She had a light patch of white flour on her chin and her neck. A plate piled with warm freshly baked cookies stood between them. He inhaled their aroma and snatched one off the plate. The chocolate was still sticky and gooey, just the way he liked them. He glanced at the empty chair next to him.

"Dad's not coming?"

She shook her head. "I'm sorry. I caught him just as he was leaving. He's heading back to the university."

"But it's Friday," Nick said. "Why is he going to work now?"

"He teaches a class on Fridays. Did you forget?" The blush on his mother's face told him that she herself had forgotten.

"Who in their right mind schedules a class for Friday night?" Nick asked. "I mean really?"

His mother shrugged and smiled. "Don't even attempt to try and figure out university administration. Their ways are strange and mysterious." The expression on her face grew more serious. "You said you wanted to talk. Do you prefer to wait until tomorrow when we're both here? Or we could talk later when your father gets home." She wrung her hands. "Although that could be quite late. As you know, he often loses track of time when he's involved in a project."

Nick paused for a moment. He didn't want to ruin tomorrow. "No, I can tell you. The messages are mainly for you."

A confused look crossed her face. "Messages? From school?"

"Not really," Nick said. "From Grandma."

Her mother's eyes widened. "Oh. From your visit with her at the hospital."

Nick swallowed. He was half-tempted to take the

coward's way out and say that the messages were from the night he went to see her at the hospital. But no, he was going to tell her the truth. That was the entire point of this although he had no idea how he was going to put his situation into words. His carefully rehearsed sentences now disappeared completely from his memory. He closed his eyes and took a breath. "No Mom. She showed up yesterday. Thursday."

A shadow crossed over her expression. "What are you talking about Nick? Yesterday was her funeral."

"She was there, and I talked to her in person." His voice cracked as he spoke but he proceeded onward, trying to get the words out as quickly as possible before she could stop him. "She told me to ask you if you remembered that afternoon when you were both in her room, and she ripped up all of Dad's letters."

Her mother drew a sharp breath. There was an incredulous look on her face "She told you about that?"

"She said to apologize to you, to tell you that she was wrong about Dad and wrong about Uncle Mitch. She understands now that Mitch was only trying to help and she appreciates the message from her husband."

She squinted her eyes. "I can't believe that she told you that. Did she tell you what Mitchell said to her as well?"

Nick nodded. She was taking this awfully well.

"She did," he said. "But she understands now that it was because he was passing on words Grandpa was telling him. He only wanted her husband's message to get to her so his spirit could go where it needed to go."

She furrowed her brow and leaned in closer to Nick. "Are you sure this didn't come from your Uncle?" Her voice was sharp, and she almost spat out the words.

"No, this came directly from Grandma," Nick said. "Yesterday."

"You mean when you saw her at the hospital," his mother said. She held up her index finger in a 'don't-say-another-word' gesture. "I don't think I want to hear any more of this. It's too soon, and I do not want to think about this right now."

She started to rise, but Nick stopped her. "Wait, Mom. Please."

She paused, looked at him with a resigned look on her face and then sat back down.

"She was at the funeral," Nick said, speaking even more quickly now. "Her ghost, her spirit or whatever you call it. She talked to both me and Uncle Mitch. She asked me to apologize to you and Dad for her. She also apologized to Uncle Mitch. You see Mom, I can see ghosts, just like Uncle Mitch. I've seen them for awhile now but didn't understand what they were. Then there was this scary man in Landon Bay who was screaming at his wife, although she couldn't see him. That was when I knew for sure what it was that I was seeing. Uncle Mitch explained it all to me."

"Stop it!" his mother snapped, before he could get in another word. She glared at him with steely eyes. "That's enough Nicholas. I don't want to hear one more word of this garbage. Did Mitchell fill your head with this crap? Is that it? Is this some kind of sick, twisted little game for him? To see how much damage he can inflict on this family?"

Nick reared back in his chair, startled by his mother's reaction. "Uncle Mitch had nothing to do with it. I told you. It was happening long before I told him. He suspected what was going on because he went through the exact same thing when he was my age. He explained it to me so I'd understand."

His mother shook her head. "No," she snapped. "I don't believe it. This is only your Uncle's crazy talk." She pointed her index finger at him. "From this point forward, I forbid you to have anything to do with that man. You will not talk to him on the phone; you will not go to his house or have any contact whatsoever with him. Do I make myself clear?

"But you've got to —"

"I don't have to do anything," said his mother, cutting him off. "Because of that man and his craziness, I almost lost your father. My mother was right that night. He's nuts, plain and simple and I can't believe that after all these years, he's still a menace to this family."

Nick felt the hot red rise in his cheeks. "Didn't you listen to a word that I said? This is happening to *me* and not to Uncle Mitch. He only helped me understand what was going on. The only reason I'm even telling you this is because I promised Grandma I would." He paused and enunciated each word. "*At. Her. Funeral.*"

"Enough Nick! You will not disrespect your Grandmother this way. Get to your room. I don't even want to look at you right now."

With that, she turned and left the room. Nick sat at the table, with warm tears streaming down his cheeks. That certainly went a lot more poorly than he had hoped. He wondered if it was worth even telling his father. No doubt he'd react the same way as Mom. It probably wasn't even up to him anyway. Nick guessed that his mother was probably on her cell right now recounting their conversation to his dad.

He thought back to the Eight of Swords card. Wasn't one of the meanings 'denial of the truth'? The card sure pegged that one right.

Nick threw his plate across the table, and it hit the buffet that was against the wall, making a loud crash as it broke into pieces. He pushed his chair aside, stormed up the steps and slammed the door to his room as hard as he could. The pile of paperbacks on his bookshelf tumbled to the floor.

Once the door was closed, he took out his phone. His

mother said he couldn't see his uncle or phone him. She didn't say anything about texting him.

Nick took out his phone and thumbed a text to his uncle.

"Told mom. All hell broke loose."

A minute later his phone buzzed. It was his Uncle Mitch.

"I was hoping they'd have come around by now."

Nick stared at the screen. He wiped his eyes with his sleeve. His heart was still ramming at his rib cage. He took a deep breath and thumbed his response.

"Didn't tell Dad yet. Mom blew a fuse."

Mitch responded a moment later.

"What did she say?" came his uncle's response.

"She said I can't see you or talk to you."

Nick waited for several minutes before his uncle texted back.

"Don't worry. I'll try to fix this."

Before he could type a response, another message from his uncle flashed.

"So sorry Nick. I never should've told you to tell them."

Nick typed his response.

"Not your fault. I did it because of Grandma."

Nick thought of his last encounter with his grandmother and smiled. He considered himself lucky that he'd been able to say goodbye to her one last time in person. Well, not really in person, in spirit. Nick knew that many people would give anything to see their deceased loved ones one more time.

His phone buzzed.

"I still feel responsible. Let me try to talk to them."

Nick thought of typing 'it's your funeral' but felt the choice of words inappropriate, especially given they had just all attended a funeral yesterday. Instead, he typed. *"OK. Talk to you l8tr."*

He stretched out on the bed and rehashed the conversation with his mom. Maybe it was all for the best. He didn't want to get involved with any of this ghost business anyway. This was a convenient way out. After all, his mother forbade him from having anything to do with it and maybe she was right. Maybe his uncle was batshit crazy. Of course, that'd mean that Nick was crazy too. Normal people don't interact with spirits.

And more than anything right now, Nick wanted to be normal.

Chapter Nine

Nick stared at the ceiling and looked again at the kitchen clock above the stove. The only sound in the room was the loud clanking of forks and knives against glass plates. Nobody spoke.

"What's up with the silent treatment?" said his sister. "Did I miss something."

"Finish your breakfast Melissa," said his mother. There was a sharp tone to her voice.

"Humph," Missy said and scooped up a forkful of scrambled eggs. "Fine. Be that way. Then I won't tell you what I saw yesterday."

Out of the corner of his eye, Nick noticed that his father kept staring at him but whenever Nick turned to look at him, his father jerked his head away and broke the gaze.

Yeah, his mom definitely had told him about their talk.

He was half-tempted to ask his father if there was something he wanted to say to him but held back. No sense getting into anything now, especially given that Gabe would be arriving any minute. His mom, on the other hand, didn't look at him or talk to him once. What did she think of him now? Did she think he was some kind a freak? An asshole? A liar?

"Tell us what you saw yesterday, honey," said Nick's dad. "We're listening."

A car horn sounded outside, and Nick breathed an audible sigh of relief. He couldn't get out of there fast enough.

"Gabe's here. See you later on." He had told his parents earlier in the week that he was spending the day with Gabe at the Renaissance Faire.

His mother jumped up and rushed to the window. Nick tensed his jaw.

"No, it's really Gabe," said Nick to her through his teeth. His voice was barely above a whisper. "I'm not so stupid as to have Uncle Mitch come to the house after the way you acted yesterday."

His mother flashed him the look of death before he rushed out of the house.

He smiled when he saw the Gabe behind the wheel of his parents' gray SUV. When Nick opened the car door, his friend's warm grin greeted him. Twin dimples displayed on his rosy cheeks.

"Sup," said Gabe as Nick closed his door.

Gabe was wearing dark green shorts which drew attention even more to his fuzzy blond legs. A tight white t-shirt hugged Gabe's well-developed body. A white and red baseball cap turned backward hid Gabe's longish blond crop of hair. His electric sapphire blue eyes twinkled as he met Nick's gaze and all at once, Nick felt his insides go runny.

Gabe's expression turned serious. "Something wrong? Dude, y'all got the strangest look on your face."

Nick shook himself and shook his head. "Nah, just my mom. She's being kind of a bitch this morning."

"Ain't that always the way," said Gabe and turned his regard back to the road. "So how are things? Missed you at lunch yesterday. I was fixin' to send out a search party." Gabe's soft southern accent melted off his tongue, the words flowing smoothly and unhurriedly like a lazy river in late summer.

Nick thought back to Friday and recalled a particularly intimidating-looking male ghost that was attached to a student who was entering the lunchroom. Nick didn't want to risk it noticing him, so he ate his lunch outside.

"Tons of crap to do," Nick said. "Had to play some catch-up since I missed school on Thursday."

"That's right. Your grandma's funeral. How was it?"

Before he could answer, Gabe continued. "I didn't mean how was the funeral. Shit, I know how funerals are. Bummer. Meant more how are you and everyone doing?"

"It's all pretty much blown over now. Things are back to normal." *Except for the fact that I now can see spirits. How about that?*

"So we're off the faire," Nick said.

"Hell yes! Glad to go this year. It's always big fun."

"Too bad Sam couldn't come," Nick lied. He was actually happy to have Gabe all to himself.

"No biggie," said Gabe. "Sam can be kind of a drag sometimes. You know what I mean?"

Nick nodded but said nothing further. He knew precisely what Gabe meant. The few times they'd hung out, Sam struck Nick as being a complainer, always seeming to find something about which to gripe or pout. Nick had privately nicknamed Sam "Sammy the Whiner'. Of course, he wasn't about to tell Gabe that, given that Sam was more Gabe's friend than Nick's. Nick had felt guilty for the nickname later on when he found out that Sam's mom had died not too long before.

They talked about school and their classes during the rest of the ride. Twenty minutes later, they arrived at the gate. Nick was surprised by the number of cars in the parking lot, considering that the faire didn't open for another ten minutes. Evidently, a lot of people had decided to take advantage of the sunny 80-degree day and come out to the Renaissance Faire. In previous years, they had always attended the faire in the middle of summer, and it had been scorching hot each time they'd gone, to the point of misery. This year, given that it wasn't even officially summer yet, the temperature was perfect.

It was too early for the official gates to be open, but there was a funny over-the-top skit taking place in the courtyard, having to do with mistaken identities, gossiping housemaids, and revolving bedroom doors. By the time a large busty woman dressed in a tight Elizabethan gown had shown up to unlatch the gates, Nick and Gabe were almost rolling on the ground with laughter.

Gabe patted him on the back. "Guess it pays to come early. That shit was hysterical."

"Yeah, this is the first time we've ever come before opening," Nick said. "Who knew they put on shows before opening?"

They walked around the park, stopping at several shops along the way. Nick felt nervous when he noticed that some of the vendors sold items such as Tarot decks, crystal balls, and other things that Nick thought of as *witchy*. There were a couple of unique looking Tarot decks that grabbed his attention as he browsed. He even picked up one one of them, and Gabe had giggled when he caught him. Nick felt himself blush and put the deck back down.

As they neared the end of the fairground, Nick pulled his phone out of his pocket and glanced at the screen.

"What time is it?" Gabe asked.

"Twenty after eleven."

"That means we only have ten minutes to find out where Marty the Marvelous is going to be."

Shortly after they had entered the gates, they noticed a

sign announcing that world-renowned comedian, juggler, illusionist and acrobat Marty the Marvelous would be on stage at 11:30 a.m. They both agreed that this was a show they didn't want to miss.

Nick pointed. "I think it's next to Sean's Kilted Treasures, right over the there."

"I do believe you're right," Gabe said. "Before we go in, I'm going to go use the privy." Privy was Rennie talk for the restroom.

"I'll be waiting right here."

Once Gabe left, Nick plopped down beneath a tree in the shade. They'd only been walking around for a little over an hour, and already Nick's feet were sore. It felt good to get off of them for a bit and sit down.

All at once, Nick had the oddest feeling that someone was watching him. There were no prickly skin or stomach acrobatics, so it wasn't a ghost. He looked around and noticed a youngish woman with bright wild red hair intensely staring at him. She sat at her table, hands tented under her chin, her eyes gazing right at Nick — or at least it looked that way. He looked over his shoulder to make sure that there wasn't someone else she was staring at but nobody else was near him. He noticed the sign above her head.

Psychic Readings by Katrina.

As he read the words, his mouth went dry. There was someone else like him. Someone who might understand. He turned his gaze back to the young woman and now she was smiling as her eyes met his. Was she smiling at him? His hands trembled as he contemplated walking over to her table. What would she have to tell him if he did? Could she see what was in his future? Gabe's voice interrupted his thoughts.

"Damn, that bathroom was packed. I swear that all of creation decided they had to drain the dragon at the same time."

"Must have been that everybody wanted to take one final whiz before seeing Marty the Magnificent," Nick said, and they both laughed.

Nick got up and kept his eyes fixed on Gabe, trying to ignore the strange psychic woman across the way. He swore that he could still feel her staring at him.

An older lady wearing a huge yellow hat and a flowery dress crossed right in front of him, and before Nick could stop himself, he plowed right into her.

Except that he didn't plow right into her. He moved right through her.

Nick almost looked up to apologize but then quickly stopped himself. He didn't want to let her know that he could see her.

"What are y'all jerking around about?" Gabe said. "For a second there, I thought you were gonna to fall."

Nick's eyes climbed to meet Gabe's. "Stumbled on a tree root," Nick said. His voice shook as he spoke.

"Oh yeah? One got me earlier," Gabe replied. "Gotta keep an eye out."

Against his better judgment, Nick stole one last glance toward the Psychic Readings booth. The woman was still gawking at him, but now she was wearing a smug smile. Had she seen the ghost too? Could she tell that Nick saw the spirit? She crossed her arms over her chest as if daring him to come over to her booth.

"Come on," Gabe said. "Show starts in a couple of minutes."

Almost all of the chairs for Marty the Magnificent's show had already been taken. Nick and Gabe found two empty seats toward the back yet still in full view of the stage.

Thunderous applause broke out for what Nick assumed was Marty the Magnificent's grand entrance. He looked up at the stage to see a tall, lanky goofy-looking man wearing a tiny black derby and riding a unicycle. Nick snickered. He tried to keep his attention focused on the show but couldn't concentrate. His thoughts kept drifting to Katrina the psychic. He needed someone to confide in, someone who didn't think he was nuts. His uncle had talked about psychics and mentioned that they could often provide guidance on an otherwise confusing situation. Maybe she'd know what to do about this ghost stuff and how he could make it go away.

Unable to stand it anymore, he leaned over and whispered in Gabe's ear.

"Gonna run to the loo."

Gabe looked at him and frowned. "Dude, you shoulda gone when I did."

Nick nodded. "Be back in a bit."

Nick made a beeline for the psychic booth. His heart sunk when he saw that it was empty. A moment later, the woman appeared from behind the curtain.

Nick approached the table. "Are you Katrina?" he stammered.

Her eyes narrowed, and she curtsied. "The one and only. And you are?"

"Nick," he said.

She looked him up and now. "I like Nicholas better. It's more fitting." She pronounced his name *nee-ko-la*.

Nick stood in stunned silence having no idea how to respond. The woman continued.

"I want to read you, young Nicholas." Her voice was throaty and low, almost seductive. She spoke with just a hint of an accent. "I have much to tell you. I saw you before with your friend and your aura was almost screaming to me."

Nick swallowed. "I'm not quite sure what much of that means."

She gave a gave a hearty laugh. "So you're a newbie, huh? Don't you fret, young one. Katrina will guide you."

"I'm not that much younger than you," Nick said, a tremble in his voice. It was true. The woman looked like she was in her 30's — early to mid probably. Although now that Nick looked at her more closely, she could very easily be older than that. She was one of those people whose age it was hard to tell.

"You're young enough. Are you even eighteen yet?"

"I'll be seventeen in a couple of months."

"To me, anyone under thirty is a mere babe. But I don't mean just your age, Nicholas. You are also new to all of this." She swept the air with her arm in a grand gesture.

"I guess so," Nick replied. "Although I'm not quite sure I know what all of *this* is."

Katrina narrowed her eyes. "You saw that spirit earlier, didn't you? The woman with the yellow hat?"

Nick sucked in a sharp breath. He was definitely in the right place. Now he was sure of it. He nodded, his excitement rising.

"I did see her. So you can see ghosts too?"

She closed her eyes for a moment and inhaled deeply. "Funny thing that. I can't always see them. To be honest, it's a rather rare occurrence for me to see a spirit. But for some inexplicable reason, whenever there's another medium nearby, their power channels to me and I'm able to see what they see. It's the oddest thing, really. So I guess you could say that I'm a medium myself except that I channel the visions of another medium." She creased her brow as her gaze locked onto Nick. "You *do* know that you're a medium, right?"

"My uncle told me only a little over a week ago. He's one too."

She clapped her hands. "Genetic mediums. I love it! It's not too often I see the likes of you." She looked him up and down and then gestured with her hand to follow her. "Come, let's go in the back. It's time for your reading."

She gestured again to him — this time with her head — and Nick followed her behind the curtain. There stood a small wobbly-looking card table over which was draped a black cloth. In the black cloth was embroidered a purple 5-pointed star, which reminded Nick of the suit of Pentacles in his Tarot deck. On top of the table was a crystal ball and next to it was a deck of cards, which Nick guessed to be Tarot although the backs were different than his deck.

"Really?" he said, pointing to the crystal ball.

She wagged her finger at him. "Don't be too hasty to judge, young one. These are all tools that we use to tune into energies. The crystal ball is used to scry. If we concentrate on an item such as a foggy crystal or a black mirror, soon the surface jumps to life with images. So tell me; have you used any tools such as a mirror or cards?"

Nick shrugged. "I've used Tarot cards. My uncle gave me one of his decks."

She snapped her fingers. "There you go. They are no different than my crystal ball. They are a tool to help a psychic to focus his or her energy." She flashed him a smile. "Here's a little trick of the trade, hon. I personally don't need such accoutrements. I get visions just from touching a client or something that belongs to a client. But instead of just staring at them while I'm waiting for the visions to appear — which they sometimes don't, by the way — these items give me something on which to concentrate. If you end up doing readings, you'll appreciate this little tidbit of advice."

Nick crossed his arms. "I don't plan on doing readings. Ever."

Katrina raised her eyebrows. "Oh?"

"Yeah. I just want this ghost thing that I have to go away."

She drew in a whoosh of air. "So *that's* why you ignored that poor spirit earlier, the one you walked through?"

Nick swallowed. "I didn't mean to pass through her. I didn't know she was a spirit at the time."

"But you didn't acknowledge her afterwards."

"No. I didn't want her to know that I could see her. I was with my friend and —"

Katrina interrupted him. "Regardless. Would you not say excuse me if you bumped into someone? These spirits are *people* too, not mere objects to be ignored. Imagine if you died and woke up tomorrow. You are the same as you are now; you have the same thoughts, feelings, hopes, and desires. You are the same Nicholas as you always were. You are the same *person.* It's the same with the spirits. Walking through them without saying excuse me is just as rude as brusquely bumping into someone and saying nothing."

Nick hung his head. "Sorry. I didn't know."

"Nicholas," she said softly.

He raised his head to look at her.

"I'm not scolding you. I'm teaching you. How do we learn anything if there is not someone there to teach us? We all started out as blank slates, right?"

Nick nodded. "I suppose so."

"Good," she said in a cheery tone. "Let's get started with your reading."

"I don't have too much time," Nick said. "I left my friend at the show and told him that I was just going to the bathroom."

"We'd best get on with it then." She rested her hands on the table, palms facing upward. "Grab hold of both my hands."

Nick did as he was told. A couple of moments later, her body jerked a couple of times. Nick couldn't help but wonder if she was just putting on a show for him.

"Shit Nicholas, you are one hell of a medium aren't you?"

Her eyes remained closed. He didn't know if he was supposed to answer, so he didn't.

"Your grandmother just passed, correct?"

"Yeah."

"I'm seeing a flower. It looks like a rose. Does that mean anything to you?"

Nick nodded. "Her name was Rose." Okay, this woman was might be the real deal. He was nearly convinced now.

"Just as you said, you come from a long line of mediums. Strange though that it's only on the male side. I don't think I've ever encountered a family of genetic boy mediums before." Her eyes flipped open. "That doesn't mean that it's unheard of, mind you. It's just I haven't yet met any until now." She tapped her chin with her index finger. "No wait, there was one I knew. A long time ago."

Nick nodded, and she closed her eyes again.

"You really don't want to be a psychic, do you?" she asked.

"I want to be normal. I didn't even know I was like this until recently. I just want things to go back to the way they were. I want to live a normal life and have kids."

"Kids, huh? And how do you think that's going to happen? By magic?"

"What?"

"Never mind. You'll figure that out soon enough." She sat silent for several minutes, nodding occasionally and saying "yes" or "okay" every now and then. She finally opened her eyes.

"Nicholas, I don't know how much you're going to like what I have to tell you."

"Is it bad? Is something bad going to happen to me?"

"No, no no, nothing like that. Here's the thing, Nicky boy. You are destined to be one of the most powerful mediums that the psychic community has ever seen. You've quite a future ahead of you, my young friend. That is if you follow the path laid out before you. From what I could gather, you shall potentially make a huge difference in the world and you will be able to help *a lot* of people using your gift."

Nick stared at her and said nothing, his brain trying to make sense out of everything she had just said. He finally broke the silence.

"What if I don't want to?" he asked. His voice was just above a whisper. "What if I just ignore it and go back to the way things were?"

"Did you not get what I was telling you? You have an opportunity to help a tremendous amount of people."

"Ghosts, you mean. Not people."

She tensed. "Here we go again. They *are* people. If you learn nothing else before you leave my booth, I want you to take this with you: spirits are folks, just like us, only they don't have bodies at the moment. Understand?"

Nick nodded. "I understand."

"Good," she said. "And about your comment about ignoring it? Well," she paused and looked upward. She appeared as though she were in deep thought. "It's pretty much your destiny Nicholas, your *raison d'être* as it were. This is what you were born to do."

"I shouldn't have come here," Nick said, his voice low.

"I don't think you had a choice," Katrina said. "The spirits pretty much guided you right to me. I got the impression I'm supposed to teach you. Who would have ever guessed? Me, teaching someone."

"Teach me?"

"I've been in this business for a long time, and while I may not be as powerful as you ultimately will be, I do know my way around the psychic world. I can at least point you in the right direction. But yeah, when I was channeling, I got the strong impression that I should serve as your guide. Help you to get your feet wet, as it were."

"So you're telling me that I don't have any choice in this? That I have to spend the rest of my life talking to ghosts?"

She shook her head. "You're seeing this all wrong. This isn't a curse that was thrust upon you to punish you and make your life miserable. It is gift given to you by The Universe. You're a gift to the world, Nicholas; a light in the darkness. It's not everyone's lot in life to be in a position where they can make such a difference in the lives of others. But you are. You are fortunate and blessed."

Nick considered this briefly. "I get what you are saying. I'm just not feeling all that blessed at the moment. This is something I never wanted. Heck, I didn't even know any of this stuff existed."

"Do you think Joan of Arc asked for her gifts of prophecy? Or that Edgar Cayce, a devout Christian by the way, wanted his gift of psychic healing? No. They didn't ask for or pray for these gifts. Their abilities were given to them, as was their destiny. You can become a great person Nicholas and accomplish extraordinary things. But in order to do so, you'll need to accept what and who you are."

"And how am I supposed to do that when ghosts scare the crap out of me? Not to mention that I'm not real fond of meeting new people and I despise being the center of attention. Judging by what my uncle told me, most of this work involves dealing with ghosts and strangers. Not a great combination, in my book."

Katrina laughed. "Oh, you'll adjust just fine. I'll let you in on a little secret. I'm afraid of ghosts too, and I'm a major introvert. Yes, you heard correctly, Katrina the Psychic is excruciatingly shy. But we learn to adapt. When we awaken to what I refer to as '*the calling*,' then we do what we must to get the job done." She flashed him a warm smile, reached out and took both of his hands. "Don't you like the idea of being a powerful psychic?"

Nick smiled back and shrugged. Maybe it wouldn't hurt to at least explore this a bit, to see what kind of instruction Katrina has to offer. "I guess it could be kinda cool."

"It is indeed cool," Katrina said. She let go of his hands. "Has your uncle given you any coaching yet?"

"Not much. He explained what it is we do and gave me a deck of Tarot cards. I don't know how much more he can show me. My mom's forbidden me to have anything to do with him."

Katrina rubbed her chin. "Ah. That must be the reason I am asked to be your guide. I was wondering about that. First of all, are you local?"

"I live about twenty minutes from downtown in Gallowspine Mountains."

"Is that North or South?"

"Northside."

"Excellent. I live not too far from you, in Landon Bay. You go to the local high school right?

Nick nodded.

"How about transportation? Do you drive?"

"I use my mom's car and take it to school most days. If the weather's nice, I use my scooter.

"Good. So here's what we'll do. I'd like to see you at least two days a week after school. More if you can swing it."

"So you're going to give me lessons?" Nick asked.

"Yeah," she said. "But only if you're open to learning and if you accept what you are."

Nick thought for a moment. He finally nodded. "Deal. I'm willing to learn more about this stuff. I might need some help dealing with a particularly nasty ghost."

She raised her eyebrows. "You've been out in the field already?"

"What do you mean?"

"You've had dealings with spirits who need help?"

"Not really. I kinda stumbled upon it by accident."

Katrina snickered. "That's usually how it happens, hon. We don't find the ghosts, the ghosts find us. Although to be frank with you, I'm not all that experienced in working with spirits who haven't crossed over. But I'm guessing that the teacher shall become the student as well." She reached into the pocket of her dress and pulled out a card. "My business card. It has my address, cell, and email. Feel free to call if you ever need to."

Nick tucked the card into his back pocket. "So how much is this all teaching going to cost? I don't have a lot of money."

She looked at him amused. "There's no charge, sweetie. This is on me. It's not every psychic who's been given the opportunity to teach the potentially strongest medium that the world has ever known." She gave him a slight bow. "It'll be an honor to be your teacher."

"Only if you promise me one thing," Nick said.

She raised her eyebrows, surprised. "And what is that?"

"Never call me Nicky boy again."

She laughed. "Done. One more question. Do you text?"

"Duh, who doesn't?" Nick replied.

"Feel free to text me then. I have a lot of appointments, and sometimes it's not easy to get a hold of me by phone."

Just at that moment, Nick's phone buzzed in his pocket. Shit, he'd forgotten all about Gabe.

WTF dude? Where r u????

Nick thumbed out a quick response.

"Be there in a sec."

He rose his head to look at Katrina. "Sorry about that. It was my friend. Gotta go."

"Gabe, is it?" She had a sly smile on her face.

"Yeah. How did you know?"

"How do you think?" she said. She tapped her forehead with her index finger and then dismissed him with a wave of her hand. "Better get moving. Don't keep your friend waiting any longer. We'll get things going next week."

Nick was out of breath when he reached the stage where Gabe stood waiting.

"Dude," said Gabe. "Where in the fuck were you? Marty was awesome. I can't believe you missed the whole friggin' thing."

"Sorry," Nick said. "Went to piss but then the situation turned out being a lot more serious than I'd originally thought." Nick rubbed his tummy for emphasis.

"You feel okay now?" Gabe asked. "Do you want to leave?"

The look on Gabe's face told Nick that he would be disappointed if they left now.

Nick shook his head. "Nah, I'm much better. I'll be fine." And for the first time, Nick felt as though things might indeed be fine. Thanks to his new friend, Katrina — although he wasn't quite sure how she managed to talk him into following through with this ghost business.

"Awesome!" Gabe said. He was looking at the schedule that he'd just taken from his pocket. "The next thing up is 'Jousting to the Death'!"

Chapter Ten

Nick sat at the desk in his room working on Monday's math assignment when there was a light tap at the door. He hoped it wasn't his mother here to give him more crap — but that seemed unlikely. Ever since he told her that he could see ghosts, she'd barely spoken a word to him. It was the silent treatment, big time.

"Come in," he said. It was his father.

"What are you up to son?" his dad asked.

"Algebra homework."

"Waited until the last minute again huh?"

"The past few days have been kinda crazy," Nick replied. The conversation struck him as odd, given that his father was not one for chit-chat and never came to Nick's room.

"School's out soon, isn't it?"

Nick nodded. "Another week and then exams."

His father smiled. "You had a nice time with Gabriel yesterday?"

Nick nodded. "It was a blast. More than I had hoped."

His father nodded and wrung his hands. "Your mother told me that you had a talk with her the other day."

Nick turned his chair so that he was completely facing his father. He nodded. "It didn't go all that well."

"So I gathered," his father replied. He brushed his fingers through his hair and sighed. "This is one conversation that I was hoping you and I would never need to have."

"It's not easy for me either," said Nick.

"I'm sure it isn't. I remember when your uncle was your age and he started to...," he paused as if looking for the right words. "See things. He told our mother, and of course, she had no idea what was going on. Father finally talked to him, and it came out that he could see these things too. At that time, Father hadn't told Mother about his ability and truth be told, I don't think he ever did. Mitch confided in me that the reason our father was gone so much was that he was out helping spirits cross over to wherever they needed to be. I never knew whether to believe Mitch or not. Father certainly never mentioned any of it to me."

"Was Uncle Mitch scared when it first started happening?" Nick asked.

"Terrified. I once found him during the middle of the day in bed with the covers pulled over his head. He told me that he didn't want the crazy ghost lady to find him. At the time, I thought that Mitch was the crazy one."

"So your mother never had a clue what was going on?"

"Not that I know of," his father said. "I could tell that Mitch was tormented by what was going on, but I felt helpless. I could neither understand nor relate to what he was going through. Then, he and Father began spending a lot more time together, but Mitch would never tell me what they were up to. It was a secret between him and Father he'd say, which angered me to no end. I suppose I was a tad jealous that they didn't include me in their outings. I felt a bit left out if you know what I mean."

Nick nodded. "Did Uncle Mitch talk to you a lot about

the spirits he saw?" Nick noticed that his father flinched at the word spirits.

"No, he stopped talking about it altogether, although he was different kid after that. More serious. Much too serious for his age, if you ask me. The topic never came up again until that dreaded Thanksgiving night when I was still dating your mother. After that, I forbade him ever to bring it up again."

"Grandma told me about it, about what Uncle Mitch said to her that night," Nick said.

"Not a very pleasant scene, I assure you. Since he hadn't mentioned it to me in years, I had hoped that Mitch was over all that ghost stuff. I thought that maybe it had gone away or that it was all in his head. But apparently, it hadn't, and it wasn't. I was never so embarrassed and furious with Mitchell as I was that night. We didn't talk for a long time after that."

"Grandma said that she tried to keep you and Mom apart.

"Indeed she did." His father chuckled. "But she wasn't very successful. Your mother and I were quite determined and continued to see each other on the sly. Eventually, your grandmother found out, and then all hell broke loose. But finally, she gave in. I imagine she realized that she wasn't going to be able to keep us apart, so she lightened up a little. I don't think she ever forgave Mitch though. They didn't see each other ever again after that."

"Mitch and Grandma made up," Nick said.

His father's eyes grew wide. "They did? When?"

"At the funeral. Grandma apologized to Mitch for the way she acted and said that she understands everything now."

His father was silent for several moments, apparently struggling with what to say next. He sighed. "So it's true. Your mother said that you saw your grandmother on Thursday."

Nick nodded. He noticed that his father avoided looking

directly at Nick. "She and Uncle Mitch talked for a few moments and then she asked me to pass on a message to you and Mom. The only reason that I told mom any of this is because I promised Grandma I would."

His father turned and met Nick's gaze. He looked visibly shaken. "She had a message for me?"

"She told me to apologize to you for meddling the way she did, trying to keep you and Mom apart. She said that she was sorry for the way she acted and she now understood why Uncle Mitch did what he did."

"Mitch still was wrong," his father said. Nick could hear the venom in his voice. Apparently, he hadn't quite forgiven Uncle Mitch either. "He had no business telling somebody something they didn't specifically ask to hear. He nearly ruined my chances with your mother."

"The ghosts can be very persistent," Nick said, recalling what his uncle had told him. "Sometimes they scream in your ear until you do what they ask you to."

His father raised his eyebrows. "So you see them all the time? Just like Mitch and our father?"

Nick nodded. "I didn't know what was going on at first. I just knew something wasn't quite right. I was nauseous all the time with a constant upset stomach."

"Ah yes. I remember your uncle telling me about those same physical symptoms when he saw one of them."

"Uncle Mitch figured out what was happening to me and told me how to deal with them. Mostly, they want help figuring out why they're still here or sometimes they have something urgent to tell someone. Some of them don't even know they're dead."

His father closed his eyes for a moment and then reopened them. "Oh, son. I never even considered the possibility that you might turn out like Mitch. I feel so bad that this has happened to you — is happening to you."

Nick shrugged. "It's okay now Dad. I'm all right with it."

"You are?"

Nick nodded. "I know that it's something that I was born with and if I can help people, that's a good thing, right?"

His father studied Nick's face for a moment. "So will you be going out with your uncle?" he said, avoiding Nick's question. Nick decided not to pursue it and let it go.

"He's not feeling too well these days. He says that I have to learn on my own."

"What in the hell is up with that?" his father said. "More like lazy, if you ask me. He hardly ever leaves the house anymore."

Nick shrugged. "I dunno. He said that his doctor told him that he couldn't get excited and had to take it easy."

Nick's dad raised his eyebrows. "Really? I had no idea that he was ill. That's how estranged we've become."

"I don't think that Uncle Mitch talks about that kind of stuff with anybody. The only reason he told me was that I insisted that he help me with a ghost. Uncle is a mysterious guy."

"That he is," his father agreed. "But hopefully he can at least explain things to you and point you in the right direction."

"He has," Nick said. "We've had a couple of nice talks, and he even gave me a deck of Tarot cards."

His father's face drained of color. "For God's sake, don't let your mother see them. She'll burn them for sure, maybe even call an exorcist, while she's at it." He laughed at his own joke.

Time to move them back into the closet, Nick thought. He'd come to treasure his uncle's cards and certainly didn't want to see his deck transformed into a pile of ash. "Speaking of Mom, she said that I couldn't see Uncle Mitch or even talk to him on the phone."

"You have to understand how she feels, Nick. She never forgave him for that night and believe you me, that woman can hold a grudge. But I think there's more to it than that. She's afraid for you."

"Why would she be afraid for me? Afraid the spirits might hurt me?"

His father shook his head. "I don't think that's it. She's seen the kind of life that Mitch has led, alone and separated from his family. Okay, I'll admit that we had a little something to do with that, but Mitch's life has not been easy."

"How so?" Nick asked. "He never talks much about his past."

"He's always been on the fringes of society, never allowing anyone to get too close to him. Come to think of it, I don't recall him ever dating anyone. A couple of times in high school perhaps, but since then, I don't believe so. Through the years, he's become more and more reclusive. Almost a hermit. I think that your mother fears that you'll end up the same way."

Nick had known that his uncle lived alone and was a bit of a loner, but he was unaware that his uncle kept others out of his life.

"I promise I won't let that happen," Nick said. "I won't keep people away."

"You know you can talk to me about any of this, if it starts weighing you down, right? We love you and support you."

"What about mom?" Nick asked. "She's okay with this now?"

His father closed his eyes for a moment and then reopened them. "We're going to have to give her a bit more time. She's having a difficult time with this. Your mother is a little rigid in her thinking, and it takes her awhile to adjust to anything new."

"Does this mean that I can see Uncle Mitch again?" Nick asked.

"If he can help you adjust to all of this, then I don't see why not. Maybe he can pass on some of the information that our father taught him although what that might be, I have no idea." He paused. "And to be truthful Nick, I don't want to know. We'll just let that stay between you and your uncle."

"Thank's Dad. I will."

"I also ask that you be careful out there. I'm not quite sure what it is exactly that Mitchell does, but I need to know that you're not going to get into anything that's potentially dangerous."

Nick thought about the angry ghost who may have been murdered by his wife. It doesn't get much more dangerous than that. Nick felt a pang of guilt as he thought about Janet and how frightened she was.

"I promise that I won't get involved in anything dangerous."

His dad smiled. "Good to hear. Oh, and if you do spend time with Mitchell, maybe it's be a good idea not to tell your mother, okay? Let's give her a little time."

"But you'll talk to her, right? Help her come around?"

His father's smile faded, and he rose. He tapped Nick's shoulder twice. "I'll do what I can. In the meantime, you might not want to tell anyone else about this. Not everyone will understand, and some people may make life difficult for you because of it."

"I don't plan on it, believe me."

His father nodded. "And make sure that this doesn't affect your school work. School comes before everything. Got it?"

Nick nodded. "Got it."

When the door snapped closed, Nick sighed. That went better than it did with his mother although it certainly was a strange conversation. Even though his father was trying to come across as being supportive, Nick got the impression that he really didn't understand, and if he did, he was not at all pleased about it. At least he gave Nick the green light to contact his uncle again. He pulled out his phone and thumbed out a text.

Dad says that I can see you again.

His uncle's response came a moment later.

And your mother?

The jury is still out. Dad said not to tell her.

Nick waited. It was a couple of minutes before his phone buzzed.

How about tomorrow after school?

Nick was reminded that he still needed to contact Katrina to set up some times to meet. He wondered how his uncle would react to Nick's sessions with her.

Sounds good. c u then.

Nick went back to his algebra, in spite of his strong urge to pull out the cards and ask them questions about what was coming. Maybe it's not a good idea to depend on the Tarot for every little thing. He'd have to ask his uncle about that when we saw him tomorrow.

IT WAS ONLY WITH THE GREATEST OF EFFORT THAT NICK kept his eyes forward as he walked down the halls of the school. It seemed that there were more ghosts than ever roaming the halls, most of them yammering away at an unaware student. Now that Nick thought about it, he'd noticed adults following students for quite some time but had never paid attention to it before. Why were there so many of them?

He remembered promising Katrina that he would help spirits whenever he came across them. But not here. Not at school. While it's true that everyone told him that this path was going to be difficult, there was no need to make it even more so. He'd limit his ghost busting to non-school hours.

One particular spirit caught his attention and Nick couldn't help but look, only because she was hovering around Gabe's friend Sam. A stately looking woman with flowing raven black hair was following him and talking in a loud, forceful voice. Her skin was a bluish color but other than that, she was lovely.

"Listen to me, Sammy. There's a small shoebox on the top shelf of my closet. In there is the address of your father. We've been keeping in contact over the years, but he wasn't ready for you to know who he was."

Sam kept walking, oblivious to the woman's presence. That only made her speak all the louder.

"You need to find your father and meet him. You need to tell him what happened to me. He doesn't know."

Judging by the way that this particular woman was talking to him, he guessed that she was Sam's mother. Nick thought back. That's right, Sam's mom had died not too long ago. How long ago, he couldn't recall. He vaguely remembered Gabe telling him that Sam's father was dead too. So why was she telling Sam he needed to call his father? Stepfather perhaps? What a pity that Gabe wasn't the one who could see spirits since Sam was closer to Gabe than he was.

Without thinking, Nick leaned against the lockers, closely watching and listening to the scene before him. The woman's head then turned, and she locked eyes with Nick. Before he could look away, the woman stood directly in front of him, only inches away.

Nick loudly drew in a sharp breath.

"You can see me! Oh my God, nobody has been able to see me. Please. You have to help me."

Nick thought about not responding, pretending that he

didn't see her but he knew that it was too late for that. She'd caught him watching her and had heard him gasp.

He looked up and noticed several people watching him. Shit. They must have heard him as well. He brought his hand up to his mouth and faked a coughing fit. He turned and began walking down the hallway in the opposite direction. She walked along beside him. Her perfume smelled of jasmine. He was surprised; he had no idea that ghosts had odors.

"Please, I beg of you. Don't ignore me. You're the first person who has even acknowledged that I'm here."

Nick held an index finger to his mouth. "Shhh," he said out of the corner of his mouth. "I'll talk to you in a moment."

She looked confused but followed along with him. He turned the corner and noticed a dark classroom. He gestured with his head to the ghost, and they both entered the room.

"Why so mysterious?" she asked.

"Because nobody can see you but me. If we started conversing in the hallway, everyone would think I was talking to myself. They'd think I was crazy."

She held his gaze. There was little doubt that the woman in front of him was Sam's mom. Nick could see Sam in her features.

"Why can you see me and nobody else can?" she asked.

"Luck of the draw, I guess," Nick said. "It's a family thing. Both my uncle and my grandpa were able to see spirits but according to my uncle, only the ones who have not crossed over."

"Well, thank heaven for that," she said. She gave him a warm smile. This spirit was completely different than James, the angry husband. Nick felt nothing but warmth radiating from her.

"Why haven't you crossed over?"

She creased her brow. "I don't know. How does one go about it?"

"There's supposed to be a light that you need to go into."

"Ah yes, the infamous yet elusive light," she said. "Nope. I never saw anything like that. I woke up, not knowing where I was or what had happened to me. It took me awhile to figure out that I had died. I'd completely forgotten about my illness. Needless to say, I wasn't happy about the situation at all."

Nick nodded. "I'm sure it must have been difficult."

"You have no idea! I wandered around for weeks — maybe even longer — confused and frightened before I figured out that I was dead. Once I realized it, I remembered that I had neglected to tell Sam something important. It was something that I had meant to do while I was alive but unfortunately, I never got around to it. The next thing I knew, I found myself by his side at school, and I've stayed with him ever since." She paused for a moment and then pointed at Nick. "Do you know my son? Do you know Sam?"

Nick nodded "We've hung out a few times. My name's Nick Michelson."

She thought for a moment. "I think I remember Sam mentioning you. Were you over the house once? You were with another kid, a good-looking boy. Southern, I think. I don't recall his name."

"Gabe," Nick said.

"That's it! You were with Gabe. So you know my Sammy! So you can tell him about his father."

"What about his father?"

She gestured to the desk for Nick to sit down. He did.

"Sam never knew his father. I suppose you could say that Sammy was a surprise baby. I was dating his father in high school in my sophomore year and unexpectedly became pregnant. Back then, I was much more unreasonable than I am now, some might say downright pig-headed. Sam's father wanted to do the right thing and offered to marry me, but I wanted nothing at all to do with him. I more or less cut him out of my life." She sighed.

"Completely?" Nick asked.

She nodded. "Utterly. It was an easy thing to do because my parents were furious with him. They'd threatened to call the police if he came anywhere near me. He was eighteen, and I was almost seventeen. Probably around your age. But legally, I was still a minor, so my parents could have gotten him thrown in jail for statutory rape."

"But he didn't rape you." Nick swallowed. "Did he?"

She shook her head. "Statutory rape means having intercourse with a minor so yes, he could have gone to prison. But they made a deal with him. They would not press charges as long as he stayed far away from me."

"So did he stay away?"

She sighed. "He did. I don't know why I was so angry with him at the time. It's not like it was all his fault. I was a more than willing partner. But you know how it is. You always blame the boy. I felt that he had ruined my life. I had plans and dreams that I would never be able to fulfill all because of him. No, I made it quite clear that I wanted nothing to do with him."

She grew quiet as if revisiting a distant memory.

"So you never saw him again?"

She shook her head. "Not until a couple of years ago. My parents made me take the year off from school. I suppose they didn't want me waddling down the hallways at school. So I stayed home during my junior year, gave birth to Sammy and then picked up with my studies the following year."

"Wow," said Nick. "I can't believe Sam's dad gave up that easily."

"Oh, he didn't give up. Even though he promised my parents that he would stay away from me, Mark called several times after I had the baby. But I refused to talk to him. I was a self-centered, stubborn little brat back then. Mark pleaded with me, begging to see the baby — his baby — but I was having none of it. I ignored the fact that Sammy was his child too. By the time I returned to school the following year, he had graduated and was off to college. After that, he never contacted me again, even after I turned eighteen."

"Sam never knew who his father was? Never met him?"

"No. Mark found me online a couple of years ago and sent me an email message. We corresponded back and forth a few times and met in person not too long after that." She sighed dreamily. "He was even more handsome than he was in high school."

"So he wasn't still pissed at you?"

"Surprisingly, no. During our talk, I learned that he'd started a successful business that unfortunately, took a downturn during the bad economy. He lost most of his wealth and ended up deeply in debt and nearly homeless."

"Yikes. That's a bummer."

She nodded. "Luckily, he bounced back from it. In fact, he'd recently begun a new venture that looked promising but didn't want to meet Sam until he was completely back on his feet. He said that when he finally met his son, he wanted to be someone that Sam could be proud of. Even though I insisted that it wouldn't matter, he wanted to wait. In the meantime, I sent him pictures of Sammy and kept him abreast of what was going on in our lives. Funny. I was getting close to telling Sam the truth about his father but I never got the chance."

"But surely he can contact Sam? I'm sure they can find each other online."

"It's not quite that easy."

"Why not? He found you."

"When Sam was little, I told him his father had died a

long time ago. Sam has no idea that his father is alive." She hung her head. "I know. You must think that I'm a terrible person."

Nick was stunned for a moment. "No, I don't think that at all. I'm sure you were confused and overwhelmed. I know I would have been. Having a baby is a lot of responsibility for someone to take on alone, especially being young. I certainly couldn't imagine raising a kid."

"I just don't want him to hate me for lying to him."

"You did what you had to do at the time. I'm sure he'd understand."

"Then you'll tell him?"

"Whoa, lady. I didn't say that."

"But you have to!" she cried out. "You're the only one who can."

"You see, there's only one problem with that," Nick said. "Nobody knows I can see spirits and I wanna keep it that way."

"Nobody?"

"Nobody except for my mom, my dad, and my uncle. My sister doesn't even know, though she's still pretty young. But definitely nobody at school."

Her voice grew more insistent. "All you have to do is to tell Sammy that there's a shoe box on the top shelf of my closet. It's behind a pile of photo albums and yearbooks. I printed out all the emails that I exchanged with his father. I also put in a letter explaining in detail, everything that happened. My reasoning was that if I couldn't find the courage to tell him in person, I could just hand him the box and let him read the contents himself. He could then decide if he wanted to forgive me."

"I don't know," Nick said. "How do I explain to Sam that I know about the box?"

She held fast onto his gaze. "I don't know. Just figure it out." She took a step back and then she was gone.

Nick blinked. This was the second time that a spirit disappeared in front of him and he wasn't sure if he'd ever get used to it.

He took a deep breath and sighed. Sam's mom was right. He needed to stop being such a mouse and do what was right. Being cowardly was not an option.

He'd survived school so far by staying under everyone's radar — by being the shy, quiet kid who stayed to himself. Truth be told, he wasn't all that shy. Okay, maybe a little, but mostly, he was terrified that people would laugh at him and make fun of him. He saw how some of the unpopular kids were treated in school and he didn't want to be one of them. So he kept his mouth shut and minded his own business, counting the days until high school was over. He also had other secrets besides the ghost thing — big secrets — and if they were known, it'd surely be the end of him. He didn't need the school to know that he was super extra freaky.

So how to tell Sam about his dad? Sam seemed like a decent kid and most people liked him. Maybe he wouldn't blab to the whole school. Or maybe he would. Either way, Nick was gonna have to do this somehow. He thought about sending Sam an anonymous email message but deep down, felt that it would be wrong. This was Sam's mom who had died, after all. No. For once, he would not take the easy way out. He would not pass on such an important bit of information through an anonymous email message. Even if he did, Sam might simply delete it, thinking it was spam or some sort of mean joke. No, he'd tell him in person, face to face.

Nick got up from the chair and looked up. "Okay, you win. I'll tell him."

Chapter Eleven

There were no more ghost sightings for the rest of the day and for that, Nick was grateful. He was especially relieved that there wasn't another run-in with Sam's mother. Nick shuddered as he recalled the promise he made to the ghost. So what exactly was he going to tell Sam?

Hey Sam, saw your dead mother today. She says hi.

No, he was going to need some time to figure out how to explain to Sam that his mom's ghost had recently paid him a visit. Nick had called Katrina earlier in the day to set up his first appointment and they'd both agreed to meet on Wednesday after school. He'd briefly considered waiting until after Wednesday to tell Sam about his mom, to see if Katrina could give him some advice but changed his mind. He didn't want to risk pissing off the ghost, should he re-encounter her. He certainly didn't need her freaking out on him while he was at school in class.

He opened his geography notebook and tried to decipher the notes he'd taken earlier today. Damn, his handwriting sucked. He wondered if there was any possibility of talking his folks into getting him an iPad when his cell buzzed, startling him back to reality.

"Nick? Oh, thank god."

"Who is this?" Nick asked.

"Janet. I know you said that you couldn't help but I didn't know who else to call. Things have gotten a lot worse since we last spoke." She sniffled, as though she'd been crying. "He's become violent."

"I'll be right there," Nick said, without thinking and disconnected the call. He briefly considered calling his uncle but decided against it. If his uncle truly was sick, Nick didn't want to make it worse.

No, he'd have to deal with this on his own.

He jumped in his mom's car, swerving around the slow-pokes on the road yet trying not to speed too much. His mother had warned him that if he got any tickets, his use of the car would come to an immediate and permanent end. He didn't want to endanger his car privileges, so he typically kept his speed near the legal speed limit — for the most part.

He parked the car in Janet's driveway and started up the sidewalk. As he neared the door, James appeared directly in front of him. Nick reared back and gasped at the sudden materialization.

The ghost's face glowed red. He stood firm, arms crossed and glaring at Nick. He seemed taller and better built than Nick remembered. In fact, he looked freakin' enormous. Or maybe it was just the smug look that he had on his face that caused him to look so menacing.

"Did you drive mommy's car?" The bastard was mocking him.

"Piss off," Nick said, trying to hold his voice steady but failing.

A thin layer of confusion crossed the ghost's face as

though Nick had thrown him off by his comment. "You made a huge mistake coming here Pee-wee. I warned you last time."

"Move aside," Nick said. "Janet asked me to come. And my name's not Pee-wee, it's Nick."

James sneered. "You're not the sharpest knife in the drawer, are you? I told you to stay out of this. It is no business of yours."

"You can't do anything to me. You're a ghost."

James raised his eyebrows gave a hollow laugh. He pointed a finger at Nick. "Oh, you think so? Wrong again."

He took a threatening step toward Nick and then the door opened. The ghost winked and then disappeared.

"Nick?" Janet said. "I thought I heard you out here. Were you talking to someone?"

Only your asshole of a husband.

"It was James," Nick said. It was then that he noticed the fresh red gash on Janet's head. From the wound hung a couple of droplets of fresh blood.

He pointed to his forehead. "What happened?"

"James," she said.

Nick felt his eyes grow wide. This was not good. "The ghost did this?" he asked. "How?"

She gestured for him to enter and then pointed to a huge brown overstuffed chair. Nick sat down. Her hands shook as she spoke.

"I don't know where to start," Janet said.

"Take your time."

She nodded and continued. "I went back to my therapist because the dark feelings that I told you about were getting worse and worse. I wasn't even sure at this point whether it really was James causing me this anguish. I considered the possibility that it was just my mind conjuring up these distressing thoughts, that perhaps I was clinically depressed or manic or even bipolar. I was desperate for some kind of help — any kind of help."

"But I told you that I saw James myself. Spoke to him even."

She nodded. "I know, but it still wasn't easy for me to believe that my dead husband was haunting me. I mean, for what purpose? I loved him, and he loved me. I can't think of any reason why he'd be angry with me." She sighed. "The therapist had me nearly convinced that my condition was all grief-related and was only in my mind — that is, until this afternoon. All morning long, that feeling of foreboding that I told you about grew stronger and stronger, and I couldn't seem to shake it off no matter how hard I tried." She pointed to a small table. "I was sitting right here on the couch trying to push those negative thoughts from my mind when all of a sudden a vase that was sitting on the end table flew across the room right at me. I didn't react quickly enough, and it smashed into my head."

"Shouldn't you have gone to the doctor?" Nick asked. "Maybe even the ER. That gash looks pretty nasty." *So much for the theory that ghosts can't move shit around.*

"And what would you have me tell them? That my invisible dead husband tossed a vase at me?"

"You could've made something up."

She shook her head. "I was just so shaken up by the whole thing. The first thing I thought of was to call you. I needed to talk to someone who would understand what was really going on." Nick had to give her points for still staying in the house. He would have bolted. No hesitation.

"And this was the first time that anything like this happened?" Nick asked. "That he physically tried to hurt you?"

Janet nodded. "This was the first time that I knew for

sure that it was him. I also smelled cigar smoke right before it happened."

"Cigar smoke?"

"James enjoyed smoking cigars in the evenings when he came home."

Nick swallowed. He glanced at the door, making sure that he had a direct route out of here if things got out of hand. He watched her, afraid to speak. It was time to come clean. "I think I know why James might be doing this."

Janet's eyes grew wide. "You do? Tell me."

"Remember last time I told you that I got a vision of James grasping his throat and his stomach?"

She nodded. "You said that he might be trying to show you that it was something else that got him. Not a heart attack."

Nick swallowed. "I think he was trying to show me that he didn't die of a heart attack. I'm fairly sure that he believes he was murdered."

Janet gasped and brought a hand up to her throat. "Murdered? But how? The doctors said that it was a heart attack."

"Not to be morbid or anything but did they perform an autopsy?"

Janet shook her head. "James had a heart condition. Arrhythmia, I think it was called. The doctor was fairly certain that this was the cause of his death. Both his doctor and I used to harp on James to quit smoking, that those damn things were going to kill him one day."

"So I take it he didn't quit."

"He did quit cigarettes several years back but started smoking cigars instead. Told me that since he didn't inhale that there was nothing to worry about." She rolled her eyes. "Did he think I was blind? He inhaled every time he smoked. He coughed worse from those damn cigars than he ever did from cigarettes. Foolish man."

Nick's mouth was dry. "Well, James doesn't seem to think it was a heart attack. He's convinced that somebody killed him."

"But who would want to harm James? He had no enemies, as far as I knew."

Nick felt himself flush cold. "Janet, he thinks it was you who killed him."

She reared back, eyes wide with surprise. "Me? No, you must be mistaken. James never would suspect me of doing such a terrible thing. He knows I loved him and would have done anything for him."

Nick was just about to respond when he was interrupted.

"Liar! Lying bitch!" James' voice was like a siren. Nick brought his hands to his ears.

"What's going on?" Janet asked. She began to get up from the couch.

But before Nick could answer, the coffee table flew up at both of them, knocking her back onto the couch. Nick felt a coldness seep into his skin. He was drenched with water.

Nick pushed the table onto the floor and turned to face Janet. "You okay?"

All color drained from her face. Instead of answering him, she leapt up and made a beeline for the front door. She was out of the house before Nick could say or do anything. His mind told him to follow her, to get the hell out of there as fast as he could.

Instead, he stood up brushed himself off, taking inventory of his body. There didn't seem to be any damage although his wrist smarted a bit. Must have happened when he was trying to stop the table from hitting the two of them. He pulled the chilly wet t-shirt away from his stomach and wrung it out. He wasn't completely drenched, only his shirt.

Nick looked up and placed his hands firmly upon his hips

so that James wouldn't see how badly they were shaking. "Okay, you made your point."

With a loud pop, James was suddenly standing there right in front of him. His green eyes bored into Nick's. There seemed to be something different about him now. He seemed calmer, and his face was no longer puffed up and red like it was when Nick had first arrived. In fact, the ghost was giving Nick a thin-lipped smile.

"And what point might that be?"

Even though James was smiling, Nick didn't trust him. Not at all. In fact, Nick was every more leery of him now that he knew James could manipulate the physical world. Nick thought of the movie "Carrie" and imagined a plethora of kitchen knives flying at him in unison from the other room, skewering him all at the same time. He knew this ghost was dangerous and no doubt he wanted revenge for what he believed to be his murder.

"That you're here," Nick said. There no was hiding the trembling in his voice. "She knows you're here now."

"Which brings me to my next question: Why can *you* see me and nobody else can?"

Nick was sure of it now. James was different than he was earlier. He was no longer the enormous and furious looking spirit he'd encountered on the doorstep. His skin tone had changed to a more normal flesh color and his face revealed a handsome man, striking actually, something Nick hadn't noticed before. This man was young; maybe late 20's with bright forest green eyes. For some reason, Nick had initially thought he was much older.

"It's a gift that some of the guys in my family have. We can talk to the dead. Well, not all of the dead — only those who haven't crossed over."

"Over to where?" the ghost asked. "You mean there's more than this?"

Nick nodded. "According to my uncle, there's a place where spirits go after they die. He calls it The Other Side."

"How do I get there?" James asked. "To this Other Side. Is there a doorway or something?"

"When you're ready, you should see a light that you'll need to go through."

He scratched his head. "Nope. I don't recall seeing any light."

"That's why you're still here. Uncle Mitch said that spirits remain here if they have uncompleted business with the living." Nick swallowed. "He also said that it's impossible for spirits to cross if they are upset or angry. And you certainly fit the bill for being pissed off."

James's eyes narrowed and Nick instinctively took a step back.

"You might say that," James said. "How else do you expect me to react? My wife murdered me."

"So you think Janet murdered you?"

"No, I *know* she did. Who else could it have been? She was in my office right before it happened. She even poured me a drink, and once I thought back on it, I recalled that she didn't pour a drink for herself; only for me. And that's not like her at all. My Janet loves her cocktails more than I do..." his voice trailed off. "Or should I say, did. Apparently, my cocktailing days are now over."

"So you didn't actually see her kill you?"

"What are you saying boy?"

Nick stood tall and thrust his chest out. "My name is Nick. And I'm hardly a boy. I'm not much younger than you."

James studied him for a moment and for the first time, he smiled. He then inclined his head politely. "Very well then. Nick. You've got balls; I'll give you that." He met Nick's eyes and held the gaze. Nick squirmed. "You look like there's something you want to tell me. Spit it out then."

"I don't think that your wife murdered you."

James rubbed his chin. "Oh? And what do you know about it? The evidence is obvious if you ask me. She was the last person in my office, and she was fiddling around with my drink canister."

"What's a drink canister?" Nick asked.

James flashed him a dark look and narrowed his eyes.

"Never mind," Nick said. He met the ghost's stare. "I don't feel that she did it. She doesn't seem to be the kind of lady who would kill someone. And moreover, your wife seemed genuinely surprised when she learned that you were angry with her. She has no idea why you're pissed at her, and when I told her that I thought you might suspect her for your murder, she was shocked. She said that you loved each other and got along well."

James intertwined his fingers. Nick was amazed at how solid he looked.

"That doesn't mean she didn't do it," James said matter-of-factly.

"And it doesn't mean she did. Sir, I get the impression that she loved you. She even said so herself. She also said that she could never think of harming you."

James stood still, staring at Nick. He folded his hands in front of him. "That's easy for you to say. You don't know the all of it, Nick."

Nick cleared his throat. "Why don't you fill me in?"

"No, it's none of your business," James snapped. He paused and tented his hands under his chin. "But still, I can't help but wonder. Could it be that I'm wrong about all of this? About her?" He pursed his lips and then shook his head. "When I first woke up — if that's what you can call it — I was confused. I had no idea what had happened to me. As time went on, I started remembering more and more clearly the events that lead to my untimely demise. Janet had come to see me that afternoon. I think we were arguing, but about what, I can no longer recall. I do remember her pouring me a drink and then she left in a huff. I had drunk maybe a quarter of it when I experienced the most agonizing burning in my throat and stomach. I remember being unable to breathe. Do you have any idea what that's like? Not being able to get your breath?"

Nick shook his head, and James continued.

"After that, I remember nothing. The more I thought about it, the more certain I became that Janet had poisoned me."

"What reason would she have had for trying to kill you?" Nick asked.

"That's the odd thing," said James. "I don't know. Insurance money, perhaps? She knew I had a bum ticker so figured maybe she was taking advantage of the situation. It was the only thing that made sense at the time. Unless..."

"Unless what?"

He narrowed his eyes. "Not important. But I am still not convinced of her innocence. Who else would want me dead? I've no enemies of which I'm aware. It makes no sense."

"Who else has access to your office?" Nick asked. "Boss? Coworkers?"

"There's one other coworker who comes to my office and that would be Matt. But we've been friends forever, and he certainly would have no reason to harm me. Hell, he'd give a guy the shirt off his back if you asked him for it, he's that type of person."

"How do you know him?" Nick asked.

"We were best friends in high school and then later on in college. I know. It's uncanny that we ended up working for the same firm. I applied first, and then he did. We're both accountants, so I suppose it makes sense. There are only so many decent accounting jobs out there." He paused and tapped his chin. "That's why we got along so well together, Matt and I. Only an accountant can truly understand another accountant."

"What about Janet? Where did you meet her?"

"Same as Matt, in high school." He squinted at Nick. "You certainly do ask a lot of questions."

"I'm only trying to figure out who might have done you in." Nick's heart skipped a couple of beats. "Everyone thinks you died of a heart attack, right?"

"I did not die of a heart attack!" The coffee table flew across the room and crashed into the far wall, leaving behind a large gash in the drywall.

Nick held up both of his hands in front of him. *It looks like someone has anger management issues.*

"Whoa. I get that," Nick said, as calmly as he could. He remembered reading somewhere that if you spoke in a calming voice and didn't overreact, then those around you would act the same way. He hoped it would work with James because this guy seemed to have an incredibly short fuse. "You misunderstand. You think that you were poisoned by the drink that your wife made for you. Correct?"

James crossed his arms in front of him. He nodded. "Exactly. I know that I did *not* pass away from a heart attack."

Nick's hopes soared. "If that's the case, then probably nobody bothered to check the booze bottle for poison. If we contact the police maybe they'll reopen the case and test the contents of the alcohol."

"Sounds like a long shot to me." James leered at him. "But I don't care how you do it. Just find out who killed me!" With that, he was gone.

"Bossy, isn't he?" Nick said out loud. He raised his head to the ceiling. "And leave Janet alone! I'll find out who killed you."

There was no answer. Nick hoped that he hadn't made a

promise just now that he wouldn't be able to keep. He took a deep breath as he left the house. What a day. Two ghosts in one day and both of them pissed off at him.

He glanced around the room. Shards of glass were scattered over the wooden floor along with a newly-broken coffee table. James had made quite a mess of Janet's living room. Nick thought about cleaning it up but thought better of it. Instead, he stepped over the toppled furniture and headed toward the door, glass crunching beneath his feet as he strode. He wanted to get the hell out of there as soon as possible.

Chapter Twelve

"**M**r. Michelson," said Ms. Schultz. "Is there something captivating about that clock on the wall? It certainly seems to be occupying your attention this afternoon."

"Sorry," Nick said. Nick heard Gabe snicker next to him.

"Then back to your worksheet."

He fought the urge to glance at the clock again but restrained himself. This day was dragging on and on, all the more so because it was nearly impossible for him to concentrate on any of his classes. He half-expected James to pop in at any moment and begin tossing furniture about the room. Nick still had not seen or talked to Sam, which was a relief as he still hadn't figured out what — or how — he was going to tell him about his mom's ghost. Earlier, he'd asked Gabe what Sam's schedule was, but he didn't know any better than Nick. Maybe they weren't as good of friends as Nick had thought.

His thoughts drifted to his appointment with Katrina on Wednesday. He had so many questions for her; so many things he needed for her to explain.

He mentally kicked himself when he remembered that

he'd forgotten to call his uncle. He'd been so wrapped up over all that had gone on over the past couple of days that he had completely neglected to tell Uncle Mitch the news of the two ghosts.

At lunchtime, Nick entered the cafeteria and looked around for Sam. The tables were half empty, and there was no sign of him. Nick must have already missed him. He moved his gaze to the cafeteria line Nick spotted him standing in line, with no ghostly mother in sight. He breathed a sigh of relief. Apparently, she'd given up shouting at Sam, at least for the moment. Maybe she was gone for good, meaning he wouldn't have to confront Sam after all. He shook the thought from his head. A promise is a promise, regardless of whether she was still here or not. It was the right thing to do. Sam had a right to know about his father.

Nick approached Sam and gestured to the petite girl in line behind Sam. Nick thought he recognized her from last year's Spanish class.

"May I please?" Nick asked in a quiet voice. "It's important."

The girl rolled her eyes and audibly sighed. "Whatever."

He thanked her and then took a place in line behind Sam. Sam turned around and upon seeing Nick, smiled.

"Sup," Sam said.

"You having lunch with anyone?"

Sam looked around the room and shrugged. "Don't think so."

"Mind if I sit with you? I need to talk to you about something."

"Me?" Sam asked. "About what?"

"It won't take long."

"Sure, I guess. Hey, did you and Gabe go to the Ren Faire on Sunday?"

Nick nodded. "Too bad you weren't able to join us."

Sam shrugged. "Had a family thing."

Nick wondered who his family was, given that his mom was dead and he wasn't aware that his father was still alive.

They walked over to a quiet area of the cafeteria near the back door. The cafeteria reeked of fried chicken which Nick thought was odd, considering that today's fare was tacos. The room was starting to clear out, much to Nick's relief. Fewer people around meant there was less of a chance that someone would come over to sit with them.

Sam and Nick plunked down their trays on the table. The nearby tables were empty. Perfect. There was nobody to inadvertently overhear their conversation.

"Who you living with now?" Nick asked.

Sam raised his eyebrows. "Huh? What do you mean?"

"I remember your mom passed away not too long ago."

"Yeah, been nearly a year already."

"I met her once when I was at your house with Gabe. I was just wondering where you're staying now."

Sam looked him thoughtfully "That's right, I forgot all about you coming to the house. That was awhile ago."

Nick nodded. "Long while."

"After that, my grandparents moved in. They were living in Atlanta but moved back here to take care of me. I guess they didn't want to uproot me after everything that had happened."

"It must be hard without your mom, huh?" Nick asked.

Sam looked at him and blinked a couple of times. "Sure it is, I miss her. I mean she was my mom." He looked away for a moment, as if looking for someone, then turned his gaze back to Nick. "So what'd you want to talk to me about?"

Nick swallowed. "You know, sometimes when people die, they keep their secrets hidden away. Like maybe on the top shelf in their closet. These might be things that they had planned on telling us at some point, but unfortunately, they ended up passing away before they got an opportunity."

"Dude, what are you going on about? You wanted to talk to me about people's secrets in their closet?" He creased his brow. "You have some skeletons in your closet that you want to talk to me about?"

Except my skeletons are ghosts. Nick sucked in a sharp breath. This was turning out to be more difficult than Nick had anticipated. He should have just sent an email instead.

"Just thinking about your mom," Nick said. "Have you gone through her things? There might be something that she meant to tell you but never got the chance to. I've heard of that happening a lot."

Sam's voice grew colder. "Nick, you are one hell of a morbid guy."

"I'm just saying that this is something that you might want to do. There might be some important information there about your dad."

Sam shot him a sharp look. "Fucking-A dude, get off of it already! You're talking crazy."

So the indirect approach doesn't work. It was worth a try.

"Listen, Sam. I have something to tell you that's gonna to sound kinda weird."

Sam scoffed. "Weirder than the stuff you've already been saying?"

Nick nodded and spoke as quickly as he could. "I don't know any easy way to say this so here it is. I just found out recently that I can see the spirits of dead people. I noticed the ghost of a lady following you around, so I talked to her the other day. She told me that she's your mom and that she'd been communicating with your dad before she died. No, he's not dead, she lied to you about that. She was planning on telling you all about it but never got the chance. All that you need to know about your dad and how to contact him, is in a shoe box on the top shelf of your mom's closet. She said it's behind some photo albums and scrapbooks." Nick took a couple of deep breaths and then gripped the arm of his chair so tightly that his knuckles turned white.

Sam grimaced and then pushed his tray towards Nick and sprang up. "Nick, that's well and truly fucked up," Sam said. "You need some major help."

"Wait, Sam," said Nick but Sam dismissed him with the one-finger salute. He turned his back to Nick and took off towards the door. Nick all at once felt a buzzing sensation on his skin and a heavy thud in his stomach. He shivered. He turned his head back toward the table. Sam's mother sat directly across from him.

"Thank you, Nick," she said softly. And then she was gone.

He looked around the cafeteria, but Sam had already left. Nick felt a hole in his chest where his heart should have been. So how long is it going to take before the entire school finds out that he's a freak?

He was totally and completely screwed.

IT WAS NEARING THE END OF STUDY HALL WHEN NICK'S phone buzzed in his pocket. He ensured that the study hall monitor was not looking his way and slowly slid the phone out of his pocket. He held it under the desk. The text was from his mother.

Call Home.

This was beginning to be a habit. After getting a written excuse along with a reprimand for reading text messages during school hours, Nick went out into the hallway to call his parents.

"I thought you should know," his mother said. "Your Uncle Mitch is in the hospital."

Nick gripped the phone so tightly that he was afraid it would shatter in his hand. "What happened?"

"He called us a couple of hours ago on the phone, and your father answered. Your uncle told him said that he didn't feel right; that he felt that something was seriously wrong with him. Your father noticed that Mitch was slurring his words so we called an ambulance."

He should have believed his uncle when he said that he was ill. "So how is he? Is he going to be okay?"

"He had a minor stroke. He's awake now but is having some trouble with memory and using certain words. The doctor says that this should be only temporary."

Nick breathed a sigh of relief. "So he'll be okay then?"

There was a pause. "There shouldn't be any lasting effects from the stroke. But your uncle's not in the clear yet. The x-rays showed that he has several potentially life-threatening arterial blockages. Once Mitch recovers, they want to do heart surgery. According to his doctor, Mitchell has known about this for quite some time and was warned that he needed to have this surgery done."

"Uncle Mitch told me that he was sick but never said what was wrong," Nick said. "Why didn't he have the surgery before?"

"No idea, you'll have to ask him that yourself," said Nick's mother. There was another long pause. "We haven't been exactly the best of friends, your uncle and I." Nick could hear her sigh into the phone. "If you want, you can go see him after school. They said that visitors would do him good. Your father's down there now. I can't believe this. First my mother, and now this."

"Uncle Mitch is not going to die," Nick said, his voice a lot sharper than he had intended.

She took a deep breath and said evenly, "Nobody said anything about Mitchell dying."

Neither of them said nothing for several moments. "I'm gotta get back in class."

"Call home if you're going to miss dinner," she said. "And give your uncle my regards."

Nick thought about skipping school and going directly to the hospital but thought better of it. He doubted his mother would write him an excuse and he didn't want to get into any more trouble.

Two hours later, he pulled his scooter into the hospital parking lot. As he walked the hallway toward his uncle's room, his stomach lurched, going topsy-turvy, inside out and upside down. This place was flooded with ghosts. Nick made sure to keep his eyes forward as he walked, focusing his attention on the clock bolted on the far wall. He didn't want to attract any unwanted attention. The hallway stunk of Pine-Sol.

Nick's father was sitting next to his uncle when he arrived in Room 502. Upon seeing Nick, his father got up and came to the door.

"He's awake and alert," said his father. "He can understand everything you say but is having a difficult time finding certain words. This is supposedly going to pass. Go on in and talk to him. He's been asking about you. I'm going to head home for dinner. You want anything from the cafeteria before I go?"

"No, I'll eat later when I get home."

His father nodded. "Don't tire him out. He's still weak from the stroke."

"And *he* can hear everything you say," said Mitch.

"How are you feeling Uncle Mitch?" Nick asked as he sat down.

"Better than earlier," Mitch said. Nick observed that his

uncle's lip on the right side of his face curved downward when he spoke. Nick had never noticed that before — must be remnants of the stroke. "School good?"

Nick nodded. "Talked to two ghosts yesterday."

Mitch raised his eyebrows. "*Two*? My, you've been a busy boy. Tell me all about it."

So Nick spent the next several minutes filling his uncle in on everything that had occurred in the past couple of days, including his regrettable conversation with Sam.

"Do you think she's crossed over to wherever it is they go?" Nick asked.

"Did she mention seeing a..a.." He paused. "That thing that... Dammit! What is the word?"

"A light?" Nick asked.

"That's it. Did she mention seeing a light?"

Nick shook his head. "I don't think so. She just thanked me and disappeared."

"It'll probably depend on whether your friend finds the box she mentioned. What was his name?"

"Sam."

"It will depend on Sam. If he doesn't find it, she'll most likely be back so be prepared for a repeat visit."

"I'm not worried. She won't find me because I'm going to have to register at a new school or maybe quit altogether. Come tomorrow, it'll be common knowledge that Nick Michelson thinks he can see spooks and the humiliation will be too great for me to bear."

"Don't you think you might be overreacting just a tad?" his uncle asked. He looked as though he were suppressing a grin.

"I can't imagine what everyone's going to say and think once the word gets out but I can tell you that it's not going to be good. Oh, I can hear it now. 'Oh, there's Nick the ghost seer. Hey Nick, seen any dead people lately?'" Nick clapped his hands rapidly. "And then come the chants. I see dead people! I see dead people!'"

Nick could tell that his uncle was trying really hard now not to crack a smile. "Here's another um...um..." he paused and looked up. "I can't get the right word. Teaching. We'll call it teaching. So I have another teaching for you. Things are never as bad as we imagine. We waste our energy and our focus by thinking about what might happen. Or we conjure up the worst case scenarios in our head, rehashing them over and over. Instead, you need to focus on the positive."

"Maybe you're right. I suppose it's possible that Sam won't tell anyone. Unlikely, but possible. I'll take your advice and try not to think about it. It's a good lesson."

His uncle's eyes grew wide. "Lesson! That's the word I was looking for."

"This must be really frustrating for you — not being able to find the right words," Nick said.

His uncle sighed. "You have no idea."

"It could have been worse. The doctors are saying that you should completely recover from the stroke."

"And then there'll be the heart surgery."

Nick nodded. "So I've heard. Did you know that you needed that surgery before this? I know that you told me that you knew you were ill. Is that what you were referring to? A heart problem?"

Mitch shot him a sharp look, and then his face softened. "Yeah, I knew about it, but I kept putting it off and putting it off. I was trying to wrap up loose ends in my life before the surgery in case things didn't go according to plan."

"Uncle Mitch! Don't say that."

Mitch closed his eyes for a moment and sighed. "Nick, you'll have to face the inevitable. I'm not going to be around forever. By the looks of it, I might be going sooner rather than later. That's why it's so important that I teach you as much as I can in the time I have left."

Nick nodded but said nothing. The beeping of the machine attached to his uncle seemed louder than it did when he had first arrived. A bag of clear liquid hung from a bedside cart.

"What's that?" Nick asked, pointing to the tube in his uncle's arm.

"IV. It keeps me hydrated." He scooted himself up in bed. "So tell me some more about this Katrina," Mitch said. There was a big grin on his face. "She sounds like a colorful character."

"She works at the Renaissance Faire and has ginormous, wild red hair. She spoke with a little bit of an accent, and she told me things that only I could have known. She knew that I saw a spirit at the fair and that I ignored it."

His uncle's eyes grew wide. "I think I know her! I wasn't quite sure at first if it was the same person. I knew her as Katie. Katie Weston. She was an excellent clairvoyant but had a most interesting additional gift. She could somehow channel the abilities of other psychics around her."

"That's what she did with me. She told me that she could only see ghosts when another medium was around."

"Well, I'll be dipped. Who could have guessed? Katie. I had no idea she was in town. So she's going by Katrina now huh?"

Nick shrugged. "I guess so. That's what she told me at least and what her booth sign said. So Katrina's not her real name?"

His uncle looked as if he were about to speak but stopped. He creased his brow and then tried again. "Dammit! I hope all of my vocabulary returns soon. This is really testing my patience. Regarding the names. Some of us work the faire circuit to bring in extra money, but for others, it's their only source of income. They work festivals, fairs, and other events as part of their psychic business." He flashed Nick a smile. "There's no money in helping ghosts cross over, and we have to pay the bills somehow. I did my share of psychic fairs back in the day. Then, I was known then as "Maurice the Mysterious."

Nick laughed. "You're shitting me, right? Maurice?"

Mitch smiled and nodded. "I'm afraid not." He rubbed his chin a few times. "Now we need to come up with a name for you."

"I think I'll just stick with Nick."

His uncle laughed again. "My boy, you must try and get into the spirit of things, so to speak. What good is being psychic if you can't have a weird multi-syllable name and wear outlandish clothing?" Mitch narrowed his gaze. "Now tell me more about this ghost who's haunting his wife."

"James," Nick said. "He wants me to help him find the person who killed him." Nick then recounted everything that had happened thus far in the James and Janet situation.

Uncle Mitch settled back into his pillows. "I don't think I like this a bit. And you're telling me that this ghost can move things around in the physical world?"

Nick nodded. "He threw a coffee table at me and gashed Janet's forehead with a vase."

"He's one of those ghosts that I told you about. Over time, some of them — especially the angry ones — can build up enough energy to manipulate the physical world. It's usually those who've been around for awhile. How long ago did you say he died?"

"I think Janet said that it happened about a year ago."

His uncle nodded. "That's not that long ago. It's rather rare that spirits ever get to the point where they can move objects around like what you just described after being deceased for such a short time. Usually, it's only the really,

really, angry ones who have been earthbound for awhile." He paused and tapped his chin with his index finger. "Although strangely enough, I've been seeing more and more of this recently." His voice was barely a whisper, and it seemed to Nick that he was talking more to himself than to Nick.

"I'd say that James definitely qualified as really, really angry. Although by the time I left, he had calmed down quite a bit. It's funny. His entire face changed after Janet left. He was like a completely different person." Nick paused. "Completely different ghost, I mean."

"And that's exactly what we do. We try to calm them down so they'll cross over."

"I don't think it'll be that easy," Nick said. "He seems pretty adamant about finding the person who killed him."

"So he no longer suspects his wife?"

Nick shrugged. "I don't know. I think I convinced him to lay off of her until we know for sure. He seemed open to the possibility that maybe someone else killed him."

"Or maybe he did die of a heart attack, plain and simple."

Nick shook his head. "No, he's pretty insistent that he did not die of a heart attack."

"You said that they didn't do an autopsy?"

"Nope. Janet said everyone thought it was unnecessary. Supposedly, James had heart disease, so his doctor naturally assumed that was what got him."

His uncle creased his brow and was silent for a couple of moments. "That does sound awfully convenient, doesn't it? No autopsy, a diagnosis of an existing heart condition — your spirit friend might be on to something."

"So what do you think I should do?"

"This is a tough one, Nick. I've never gotten myself heavily involved in a murder case before. Mine have been mainly accidents and suicides. My father once told me that it's rare for a ghost to tell you who murdered them so it's kind of strange that this particular spirit is so hung up on it. I think there might be something else going on here."

"Like what?"

His uncle sat upright in the bed. "Not sure. Something just doesn't ring true. Although you're asking the wrong person seeing as I haven't dealt much with murder investigations."

"I thought you said that some of the ghosts you helped were murdered?"

"That's true, there have been a few. But those spirits knew who had killed them, and most of the time, their killer was already in jail. They weren't seeking justice or revenge for their death but rather closure. The only thing keeping them here was a need to pass on a message to a loved one. There was never any mystery surrounding their deaths."

"So what do you think I should do?"

"Maybe Katie has some experience with this and may be able to offer some advice. She might be able to get some information psychically. In the meantime, I don't want you to get involved with this one. An unsolved murder could prove to be dangerous, especially if you dug up something that pointed a finger at the killer."

"Got it," said Nick. "I'll stay away from the case until after I talk to Katrina."

His uncle breathed an audible sigh of relief. "Thank you. I'd worry about you and would feel responsible if anything happened to you. After all, it was I who got you into this."

"How do you figure?" Nick asked. "I'm one one who stumbled onto James."

"True, but I kinda pushed you into this odd, frightening world of restless spirits."

"I made my own decision about doing this," said Nick. "I wasn't going to, you know. I'd planned on completely ignoring this ghost thing and was gonna pretend that I couldn't see them. I figured that if I did that long enough, that maybe eventually I'd stop seeing them."

Mitch raised his eyebrows. "So what changed your mind?"

"Things that both you and Katrina said, about doing what's right and about making a difference. I guess I was given this ability for a reason and that's to help others."

"You're a wise young man Nick," said Mitch, a warm smile on his face. "I had a feeling you'd come around. Now down to business. I don't suppose you brought that Tarot deck with you by any chance?"

Nick smiled. "Yup. I was afraid Mom would find it so I put it in my backpack. Why?"

"It's time to continue your lessons. You're not getting off the hook that easily."

"But you just had a stroke."

"Posh," said Mitch, waving his hand in the air. "Minor details. Like I told you, I want to pass on as much as I can to you while I'm still here to do it."

Nick was about to interject, but his uncle waved his index finger back and forth, cutting him off. "Don't interrupt me. I won't be here forever. Maybe I'll be here twenty years from now; maybe I'll be gone tomorrow. Who in the hell knows? The date of our death is the one thing that the cards won't tell us. But I will say this. The sooner you learn your way around the psychic world, the easier your job will be out there when you encounter spirits. So are you game?"

Nick smiled and nodded. "You're the boss."

"Yes, I am and don't you forget it." He grinned. "Now bring out those cards, and I'll tell you about the time I ran into the ghosts of three little kids who died in a fire."

Nick shuddered. "Yikes! Did it have a happy ending?"

Mitch smiled. "It always does."

Chapter Thirteen

"Why are you moving so slowly this morning?" asked his mother. "You're moping around here like you've just lost your favorite puppy. You feeling alright?"

Nick pushed his breakfast plate away from him. He considered lying for a moment, telling his mom he was sick so he wouldn't have to go to school but thought better of it. Tomorrow, the question would still be dangling out there like a hangman's noose, and it would be one more day of torture he'd have to endure — one more day of not knowing. No, he needed to know today whether Sam blabbed. He needed to know if it was all over the school.

He needed to know if his life was ruined.

Nick gulped down his orange juice. "I'm fine. Just a little distracted."

His mother nodded and took a sip of her coffee. "I imagine you're worried about Mitchell." She placed the cup on the table and folded her hands in front of her. "I'm sure he'll be fine. From what everyone at the hospital says, things look promising."

"Do you have any idea how long they'll keep him there?" Nick asked.

"Your father was at the hospital this morning before he went to work," his mother said. "They're going to keep Mitchell there until after the surgery. They want to operate as soon as possible, but first, they need to ensure that he's strong enough to handle it. Right now, his white cell blood count and his oxygen level are not quite where they'd like them to be. Should be a few more days yet."

"Sounds scary. All of it."

"Cardiac surgery certainly isn't without its risks. But your uncle is more at risk if he doesn't have this operation."

Nick nodded and stood up. "Is it okay if I stop by and see him after school."

She nodded and then pointed at his plate. "Aren't you going to eat your pancakes? You only took a couple of bites."

"Not hungry," Nick said, as he scooped up his backpack. He leaned over and kissed her on the cheek.

"Are you sure you're feeling all right? It's not like you to skip a meal."

"I'm fine, really," he lied. He gave her one final wave and was out the door.

His hands shook as he drove to school and the closer he got, the more his heart raced. He tried not to think about it — about what everyone would say once they found out. Funny, he'd completely forgotten about school last night while he was at the hospital. His uncle had distracted him, first with Tarot lessons and then with stories about some of the spirits he'd encountered over the years and what he did to help them to cross over. Nick was amazed at how many people's lives his uncle had touched. Could he ever hope to be anything like his uncle? His uncle thought so. Nick wasn't so sure.

He pulled in the parking lot and turned off the car. The

saliva in his mouth dried up and his tongue felt like an old piece of wood. He sucked in a deep breath, got out of the car and trudged toward the door. Once near the steps, his legs involuntarily screeched to a halt.

He did not want to go inside.

He willed his heart to slow down and thrust his trembling hands in his pockets. How was he supposed to face everyone?

What would he tell them when they asked him if he really thought he could see ghosts?

He could say, 'why yes, I can see spirits, and there's a very ornery fella haunting you right now.' Or maybe, 'your grandma knows that you have a wank in your room every day after school.'

Would he become the laughingstock of the entire school?

He opened the school doors and keeping his eyes affixed to the floor, scuttled to his locker. Gabe was there waiting for him. His heart jumped an extra couple of beats. How had he forgotten about Gabe?

"Dude, you're almost late. Where y'all been?"

Nick studied Gabe's face for any indication that Sam had told him about their conversation. There was none.

"Family breakfast talk," Nick said. "It went on and on and on."

Gabe shuddered. "I feel for you. I know what those mornin' family talks are like. Say, you wanna head into town after school? There's a new burger place next to the car wash that I've been wanting to check out. Heard some good things about it."

Nick smiled when Gabe didn't act any differently than usual. He thought about Gabe's offer for a moment, half-tempted to accept. "Sounds like fun but I can't. My uncle's in the hospital, and I promised I'd go see him."

"Really? Your Uncle Mitch is sick?"

Nick nodded. "He had a minor stroke, but he's doing okay. He has to have surgery in a few days though."

"That's tough. Your family hasn't had the best of luck lately, have they?"

"Not so much," Nick said. He looked around. Nobody appeared to be giving him strange looks. Nobody seemed to be paying him any extra attention at all.

"Have you seen Sam this morning?" Nick asked.

Gabe shook his head. "Nah. He's not coming to school today."

"How do you know?" Nick asked.

"Dude texted me this morning. Said he had something important to do today and wouldn't be around. We have World History together so I told him I'd take good notes and text him the assignment." He narrowed his eyes. "Why are you looking for him? I didn't know you two hung out."

"We don't. I just realized that I hadn't seen him for awhile."

"I'm pretty sure he was here yesterday."

"Must have missed him." Nick glanced at the clock on the wall. "We better get a move on. It's almost 8:30."

Safe for at least one more day, or at least until Sam comes back to school — but that meant one more day of not knowing whether or not Sam planned on revealing Nick's secret. Did Sam's absence have anything to do with their talk yesterday? It was almost too much of a coincidence. The good thing about Sam not being in school today, however, meant his ghostly mother wouldn't be here either.

When the final bell rang at the end of the day, Nick dashed out the door with the intention of going directly to see his uncle. He was on his way to the hospital when his phone buzzed. It was Janet. He'd not heard from her since the day when he had talked with James at her house after she hightailed it out of there. Nick had no idea where she was or whether James had kept his promise to stop haunting her.

Can we talk?

Nick read the text and took a deep breath. Even communicating with her made him nervous, knowing that she could be a murderer. He pulled over to the side of the road and thumbed back a one-word response.

Where?

She texted back an address and room number of a Day's Inn motel. He seriously considered making up an excuse not to go, and it wouldn't have been a lie. He had, after all, promised Uncle Mitch that he'd see him after school and truthfully, he didn't relish the idea of being alone in a motel room with her.

He should at least tell someone where he's going. His mother? Not after the last conversation they had. No, telling his parents wasn't an option. He hadn't told them anything about the Janet and James situation and wasn't about to spill it now. Did his uncle have his cell with him at the hospital? Nick couldn't remember whether he saw it when he was there yesterday. He typed out a text to his uncle.

U have your cell with u?

Nick stared at the screen for a couple of moments. His phone finally buzzed.

Yes. What's up? You still coming today?

Nick responded. *Yes. Forwarding u some Janet messages.*

Nick then forwarded the texts he'd received from Janet to his uncle.

Should I go?

It was nearly two minutes before his uncle responded.

Up to u. If u do, make sure u tell her that I know where u r.
I'll come by afterward.
BE CAREFUL!

Nick smiled at his uncle's response and then typed out a response to Janet.

Will be there in 10.

Nick fired up the navigation app on his phone and pasted in the address that Janet sent to him. He was at the motel ten minutes later.

He knocked on Room 207.

"Thank you so much for coming," Janet said as she gestured him into the room.

Nick gave her a slight nod and walked in. His eyes glanced around the room. No weapons in sight or anything else too threatening. He heard the door click behind him. Janet walked past him and sat down on the bed. Nick stayed close to the door.

"Have a seat," she said.

"I'm good," Nick replied. "I can only stay a couple of minutes. I have to go to the hospital to visit my uncle."

"Is that the uncle that you told me about? The one who...," She paused for a moment as if searching for the right words. "The one who's like you?"

Nick nodded. "That'd be the one."

She looked down. "I hope it's not anything serious."

"We don't know yet. He's supposed to have heart surgery in a few days."

Janet nodded. "That can be scary. They told James that he'd eventually have to have surgery." She closed her eyes for a moment and tensed her lips. "Unfortunately, it never came to that point."

"I texted my uncle before I came. He wanted to know exactly where I was going."

Janet creased her forehead and then raised her eyebrows. The realization about what Nick was trying to say slid over her expression. "You can't seriously think that I had anything to do with James's death?" She crossed her hands chastely in front of her.

Nick studied her face for a moment. "I only know what you and James have told me." Then, seeing her expression, he added, "and no, not really. You seem like a nice lady — not the kind that would kill anyone. Course, I don't think I've ever met a true murderer."

Janet stared at him for a moment and gave a curt nod. "I apologize for leaving so abruptly yesterday. It all was too much. I was so terrified. I had to get away from him."

"No problem. I was kinda scared too. It's not every day that furniture comes flying at you on its own."

She hesitated, then blurted out the question that probably had plagued her since she hightailed it out of the house. "What happened after I left?"

"James and I had a talk," Nick replied.

"You had a conversation with him? A civil one?"

Nick nodded. "He calmed down after a bit, and we were able to have a proper conversation. He's not a bad guy once you get to know him."

"He was the nicest person you'd ever want to meet. That's why his behavior is so surprising. It's really out of character for him."

"He's still kind of scary though."

Janet's eyes never left Nick's. "So what did he tell you? Does he still think that I killed him?"

Nick thought it prudent to tread very carefully. "He might still believe it. I think I convinced him to leave you alone until we can find out the truth. He was open to the possibility that someone else might have been involved with his death."

"Thank God for that. I still have no idea why on earth he would suspect me. I've never done or said anything that could have given him cause to think I'd want to hurt him."

From out of nowhere, a vivid image popped into Nick's

mind. It displayed a man wearing a little red hat and carrying a bunch swords. It looked like he was on tippy-toes and from what Nick could see, there were a bunch of tents behind him. Nick got the impression that the swords belonged to whoever was in the tents and that the man was stealing them. The image seemed familiar like Nick had seen it somewhere before. But right now, he couldn't place it. Janet's voice interrupted the vision.

"Nick, are you listening to me?"

Nick shook himself. "Sorry. I must have drifted off. I haven't gotten much sleep lately."

"So what now?"

Nick was about to tell her about the booze carafe when he stopped himself. He didn't want to give her an opportunity to get there first. Just in case, by some miracle, it was still there.

"I'm not sure. I told your husband that I'd help him find out what really happened. I'm gonna see a friend of mine on Wednesday who's good that these types of things."

A look of bewilderment crossed over Janet's face. "Is he like you too?"

Nick nodded. "She. Yes and no. She doesn't see ghosts, but she is psychic. She might have some ideas."

Nick carefully observed her expression for the slightest falter, but nothing gave her thoughts away. "I now realize that not having an autopsy done after James's death was a mistake. Maybe that would have given James some peace." Her eyes narrowed. "So he's genuinely convinced that someone did him in?"

Nick felt his stomach flip. *Shit*. "Yes. He seems fairly certain of it."

"But why did he wait so long to make his presence known to me?"

Nick considered this briefly. "He told me that when he

first became aware — or awake or whatever it is you become after you die — he had no clue as to what had happened to him. He couldn't remember a thing. Then slowly, he recalled bits and pieces. Eventually, he was able to remember the moment of his death. He emphasized that it was not a heart attack that killed him. He's positive somebody poisoned him."

She watched him with an expression that bordered on awe. "He told you all of that? It's truly incredible what you can do. I can't believe how fortunate I was to stumble upon you."

Nick smiled. "Actually, I think it was me who stumbled upon you."

She nodded. "Let's say we stumbled upon each other." Her expression became serious. "So James thinks he was poisoned? What makes him think so?"

Nick remembered the vision of the glass of alcohol but again, felt hesitant to tell her. "It was just the way he described his death. There was no chest pain. It was all in his stomach. And he said he couldn't breathe."

She hesitated, and then blurted out, "I still think I'm going to stay here a little bit longer. I'm not ready to return to the house."

"Why?" Nick asked.

"Just in case he's still angry at me or still suspects me. I don't want to go through yesterday's ordeal again anytime soon, especially now that I know he's capable of physical violence. He nearly scared me to death."

Nick wondered if he should tell her. Probably would be for the best. "Um," he started and then looked in the corner.

"What is it?" Janet asked.

"James is here now."

Janet jumped to her feet and backed herself against the

wall. She brought her hand up to her throat. "What? He's here? How can that be possible? He was at the house."

James sniggered in the corner like a naughty child. Nick couldn't help but flash him a dirty look. James bowed mockingly.

Nick remembered something his uncle had mentioned the previous evening. "Janet, there's a misunderstanding that many people have concerning ghosts. Ghosts don't typically haunt buildings. I mean maybe some of them do. Maybe. But mostly, they haunt people."

Her eyes grew wide. "What are you saying? That there's no way to get rid of him? That he can follow me around no matter where I go?" The pitch of her voice rose as she spoke until it sounded like a siren.

Nick took a deep breath. He had to try to calm her down.

"Tell her, Nick," said the ghost in the corner. "Tell her that she's stuck with me."

Nick turned to James. "You be quiet."

"You're talking to him now, aren't you? He really is here." Her body grew limp. She stumbled back to the bed and fell backward, defeated. The bright orange bedspread glowed next to her pale skin.

"Yeah, he is," said Nick, in as quiet a voice as possible. "But he promised he wasn't going to bother you. He only wants to find out what happened."

"So what's he doing here?"

Nick narrowed his eyes and looked at James. "I was wondering the same thing."

James held out both of his hands, palms up. "I just wanted to let her know that she can't outrun me. If she did kill me, I'm going to see to it personally that she pays."

"You promised you'd leave her alone."

James' bright green eyes narrowed and sharpened. "And I've kept my word. I have done nothing to harm her. I never promised, however, that I wouldn't be watching. There's more to this that you don't understand."

"Then what? What are you keeping from me?"

The spirit slowly shook his head. "No, not yet. Not until I know for sure. I suspected when she was alive. I need to know."

Nick let go of an exasperated breath. "What is it then? Just tell me."

James disappeared. Nick growled. What a dick. This ghost was frustrating him to no end. Now he's talking in riddles. How was Nick supposed to figure this out if the ghost was keeping essential information from him?

"What did he say?"

With an effort, Nick stilled his thoughts. "He vowed that he wouldn't hurt you but wanted me to tell you that he's watching."

"Watching for what? Is he expecting me to confess to someone that I poisoned my husband?" Her expression was wild and panicked.

"I dunno. He didn't say. Maybe he's hoping to discover some clues about his death."

She jumped to her feet and looked at the ceiling as she shouted. "Well, you can tell James to look elsewhere! I hate to disappoint him, but I did not kill him. He'll have to look somewhere else to find his murderer."

Nick swallowed. "He's gone now."

"Oh," she said. Her lips broke into a weak smile. "That's good. I hope he stays gone."

"I can't make any promises about that. As soon as I find out what my friend says, I'll let you know." He walked over and sat down next to her. He took her hand in his. "Call me if he bothers you in any way. I'll come down and talk to him."

She blinked and nodded. "I suppose I might as well go

back home. It doesn't make any difference where I am, does it? He'll find me anywhere, no matter where I go."

"I'm afraid so," Nick said. "But on the bright side, you get to go back to your own house." Nick rose. He let go of Janet's hand. "I'll talk to you soon."

"Bye Nick — and thank you."

As he walked to his car, he passed a young man with blond hair scuttling down the sidewalk at a rapid pace towards the hotel. The man was so focused on where he was going that he would have plowed right into him if Nick hadn't moved out to the way to let the man pass. Nick stopped and turned around.

The man was knocking on the door to Room 207.

Chapter Fourteen

"He's still sleeping, and I'd prefer not to wake him up," the nurse said to him. She had stepped directly in front Nick in the hallway, arms extended as he was heading towards his uncle's room. "He had a restless night last night and with all the tests, didn't get much sleep today."

Nick nodded. He wondered if his uncle's uneasy night had anything to do with the fact that this hospital was rife with ghosts. They roamed the halls, popped in and out of rooms, and constantly attempted to get the attention of the nurses. It was only with the greatest difficulty that Nick was able to keep his eyes forward and pretend he didn't see them.

"I'll come back tomorrow then," Nick said. "But you'll tell him that I was here when he wakes up?"

"Of course," the nurse said. Nick noticed that her name tag said 'Ashley.' "Hopefully, he'll feel better tomorrow."

"Thank you, Ashley," Nick said.

Ashley brightened at the mention of her name. She didn't look to be much older than Nick. Probably fresh out of nursing school. She certainly was friendlier than the older snarky nurse who was here yesterday.

"Tell him he can call or text me when he wakes up."

When Nick pulled into his driveway, he noticed the silhouette of someone sitting on the porch, and it looked to be neither his parents nor his sister. He got out of the car, and as he came closer to the house, he recognized the person.

Shit. He so did not want to deal with this right now.

But better here than at school — best get it over and done with.

His feet crunched on the gravel in the driveway and Sam snapped his head up.

"Hey," Sam said. "Thought you'd be here right after school."

"You've been waiting here that long?" Nick said. He studied Sam's face for any indication of why he was sitting on Nick's porch, but his expression was emotionless.

Sam shook his head. "Only about fifteen minutes. Your mom said that you might stop off and visit your uncle at the hospital, but I decided to wait anyway. Sorry to hear that he's sick. How's he doing?" There was no hostility in his voice. That was a good thing. So what was he doing here?

"Dunno," Nick said. "He was sleeping when I got there, and the nurse wouldn't let me see him. I'll probably phone him later on."

Sam nodded and was silent for a couple of moments. He gestured to the step next to him. "I need to talk to you. Wanna sit down?"

Nick didn't want to risk his parents coming out or over-hearing their conversation. His mom would pitch a hissy fit if she knew he had told someone at school about his abilities. Not that Sam's mom had given him much choice in the matter.

"How about we sit inside the screen porch out back? It'll be more private."

Sam nodded and followed him out back. Nick plopped down on one of the cushy lawn chairs. Sam sat next to him.

"You weren't in school today," said Nick. "You okay?"

Sam smiled. "I was with my dad."

Nick raised an eyebrow. "Your real dad?"

"Yeah," Sam said. Excitement welled up in his voice, and he rocked back and forth in the chair. "I emailed him and responded, asking if I wanted to spend the day with him, to get to know him."

Nick straightened and locked eyes with Sam. This was not at all how Nick thought this would go down. "So I take it you found the box?"

Sam nodded. "It was there, just like you said it'd be. I had a hard time believing it at first, but sure enough, there it was. Mom had printed out every email that my dad had sent to her as well as the ones she sent to him. I had no idea that she was so messed up."

Nick took a deep breath. "Yeah, your mom gave me the impression that she had some issues when she was in high school. She certainly didn't treat your dad very well at the time."

Sam gave him a weak smile. "I know. It kind of hurts that she lied to me all these years."

Nick's skin prickled, feeling like thousands of tiny pins and needles were poking him simultaneously and he knew that Sam's mother was behind him. He glanced over his shoulder. Sure enough, there she was, standing behind his chair. She was gazing lovingly at her son.

"Something wrong?" Sam asked.

Nick cleared his throat. "Um yeah. Your mom's here."

Sam's eyes grew wide. "She's here? Now?"

Nick nodded. He kept his gaze locked on Sam, trying to figure out whether or not Sam believed him.

All at once, the spirit stood in front of Nick.

"Thank you for telling him," she said to Nick. "This is all that I wanted — Sam to reunite with his father. Tell Sam that I'm sorry I lied to him and that I love him very much."

"I will," said Nick.

"What's she saying?" Sam asked. His gaze swung back and forth around the room, and he squinted his eyes as if that would help him to see her.

"She said that she's sorry she lied to you. She also says that she loves you very much."

"Where is she?" Sam asked. "She's still here?"

"She's standing right next to you," Nick said in a voice that was barely above a whisper.

"Tell her I said thank you for getting the message to me."

"She can hear you, Sam. You can tell her yourself."

"Mom, I love you too," he said. His voice crackled as he spoke. "I miss you so much."

Nick noticed that a streak of tears left a wet trail down Sam's face. Nick almost felt as though he should leave, as though he were invading a private family moment.

"Sammy, please don't be angry with me. I planned on telling you the truth. I know I kept this a secret for way too long. But the longer the lie went on, the harder it became to tell you."

"She doesn't want you to be angry with her," Nick said. "She said that because so much time had passed, it became more and more difficult to tell you. She was gonna to talk to you but didn't get the chance."

Sam looked up. "I know Mom. I was pissed at first, but then Dad told me everything, about how confused you were when you first found out you were pregnant, how Grandma and Grandpa threatened to report him to the police and how you lost touch with him after that. He told me that it wasn't all your fault. He was to blame as well for giving up too easily." Sam took a deep breath and continued. "Dad's really nice, Mom. I think you'd like him. He told me that I can even come live with him if I want."

Nick watched her as Sam spoke. He would never have imagined that a ghost could cry but this one certainly could, reinforcing everything his uncle and Katrina had told him — that ghosts weren't that much much different than living people. They could feel, they could hurt and apparently even cry. They just didn't have bodies.

"That's wonderful," his mother said through her tears. "I wanted nothing else except for your father to be in your life."

Nick repeated his mother's words to him.

"He'll never replace you Mom," Sam said. "I miss you so much; sometimes I can't stand it."

"Tell him…tell him that he'll be fine. Tell him that I want him to love his father as he loved me," she paused. "And that everything will be okay."

Nick told Sam what his mother had said. Sam nodded, unable to speak.

His mother's head turned to the right wall. "What's that?"

Nick followed her gaze. "What? I don't see anything."

"That light." A blazing smile broke out on her face, and her eyes twinkled. "Is that for me?"

Nick nodded. "That must be your light. Nobody can see it but you."

"What's up?" Sam asked. "What's going on?"

Nick narrowed his eyes as he turned his gaze to Sam. "She's getting ready to leave."

Sam flew to his feet, a panicked look on his face. "Go? Go where? No, you can't go!"

"Sam," Nick said quietly. Sam turned his head toward Nick. "It's her time to go. My uncle said that when people pass on, they cross over to begin the next stage of their journey. The only reason they hang around here is that there's something that they need to do or a message they need to give to a loved one. You mom wanted to make sure that you found your dad. Now that you have, she can move on."

"No! Mom, stay, please!"

"I can't honey. He's right. It's time for me to leave." She gazed at the wall again and then brought her hand to her mouth. "Oh my god, it's my brother! He's waiting for me."

"What's she saying?" Sam asked.

"Her brother is in the light," Nick said. "He's waiting for her."

"Uncle Kyle," said Sam. "He died a couple of years ago in a car crash."

As Sam's mother walked closer to the wall, her entire body took on an ethereal glow. She turned toward them, blew a kiss to Sam and then held out her right arm as if she were holding hands with someone. She then disappeared.

Nick immediately noticed that the sensations he typically experiences when there's a spirit around were gone. He reached out and touched Sam's arm.

"She's gone, Sam."

Sam sunk back down into his chair and rested his head in his hands. Nick got up, walked over to Sam's chair and sat down next to him. He wasn't sure what to do or say. He put his arm around Sam.

"She was a sweet lady, Sam, your mom. You're lucky you got to talk to her one more time. Most people never get that opportunity."

Sam looked up. "You're right Nick. I am lucky. And now I have my dad, someone who I thought was long dead."

Nick smiled. "Maybe I'll get a chance to meet him sometime?"

"For sure. That'd be great."

"Did you tell him about me and the ghost thing?" Nick asked.

Sam shook his head. "No. I told him that I came across the box while going through Mom's stuff. I don't know him well enough to know how he'd react to something like that."

Nick breathed a sigh of relief. "Don't tell him, okay? I'd prefer that nobody else knows."

Sam smiled. "Don't worry. I won't. Promise"

Nick nodded. "And thanks for not telling anyone at school."

Sam's face instantly reddened. He looked down and fell silent.

"Oh shit. You told somebody, didn't you?" Nick asked. His voice came out sharper than he'd intended. His heart slammed against his ribcage. "Please don't tell me that this is going to be common knowledge all around school tomorrow."

Sam slowly raised his head and met Nick's gaze. He nodded. "I only told one person."

"Who?" Nick asked desperately. "Who did you tell?" Nick needed to know the answer to the question, and yet he didn't want to know.

"Gabe Griffin."

Nick felt stricken, and his mouth grew dry. Of all the people at school, he especially didn't want Gabe to find out. He didn't want Gabe to think he was a freak of nature. But now, it was too late for that. He winced at the thought.

"When did you tell him?" Nick asked as softly and evenly as he could. He was trying to keep his voice calm, which was not an easy feat. He was pissed at Sam — super-pissed — but didn't want Sam to know it. Not after what he'd just gone through with his mom.

"Last night. Listen, I'm so sorry. Gabe's my best friend, and after finding the box, I was so excited that my dad was still alive and that I was going to see him. So I called Gabe to tell him the news. I didn't mean to rat you out. I just kinda blurted out the entire story without thinking it through. Gabe was incredulous but seemed okay with it. With you, I mean. I don't think he'd tell anyone."

Nick straightened. *He's not your best friend. He's my best friend.* "You told him last night?"

"Yeah, after I found the box and got the call from my dad," Sam said somberly. "I wasn't thinking. I didn't mean to spill your secret. But Gabe's cool with it. Really, he is."

Nick wouldn't have cared if Sam had told anyone else. But of all people, he had to tell Gabe. Funny that Gabe didn't mention it at all during school; although he had caught Gabe giving him a strange look once or twice. But mostly, Gabe hadn't treated him any differently than usual. Maybe Sam was right. Maybe Gabe was cool with it.

"I swear I won't tell anyone else," Sam said. "Promise."

Nick turned his gaze to meet Sam's, and Sam lurched back. Sam's face was still red, maybe partly from crying earlier. His jaw tensed and his entire body stiffened like he was afraid Nick was going to hit him.

"It's okay Sam. I probably would've done the same thing." He reached over and touched Sam's arm. "I'm not pissed." Strangely enough, it was the truth. The anger had passed once he realized that Gabe had discovered his secret last night and had said nothing. Maybe Sam had done Nick a favor instead of a disservice. Now he wouldn't have to lie to Gabe.

"How did Gabe react when you told him? What did he say?"

"I don't think he believed me at first, about you being able to see ghosts. So I told him the whole story, and he was convinced at the end. I don't think he'll have any doubts after I tell him what happened today." He stopped and studied Nick's face. "You don't mind if I tell him about today, do you? I mean he already knows about you. It's just that he was there for me when my mom died, and he's the only person I feel comfortable talking about shit like this with."

Nick nodded. "Sure, since he already knows anyway."

Sam reached over and squeezed Nick's shoulder. "I can't even begin to thank you for everything you've done for my mom and me. I didn't even believe in this stuff a couple of days ago. Ghosts. Who'd a thunk it?"

Nick laughed. "I didn't even believe it either. This kind of started happening to me a couple of weeks ago all at once, without any warning. Although from what I know now, it's probably been going on for awhile. I just didn't realize it."

"So you can see the ghosts with your eyes? It's not like in your head?"

"They look like normal people."

"Really? So how can you tell them apart from living people?"

"It's not easy. But when I'm around a spirit, my skin gets this weird tingly feeling, and my stomach feels weird, the kind of stomach you get when you're nervous or extra scared. I didn't pay any attention to it at first. My uncle finally told me what was going on. Oh, and another thing — the moment they catch you looking at them, they freak out and get all excited that someone can finally see them."

"It must be pretty lonely wandering around with nobody being able to hear you or see you."

"I imagine so. I hope when I die, I cross over right away."

Sam locked eyes with Nick and held the stare for a few moments. "That makes what you do super important Nick. I wouldn't be able to stand it if I knew that my mom was in that situation — stuck on earth forever with nothing to look forward to or nobody to talk to. How badly would that suck?" He shuddered. "We were fortunate that you were around."

Nick felt the tears behind his eyes. "I'm glad I could help. She was a nice lady — although a bit scary at first."

Sam raised his eyebrows. "My mom was scary? Like Friday the 13th Michael Meyers kind of scary?"

Nick chuckled. "Nah. To me, all the spirits seem scary, especially when they figure out that I can see them. They're so desperate for someone to help them, that they come across kinda strong. My uncle says that sometimes they'll even make threats so that you'll help them. Most of them can't hurt you though." Nick thought about James and the flying furniture. He hoped that James had kept his promise and not harmed Janet.

Sam smiled. "I'm happy my mom didn't scare you away then." Sam pulled out his phone from his pocket and pressed the home screen button. "I gotta get going. I'm meeting with a bunch from school to work on a group paper."

"You gonna get into trouble for missing school today?"

"My dad wrote a note," he said, smiling. "Oh, and one more thing."

"Yeah?"

"Sorry I was such a dick to you at school yesterday."

Nick chuckled. "I understand, believe me. I'm sure I sounded like a crazy person."

After Sam had gone, Nick stayed in the screen porch and texted his uncle.

U awake?

A moment later his phone buzzed.

Yup. But a bit groggy. What's up?

Nick typed his response.

Crossed over my first ghost today.

His uncle's reply came right away.

Really?? Who? James?

No. A friend of mine's mom.

It took nearly a minute before his uncle replied.

The boy you told me about yesterday?

Yup. Sam.

So ur not worried about it getting around school?

Nah, I trust him. My best friend knows too.

Gabe knows? his uncle typed.

Yeah.

So you told him???

No, the guy whose mom I helped did.

Ah. I hope it doesn't get out at school.

Nick took a few moments before deciding what to type.

I think it'll be okay.

U coming tomorrow?

L8tr on. Meeting Katrina after school.

One last text came from his uncle.

OK. Can't wait to hear about it. c u.

He was excited about meeting with Katrina, wondering what she was going to teach him. He hoped that she might have some insight on how to proceed with the James and Janet situation because as things stood right now, he had no idea whatsoever about what he should do next.

Chapter Fifteen

K atrina opened the door and then clapped her
hands, delighted. "Nicholas, you came!"

"Did you think I wouldn't?" Nick asked. A
wave of patchouli drifted out of the room and into Nick's
nostrils. A strong odor of the incense then blasted his eyes.
He rubbed them, to help relieve the stinging.

Katrina gestured him in. She was wearing a large flowing
dress, patterned with various yellow and red spring flowers.
Over her shoulders was draped a thin red silk scarf which was
clasped at her throat by what appeared to be an antique
broach. Her numerous bracelets clinked and clanked as she
pointed.

"I never assume anything with anyone," she said. "You'd
be amazed at the number of clients who make appointments
with me but fail to show up. I suppose they get cold feet or
perhaps they are afraid of what the Lady Katrina will tell
them." With that, she chuckled and pointed at him. "You
were like a little fawn when we first met — so timid and
unsure of yourself. And more than a bit wishy-washy about
your abilities. I was uncertain that I'd see you again."

Nick raised his eyebrows. "Wishy-washy?"

She laughed. "I recall at the faire. You were all set to admit defeat and turn your back on your abilities. But since you're here, I take it that you've changed your mind?"

Nick nodded. "I've been doing a lot of thinking lately, and you were right. I can help a lot of people. If it's my destiny, who am I to argue with that?"

"You do know you are not forced to acknowledge your gift, correct? While it is true that I told you that this work — referred to by many as *The Great Work* — is your life's purpose, it is not meant to rob you of your free will. You always have the final say-so about what path it is you choose to follow. Yes, you can certainly make a huge difference with your talents. But I do not want you to proceed because you feel it is something that you *must* do. If your heart's not in it, then it's not your path." She narrowed her eyes. "This work can be draining, frustrating, disheartening and even frightening. You must be willing to dedicate yourself completely to it."

He was silent for a moment, struggling with his thoughts. "What do you mean by *completely*?"

"What I mean my dear boy," she said, waving her index finger back and forth, "is that there cannot be any doubts. You must be certain that *this* is the road that you want to follow."

"But I can still go to college and get a job, right?"

She looked amused. "Why of course! We all have to eat and pay the bills. The ghosts certainly are not about to pay us for our time." She chuckled at her own joke.

He breathed out a sigh of relief. "When you said I had to dedicate myself completely, I thought you meant that as excluding everything else."

"Not at all, silly," she said smiling. "Although I have known some psychics over the years who have estranged themselves from their family and friends, focusing on nothing but The Work. Not good. People who do this soon find themselves cut off from everyone and everything. They end up with overblown egos and exaggerated views of their importance in the world, which then leads to difficulty in empathizing with their clients. When this occurs, the psychic becomes ineffectual. We must always remember that our only purpose in doing this type of work is to help others. If your client is not in a better place when he or she finishes with you, then you have failed."

"Got it," said Nick.

She offered him an easy smile. "As you will learn, I tend to veer off on tangents. Take only that which resonates with you and leave the rest. This is true with any teaching." She gestured to a small table situated in front of the living room window. Nick could see a deck of cards resting in the center of the table. "Shall we sit?"

Nick's mouth grew dry, and his body began to tremble. She seemed so knowledgeable, so strong, so confident. No doubt he was going to make a fool of himself in front of her. Come to think of it, he did feel like a fawn after all.

He wedged himself into the tight space between the chair and the table and took a deep breath, trying to calm his shaking hands. He recognized the pattern of the cards on the table. They belonged to the same kind of Tarot deck that he now owned. At least he'd be a little familiar with something and wouldn't make a complete ass of himself — unless she quizzed him on the cards. He prayed that she wouldn't.

She looked at him and widened her eyes. "My goodness, what is it?" she asked.

"What do you mean?"

"I am getting wave after wave of anxious energy from you. What on earth is wrong? Are you afraid?"

Nick swallowed. "A little nervous, I guess."

"Oh honey, there's nothing to be nervous about. I'm the one who should be nervous around you. You're one of the most gifted psychic mediums I've ever encountered. Or at least, that's what my instinct is telling me. Now what we need to do is to get you to hone those abilities and control them — bend them to your will, as it were." She paused and gave him a sweet smile. "So when you come in here, leave your fears, anxieties, and burdens at the door. Okay, sweetie?"

Nick nodded. "Okay."

"Good. So tell me about your week."

"I crossed over my first ghost."

Her eyes twinkled, and she clapped with a burst of enthusiasm. "And we haven't even had a lesson yet! How exciting! Tell me all about it."

Nick recounted all of the events that led up to the encounter on Nick's porch with Sam and his mother.

"That is absolutely wonderful. Now you understand, don't you? You now know the importance of our work, how essential it is."

Nick nodded. "I do."

"This event with your friend's mother taught you more that afternoon than I could teach you in weeks of lessons. You see Nicholas, through our work we bring order and balance in the world in our own little way. By helping these people — in your case, those spirits who haven't crossed over — we bring joy as we relieve their suffering. But it is not only the spirits to whom we are of service. It is their loved ones as well. You saw this with your friend Sam, did you not?"

"I guess so. He did seem awfully grateful afterward."

"Certainly he was. Think about it, Nicholas. Not only did you bring peace to his mother, but you allowed him to communicate with her one final time, to say a proper good-bye. Moreover, you also succeeded in reuniting him with his father. Think of the implications that just this fact alone will have on your friend's life. You see now?"

Nick nodded. "I understand. It's not just the ghosts that we are helping but everyone else involved."

"Exactly!" she shouted. She laughed when Nick jumped in his chair, startled at her enthusiasm. "Sometimes we help the families more than the ghosts. You will undoubtedly encounter spirits who are still here, not because they've unfinished business per se, but rather because their husband, wife, boyfriend or girlfriend won't let them go. Some people hold on so desperately to their grief that they end up binding their deceased loved one to them, here in the physical. In these types of cases, it is the loved one whom you must heal, not necessarily the ghost."

"I thought you didn't see ghosts," Nick said.

"I don't," she said in a light voice, smiling pleasantly. "At least, not in the way you can." She pointed to the deck of cards on the table. "Did you know that you can communicate with spirits through Tarot cards?"

Nick's eyes widened. "So I could talk to James through the cards?"

She shook her head. "Not exactly. Your gift is to see and converse with spirits who haven't crossed over. But by using the cards, you can sometimes communicate with those on the Other Side. That is to say, those spirits who are no longer here on earth but who have crossed over into the light. When grief-stricken clients come to see you, messages for their loved ones often come through during a reading. It's a strange process actually. Instead of physically seeing the spirits with the eyes like you do, I get flashes of images and a string of thoughts that go with those images. Often, it's the picture on a card that sets it off."

"I had no idea," Nick said. "My uncle never told me that."

"Perhaps he doesn't even know that himself," Katrina said.

"From what you tell me, he's a whisperer like you." She tapped the side of her head. "No doubt, most of his work involves assisting ghosts that he can see with his eyes to cross over. My work, however, involves performing readings for clients, in which I use my talents in an entirely different way than you or your uncle."

Nick studied the deck of cards for a moment and then shifted his regard to Katrina. "Is this something that I could do?"

She creased her brow. "I don't know. Possibly. When I read you the other day, I sensed that your abilities are strong, although it'd be unusual for someone to be both a medium and a whisperer. But it's not unheard of. But first, let's work on the abilities that we *know* you have, okay?"

Nick nodded. "Deal."

Her eyes held him. She folded her hands and rested them on the table in front of her. "There's something you want to ask me, correct?"

Nick smiled. "You really are psychic."

She laughed. "Nick, one does not need to be psychic to see you squirming in that chair like an overexcited child. Now tell me what's on your mind."

"It's about that case I told you about. James and Janet."

She nodded. "Ah, the ghost who is haunting his poor wife."

"According to his wife, he died of a heart attack. Since the last time we spoke, I've had a conversation with him, James. He swears that he didn't die of a heart attack but rather was murdered by his wife. I talked him into laying off of her for the time being until we know for sure, but I don't know how long he'll leave her alone. He was spitting mad."

Katrina creased her brow and locked gazes with him. "What does your intuition tell you?"

"Huh? What do you mean."

"Your gut Nicholas. Use your intuition. What does your gut tell you?"

"I believe him. I don't think that he died from a heart attack. I think he was murdered, but I don't see the wife as the murderer."

Katrina raised her eyebrows. "Now that is interesting. What makes you think so?"

Nick shrugged. "Just my gut I guess. When talking with Janet, she seemed genuinely confused as to why James was angry with her. If she had killed him, wouldn't she have figured out that this was the reason he was so pissed off at her?"

"So one would think," said Katrina. "But people can be convincing actors when the need arises. So what was your question for me?"

"I wanted to know if you could help me to figure out who killed James and what I should do next. I promised I'd help him but I don't know how. My uncle doesn't want me to get involved too deeply. He's afraid it's too dangerous."

"He has a point," said Katrina. "There's certainly a risk when getting involved with murderers — and you shouldn't make promises to people unless you know you can keep them."

"Can you do a reading about it?" Nick asked.

Katrina smiled. She reached for the cards and then pushed them toward Nick. "How about if *you* do a reading on it? You're the one who is the student, correct?"

"But I'm not good enough," complained Nick. "I don't know all the meanings of the cards yet. I want to make sure that I get it right so I know what to do."

She crossed her arms and heaved an icy glare at him. "Nicholas," she said slowly. "If you are going to be successful in this work, you have to trust yourself. Do not compare your abilities to others or think that someone else can do better.

You must trust your own interpretations and your own judgment. What makes you think I can do a reading any better than you? Because I have more experience? Blah! We all have different gifts, different insights, different strengths and different weaknesses. But one weakness that you must *not* have is that of self-doubt." Her gaze softened. "That is one weakness that will cause you to fail. Okay?"

Nick reared back a bit in the chair and then nodded. "What do you want me to do."

"Have you done a reading yet on this?"

Nick took a deep breath and nodded. "I asked my cards if James was murdered."

"And what was the result of the reading?"

"The card that came up was the 10 of Swords."

She straightened and looked at him. "And what message did you get from that?"

"It's a scary card, that's for sure." Nick swallowed. "The guy on the ground with all the swords sticking in his back made me think that James was right — that he was murdered."

"I feel that you're on the right track. I most likely would have reached the same conclusion. So we've got at least a part of this nailed down. So let's assume that the cards were right and that somebody killed James. What else do you want to know?"

They exchanged looks. "Who murdered him, I guess. I'd want to know who killed him and why."

She pointed to the cards. "That's a good start. When doing a reading, you always want to decide beforehand on what questions you wish to ask. Get the questions entrenched in your mind as firmly as possible. I like to visualize them written out on a giant blackboard in my mind's eye. I close my eyes and study the questions as I shuffle. Okay, what else?"

Nick thought for a moment. He glanced at the cards and then back at Katrina. "What should I do about it?"

She took a deep breath. "Another lesson Nicholas. You never ask the cards a question that has the word 'should' in it."

Nick creased his brow. He vaguely remembered his uncle telling him the same thing but couldn't remember why. He should have been paying better attention. "How come?"

She smiled. "You tell me."

Nick sat silent for several moments, desperately trying to remember what his uncle had told him. He finally gave up. "I have no idea. Because it's asking for advice? But if you can't ask the cards for advice, then what good are they?"

Katrina shook her head. "Not exactly. When you ask the cards questions that begin with "should," you are taking your responsibility and placing it somewhere else. That is to say, you are giving someone else or something else your power."

"I don't get it."

Okay. Imagine I ask the cards the question: 'Should I marry Rick?' and the Hierophant card comes up. Do you know what the Hierophant card signifies?"

"It has to do with religion, doesn't it?"

She nodded. "But it's also associated with marriage ceremonies. In fact, some call it 'the marriage card.' With that in mind, I might take the answer as a yes — I should marry Rick. Even though I might not love Rick, the cards said that I should marry him. So I do. And where do I end up? Unhappy, in a loveless marriage. In this situation, I gave away my power to the cards."

"So what kind of questions can I ask then?"

"Try something like 'what would be the outcome if I took this path' or 'what advice do the cards have for the next step.' These types of questions are always preferable to those that include the word 'should'."

"I think my uncle mentioned something about this."

She smiled. "It's also worth noting that just because the cards give advice, doesn't mean you have to take it. Likewise, if the cards show you an undesirable outcome, you make changes in your life to avoid that outcome. You might draw additional cards to see what you can do to avoid that particular outcome or at the very least, soften the blow when it arrives. Do you see where I'm going with this?"

Nick nodded. "I think so. I will avoid the word *should* from this point forward."

She flashed him a warm smile. "So back to our issue. We want to find out who murdered James and what to do about it. So what question can you ask?"

"What steps can I take to help James?"

She clapped her hands excitedly. "Excellent! What else do you want to know?"

"Is this case dangerous for me?"

"Not bad, but Tarot is not that great at answering yes or no questions. It's best to avoid them if possible."

Nick brushed his hands through his hair. "There certainly seems to be a lot of rules."

"They're not rules per se but more like best practices. So back to the questions. How else could you rephrase it?"

Nick thought for a moment. "What do I need to know about the dangers of this case?"

She nodded. "Perfect. Okay, that's at least three cards." She pointed to the deck. "Visualize your questions and shuffle.

Nick thought of four questions and tried to imagine them written out on the blackboard, just as Katrina had recommended. At first, he couldn't do it. He'd bring the blackboard into view and then *poof*; it would disappear. After a couple of tries, he finally got the hang of it and could visually see his questions.

Then, Katrina taught him how to split the deck into three piles and then reassemble them. He dealt out four cards.

"So what was the first question?"

"Who murdered James," Nick said. He turned over the card.

"It's the Three of Pentacles," Katrina said.

Nick looked at the card and crossed his arms. "That's not very helpful."

"Don't be so hasty. Look at the image. What do you see?"

"There's a guy working, and it looks like there are two people watching him. One of them is dressed like a monk. The monk might be talking to the person next to him, maybe commenting on the guy's work."

"What might this be telling you?" Katrina asked.

"That he was killed by a priest?"

She chuckled. "I suppose it's possible, but unlikely." She tapped the card with her index finger. "What do you know about the suit of Pentacles?"

"They have to do with health and money, right?"

She nodded. "Anything else."

Nick glanced at the card again and all of a sudden it came to him. "Work! Someone at work killed him!"

Katrina stared at the card and nodded. "Maybe. Or it could be stating what we already know, that he died at work. What was your next question?"

"Why. Why did he kill James?"

"Or she," Katrina added.

"Right," Nick said. He turned over the next card.

"Seven of Swords," Katrina said.

"I've seen that card before," Nick said. "I saw it in my head, I think."

"In your head? You mean you visualized it?"

Nick nodded. "Yeah, it just popped into my thoughts."

"That's a sign that you need to pay special attention to it. Do you remember what the card means?"

"I looked it up. It means deception." He pointed at the card. "The guy in the card looks like he's stealing those swords so it could also be thievery."

"Good. Stare at the image for a moment and then close your eyes. See if anything else comes to you."

Nick did as he was told. He saw the card in his mind's eye, saw the curly-haired man sneaking off with the swords. Then out of the blue, another card popped up in his mind. He opened his eyes.

"I saw another card!"

Katrina looked confused. "What do you mean another card?"

"I'm pretty sure it was the Queen of Cups," Nick said. "While I was thinking about the Seven of Swords card, the picture in my mind changed to the lady on the throne holding a large golden cup. I remember the Queen of Cups because my uncle said it was one of his favorites."

Katrina creased her brow. "So the card just showed up in your mind?

Nick nodded.

"Does this happened often?"

Nick creased his brow. "No, only once before today."

She stared at him for a moment and then smiled. "I am impressed, especially since you haven't been working with the cards all that long. You're beginning to think symbolically. Okay, so what does the Queen of Cups tell you, if paired with the first card?"

"The first thing that I thought of was an affair. He's sneaking around with a woman."

She considered this. "You might be onto something. The Seven of Swords can sometimes represent an affair, someone cheating on their spouse."

"What does that have to do with who killed James?"

Katrina shook her head. "That's something you'll have to work out for yourself. So what's the next question?"

"What can I do to help James," Nick said. He turned over the card.

"The Hermit?" asked Nick. He frowned. "I don't get it. What am I supposed to do, become a recluse? How's that going to help James?"

Katrina laughed. "Don't take the card so literally. The Hermit in this instance could take on any one of several meanings. First, you might need to spend some time alone, thinking upon and contemplating the question. Sometimes a bit of inner-reflection can help us find the answers we are looking for."

"You said it has several meanings," said Nick. "What else could it mean?"

"Think of the Hermit as a wise elder, a counselor or even a mentor. This card might be advising you to seek guidance from someone else."

Nick stared at the card and blinked. "You know, this could represent my uncle. He's kind of a hermit and pretty much sticks to himself at his house. He hardly ever goes out. Do you think it means him?"

Katrina nodded. "It's certainly a possibility. Why not talk to him and see if he can recommend some ways in which you can help James?

"Okay. One more card. This was my question about danger." Nick turned over the card.

"Three of Swords," Nick said. The image depicted a red heart punctured by three daggers. "This doesn't look good at all. So someone's going to stab me in the heart?"

Katrina took a deep breath and then sighed. "At first glance, I can see how you might interpret this as the death of someone and it is true that the cards can sometimes provide a literal meaning. Traditionally, however, the Three of Swords signifies a broken heart — stormy weather for the emotions, if you will."

"Ah, hence the swords stuck in the heart."

She nodded. "You often see this card come up when someone has just broken up with their partner or has asked about the possibility of a reconciliation with an ex-lover. I've also seen it appear in situations where there's been cheating in the relationship, and the result of that deceit is shattered emotions of all those involved. So don't be too quick to jump to conclusions. You might have to wait a bit until this one plays itself out."

Nick raised his eyebrows. "So what do you think? Do you feel that there is danger for me?"

Katrina smiled. "Honey, I don't need the cards to tell me that. Anytime you find yourself involved with a murder, there's bound to be the possibility of danger." She scratched her head. "I find it curious that the theme of cheating and betrayal came in for two different cards." She tapped her finger on the 7 of Swords. "This message might be something you want to pay attention to."

"Do you think James was cheating on Janet?" Nick asked. "That could be why she killed him."

"It's possible. But you have to know for sure before you make any accusations."

"That's exactly what my uncle said."

She smiled. "Then he is indeed a wise man." She scooped up the cards. "You'll need to do some legwork on your own to come up with the answers you're looking for. Maybe use some of that Hermit energy and reflect on the situation. See what you come up with."

"Or go ask my uncle."

Katrina shook her head. "The easy way is not always the best way, Nicholas. Simple reflection can often provide the answers for which we're searching. I've solved many a complex situation during a meditation session." She stuffed the cards back into the deck and gave him a smile. "I have another client coming in a few minutes, so we'll have to end our session for today. I will say that you did very well. You're a fast learner."

Nick thrust his backpack over his shoulders. "Thanks for everything. You taught me a lot."

She wagged a finger at him. "Just be careful. Don't do anything until you've talked to me or your uncle first. Otherwise, I'll worry."

Nick flashed her a grin. "Promise. See you on Friday."

As Nick walked to his car, he thought more about the Three of Swords card. Was James cheating? Did he dare ask James that question? He already knew that the ghost had a temper. He'd seen it in action. Maybe Katrina was right. He'd best wait and talk to his uncle before confronting the ghost again.

Chapter Sixteen

"So let me see if I got this right," his mother said. Her arms were crossed in front of her, and she glared at Nick across the table. "You met a woman at a psychic fair —"

"It was the Renaissance Faire and her name is Katrina," Nick interrupted.

"Katrina," his mother repeated, "who said that she could teach you to talk to ghosts. Except that she can't see ghosts herself."

Nick nodded his head but kept silent.

"And that's where you were after school?"

Nick nodded. "She's giving me lessons a couple of times a week. She's going to help me develop my abilities."

His mother cringed. "Of course she is." She shot a glimpse at his father who was rocking in the recliner and hiding behind a photography magazine. She turned back to Nick.

"And what was the reason that you didn't bother to tell us where you were going?"

Nick shrugged. "I assumed you didn't want to know." He pushed his cereal bowl away from him. "You made it crystal clear the other day that you didn't want me to ever mention it or talk about it in your presence. So I didn't."

His mother slammed her fist down onto the table. His father lowered the paper. "I never said that!"

"Um...yeah, you did? If I remember correctly, you told me to shut up and that you didn't want to hear any more of what I had to say. So I complied. I shut up."

"You will not use my own words against me, young man."

"You're the one who said them."

"Regardless, that doesn't give you the right to go out gallivanting with strangers without telling your father or me where you are."

"She's not exactly a stranger. She knows Uncle Mitch."

"Well, imagine my surprise!" her mother said. "So your uncle knows another crackpot."

Nick stiffened.

"So what, you think I'm a crackpot too?" Nick felt tears try to push through his eyelids, but he fought them off. This was exactly the kind of reaction that he feared. This was why he'd never wanted to tell his parents in the first place. He tensed his jaw, determined that he was *not* going to let his parents see him cry.

"That's enough!" his father said. Both Nick and his mother reared back. He threw his magazine on the floor. "This conversation ends now."

"Don't you even think about telling me what to do John," his mother said through clenched teeth. "It's because of *your* family that we're even talking about this."

His father pursed his lips and sighed loudly. "Liz, this is about our son, not about my family. Let's talk about this like the rational adults that we are." He turned his gaze to Nick and gave him a slight nod. "Isn't it time for you to be getting off to school?"

Nick nodded but said nothing. This was one conversation

in which he did not want to get involved. He grabbed his backpack, scooped up his car keys from the counter and dashed out the door without saying goodbye.

He'd hate to be his dad right about now.

~

NICK'S BREATH FLEW RIGHT OUT OF HIM WHEN HE TURNED the corner and noticed Gabe standing at his locker. Gabe's locker was only a couple away from Nick's, so there was no more avoiding him.

Gabe was rummaging through his locker when Nick approached.

"Hey," said Nick.

"Nick. Been looking for you. Y'all not avoiding me now, are you?"

"Course not." He turned toward his locker.

"Talked to Sam earlier and he said that he hadn't seen you. Thought you might be having lunch with him."

Nick was silent for a moment, struggling with the words that couldn't find their way out of his mouth. "I never have lunch with Sam. He's more your buddy than mine."

"I just thought that with everything that happened and all. Sam thinks mighty highly of you now, you know. He appreciates everything that you did for him."

Nick looked down. "I really didn't do all that much."

"Now don't you go and get all modest on me, Nick Michelson. What you did was enormous, unless little ol' Sam is playing tricks on me and telling me some tall tales." He crossed his arms in front of his chest.

Nick looked up and met Gabe's eyes. Gabe had an odd smirk on his face that made Nick uncomfortable.

Nick broke the gaze and dialed the combination to his locker. He pulled on the lock. Damn.

"You been keeping secrets from me, huh?" Gabe said. The tone of his voice had suddenly turned frosty.

Nick was hoping that Gabe wouldn't go there. But now that he was there, there was no turning back, although he wished it didn't have to be at school.

"I didn't intend to," he said. "Keep it a secret, I mean. It all happened so fast. I didn't even know I had these abilities until about a week ago." As the words left Nick's mouth, he thought about how lame his excuse sounded. This was Gabe he was talking to, not some stranger.

Gabe raised his eyebrows. "Really? How could you not know? I think I'd know it if I saw ghosts."

Nick turned his head to make sure that nobody was looking. He moved in closer to Gabe. He took a deep breath and inhaled. Gabe smelled like sweet chocolate. "It's not easy to tell them apart from living people. They look just like anyone else, except they're usually shouting at someone."

Gabe looked over his shoulder. "I don't have any ghosts hovering around me, do I?"

Nick punched his arm playfully. "Not that I can see."

Gabe frowned, and his expression grew even more serious. "Why didn't you tell me about it, Nick? I thought we all were friends or was I mistaken?"

Nick tugged at his shirt. "Come on Gabe. You know you're my best friend."

Gabe shook his head and took a step back. "So why did I have to find out about it from Sam and not you. I mean WTF Nick?"

Ah shit. Gabe was pissed at him. Nick didn't see that coming at all.

Nick dialed the combination again and his locked clicked open. He pulled out his World History book and closed the locker. "I wasn't planning on telling anyone, not even my parents. I was gonna ignore all of it. I didn't want anybody to know."

"But you told Sam," Gabe said. "So why'd you change your mind?"

Nick shrugged. "I dunno, there were a couple of reasons I guess. First of all, my grandma showed up at her funeral and made me promise that I'd pass on messages to my parents."

"What else?" Gabe asked. The tone of his voice was sharp.

"Sam's mom. She wasn't going to let it go once she figured out that I could see her. Boy, was she pushy!"

Gabe let loose with a short chuckle that sounded forced; then his face grew serious again. "I wish you felt that you could have told me. I mean this isn't the kind of thing a body should face alone."

Nick swallowed and felt the heat rise in his face. "I didn't think you'd understand. I was afraid that you'd think that I was some kind of a freak show."

Gabe took a step closer to him, so close that Nick could smell the mint on his breath. "I thought you knew me better than that. You think I'd ever desert you or make fun of you? Really Nick? After everything we've been through? I thought we were real friends, you and I. True friends."

"We are," Nick said. "You have to understand that this isn't an easy thing to tell anybody."

"I'm not just anybody, now am I? I'm supposed to be your best friend. I mean what the hell?" He glared at Nick now. "So y'all were never planning on telling me?"

Nick hesitated before responding. Gabe's southern accent came through much more when he was upset. Like now. "No. I wasn't going to tell anybody. Ever. Not even you. I didn't want to risk it getting around."

"Isn't that just great!" Gabe turned his back to Nick, grabbed a book and a fat paper notebook from the locker and then slammed the locker door.

"Gabe," Nick said, but Gabe held up his hand behind him in a don't-talk-to-me gesture. Without saying a word, he took off down the hallway.

Stunned, Nick watched his friend disappear into a classroom and felt a hole in his chest like somebody had punched him. How in the hell did he end up pissing off Gabe? Seeing ghosts was okay, but keeping it to himself wasn't? Nick was relieved that he didn't have his last class of the day with Gabe. He didn't think he could take Gabe staring bullets at him for an entire hour — or worse yet, ignoring him. He was gonna have to fix this with Gabe somehow, make things right. He couldn't take his friend being mad at him. Anyone else, but not Gabe. Definitely not Gabe.

The last bell rang, and he took off running down the hallway.

Chapter Seventeen

"You look a lot better today," Nick said. "Not quite as pale as yesterday. It looks like your color's coming back.

His uncle scooted himself up against the bed board. "Feeling better too. I think I even have all of my words back, as far as I can tell."

"I noticed that last night. I don't think you stumbled once. Although we didn't get much of a chance to talk."

"Yeah, I'm sorry about that. Whatever they're giving me makes me loopy and tired. I think all I've done since I've been here is sleep."

"Isn't that what hospitals are for?" Nick asked. "To get rest?"

Mitch reached over to the bedside table and took the glass of water that was sitting on it. The straw slurped as he sipped. "You'd think so, right? Unfortunately, that's not the case at all. I'm lucky if I got three hours of sleep the night before. That's why I was so out of it last night. The nurses come in every hour or so to wake you up and take your vitals.

Then there are the people screaming and shouting all night long."

"Shouting and screaming? Really?"

"The night nurse told me that whenever someone comes into the emergency room, and the hospital decides to check them in for the night, they bring 'em here." He raised his eyebrows. "Lucky me, hey? Needless to say, there's no shortage of drama to be had here at night."

"I'm sure all the ghosts around here don't help either."

His uncle raised an eyebrow. "Really? I haven't seen one since I've been here."

"You kidding, right? How can you not have seen them? They're everywhere, and some of them are creepy as hell."

"That's one advantage of being sick. Your psychic side tends to shut down as your body heals." His uncle narrowed his eyes. "So you say there are lots of them around?"

Nick noticed the ghost of a young woman walked past his uncle's room. She said, "Excuse me, have you seen my doctor?" to everyone who passed by, ghost or human.

"You have no idea."

His uncle laughed. "I think I do. Regrettably, I've spent my share of time in hospitals."

"Bet you're looking forward to getting out of here, huh?" Nick asked, to change the conversation.

"And how." He locked eyes with Nick. "I hate to admit this, but I don't remember too much of our conversation last night. I was rather high from the meds."

Nick smiled. "There's not much to remember really. I wasn't here too long before you dozed off. I could tell that you were flying on something. You repeated everything like six or seven times."

His uncle grinned. "So you got here late yesterday?

Nick nodded. "I had a session with Katrina."

His uncle snapped his head up, and his face brightened. He patted the pillow next to the rail and stuffed it behind his head. "I forgot all about your meeting with Katie. How did it go?"

"It was interesting."

Mitch laughed. "Sessions with Katie always are. Did you tell her that I'm your uncle?"

Nick grimaced. "Whoops. It completely slipped my mind. Sorry — I'll make sure to do it next time."

Mitchell dismissed him with a wave of his hand. "No biggie. I just thought she might give you a deal if she knew that I was your uncle." He rubbed his chin. "Or come to think of it, maybe she'd charge you more."

Nick smiled. "She's not charging me anything."

His uncle's eyes grew wide. "Really? That certainly does not sound like the money-grubbing old Katie that I know. What gives?"

Nick shrugged. "Dunno. She said that she wanted to be a part of training the most powerful medium the world has ever known."

His uncle laughed. "My, my Nick. You've certainly have gotten full of yourself since we talked last."

"Hey, those were her words, not mine. I'm still as humble as ever." He bowed his head and closed his eyes in mock reverence.

"That remains to be seen." He pointed to the pitcher on the stand. "Can you pour me another glass of water? It's a bit tough to reach it from here."

Nick filled his uncle's glass and then handed it to him.

"So tell me," said Mitchell. "What did you and Katie talk about? Did she teach you anything new?"

"She goes by Katrina now, not Katie."

His uncle nodded and gave Nick a tight-lipped smile. "Ah yes, the Lady Katrina. I forgot."

"We worked some more with Tarot yesterday. She taught me the proper way to ask questions of the cards."

His uncle nodded. "That's essential to know. What else?"

"We did a reading about the James and Janet situation," Nick said. "I wanted to see if I could find out more info about it, maybe figure out what is truly going on."

"I was gonna ask you what was going on with that. Have you been back at their house since that day at the hotel?"

Nick shook his head. "I haven't talked to either of them since then. I wanted to talk to you and Katrina first."

"So tell me what the cards said."

Nick told him the results of the reading and how the cards hinted at an affair or betrayal of some sort.

His uncle scratched his head. "That's not surprising based what you've told me. You were pretty much already convinced that he was murdered." He folded his hands in front of him. "So you don't think it was the wife who did it?"

Nick shook his head. "Katrina told me to trust my intuition and listen to my gut. Well, my gut tells me that Janet didn't do it." He hoped that he was right about this. Otherwise, he could find himself in a mountain of trouble.

"I don't suppose your gut is hinting at who might have killed him?" There was a twinkle in his eye.

"You're not making fun of me, are you?" Nick asked. He crossed his arms in front of his chest and flashed a fake dirty look at his uncle.

"I would never do such a thing," said his uncle. "I'm genuinely interested in what's going on here, seeing that this is your first case."

"Second," Nick said.

"What do mean second?"

"Remember — I texted you the other night and told you that I got Sam's mother to cross over."

His uncle creased his brow. "Who is the hell is Sam?"

"A friend of Gabe's from school. I told you about him."

"Gabe," his uncle said, nodding his head. "Now that's a name that's familiar. So back to your ghost and his presumed innocent wife."

"So Katrina and I did another reading, and one of the cards suggested that maybe someone from work murdered James."

"What kind of work did James do? Hitman? Drug dealer? Mafia Godfather? Arms smuggler?"

"I think he's an accountant," Nick said.

"Accounting must be one tough gig. Any other hints? Boss? Coworker? Client?"

Nick shook his head. "None of that came out. But there were a couple of cards that caught our attention, that suggested an affair. The Queen of Cups came up next to the Seven of Swords." Nick creased his brow. "Wait, that's not quite the way it happened. After I had turned over the Seven of Swords, the Queen of Cups popped into my mind.

"Popped in your mind? How?"

"It was like one of those vision things I had. Sometimes, a card pops in my mind out of the blue."

His uncle scratched his chin. "And this happens often?"

"Only a couple of times."

"That makes me think that you're starting to think in symbols."

"That's what Katrina said."

"She's a bright one, that Katrina. So the Seven of Swords triggered the Queen of Cups. Hmm...you might be on to something with your hunch about an affair," said his uncle. "Jealousy's a common motive for murder."

"So much for Janet being innocent. If James was having an affair, then Janet could have been the one to kill him. Pissed off wife poisons husband."

Mitch creased his brow as if in deep thought and

drummed his fingers on the table. "Not necessarily," he said finally.

"How so?"

"What if it wasn't James who was having an affair? What if it was Janet?"

Nick reared back. "No way. Janet's such a nice lady. She'd never do that."

Mitch laughed. "You considered her a murder suspect a few moments ago. She couldn't be *that* nice. Besides, it's not only mean, rude ladies who cheat on their husbands. Come to think of it, who'd want to have an affair with someone who's ornery or off-putting?"

Nick shrugged. "I still don't see Janet cheating on James. She doesn't seem to be the type."

"And what type of disposition does a person need to have in order to cheat on one's spouse?" his uncle asked, a half-smile on his face. "We've already eliminated nice people."

Nick growled at him. "You're making fun of me again."

"Am not."

"Am too.

"Well, perhaps a tad." His uncle had a mischievous grin on his face.

"I've never met anyone who's had an affair, so I guess I don't know if she's the type or not."

His uncle laughed. "Ha! I bet you've met plenty of people who have had affairs, Nick. You just never knew about them. Sleeping around on your spouse is not something that someone's going to blurt out and tell you."

"So do you think Janet did have an affair?"

"What do you think?" his uncle countered.

Nick thought about it for a moment. "I have no idea. I suppose it's possible. I haven't known the lady for very long, so I have no idea what she's capable of."

"I have an idea. Why don't you go ask her?"

Nick widened his eyes. "What, are you crazy? You want me to go ask Janet if she cheated on her husband while he was alive?"

Mitch nodded. "Why not? She knows you can see spirits and she knows that you're trying to help James. It's a valid question."

"Not coming from me — a high school student!"

"I still feel that it's worth a try. By now, Janet must be quite desperate to prove her innocence to James, so I'm guessing that she won't object to you trying to cover all the bases." He folded his hands under his chin and rested his head on them. "She needs to understand that to get James crossed over, you'll need to find out what happened to him and that might involve some delicate and embarrassing questions."

"If it will get rid of this ghost, then I'm all for it." He paused. "I think." Nick's mouth went dry at the mere thought of asking Janet if she was, by any chance, sleeping around on her husband.

"It doesn't sound like James will cross over until he knows for sure who killed him."

The cards hinted so strongly at the idea of an affair that Nick couldn't get the notion out of his mind. James could have had an affair and Janet could have killed him in anger or jealousy. Now if it was Janet who had an affair, what would be the reason to kill James? Unless James found out about the affair and rather than face his anger — or a divorce — she murdered him. Nick knew firsthand how pissed-off James could become. Or maybe Janet and her lover planned on killing her husband and then running away together with the insurance money. Nah, too cliché.

Nick then remembered something that he had completely forgotten.

"Uncle Mitch," Nick said. "There's something else. The

day that I left the hotel room, I passed by a guy. When I turned my head, he was knocking on Janet's door. At the time, I didn't think much of it, figured it was just a friend. But maybe he's more than a friend."

His uncle was quiet for a moment. "Now you're on to something."

"And I'll ask James, too," said Nick.

"Ask him what?" asked his Uncle. "If he had an affair?"

Nick nodded. "If James were sleeping around, then she'd have a strong motive."

"And if it was Janet who was sleeping around?"

"Dunno," said Nick. "She still might have killed him. Maybe she was afraid of what he'd do if he found out. Or maybe she was in love with the guy and wanted James out of the way."

"Possibly." His uncle's expression grew serious. "But you might want to tread extra carefully around James. From what you've told me, he seems somewhat volatile. I'm concerned, more so now that we know he can move physical objects."

"Janet's not the only one who's desperate here. James is pushing me pretty hard to help him so I bet he'd be willing to answer just about any question I might have, even a delicate one," said Nick.

"I hope you're right," said Mitch. "So the ghost thinks it's poison that did him in?"

"Yup," said Nick. "Shortly before he died, Janet had fixed him a drink. He'd consumed a good portion of it when without any warning, a horrible stomach pain took hold of him. That's the last thing he remembers."

"What about the glass or the liquor bottle?"

Nick slapped himself in the head. "Shit! I forgot all about that. I was going to ask someone to check it out."

Mitch reached over and touched Nick's arm. "Good plan.

If everyone thought he died of a heart attack, then it's very likely that nobody bothered to check the booze bottle."

"I think James mentioned that the booze was in a canister of some kind. Or maybe was it a carafe." Nick pursed his lips. "You think it might still be there?"

"Doubtful. If the killer had any brains whatsoever, he or she would have gotten rid of it by now. But what if they neglected to wash out the container? If they didn't, then there still could be some poison residue left." His uncle's expression grew serious. "Now Nick, this is one of those times where you have to be careful when approaching the police. If you stroll in there and ask them to check James's office for poison, you could very likely become a suspect yourself."

"Not if I explain to them," Nick said.

"And what exactly are you going to explain to them?" asked his uncle. "That the ghost of the victim came to you and told you that somebody poisoned him?"

"Oh, right." Nick rubbed his forehead. "So what do you suggest?"

"You make an anonymous call or send an anonymous email. I've done it many times." He creased his brow and tapped his chin. "Too bad we weren't in Chicago. I had a friend there who worked in homicide and who knew all about my line of work. But since we have no such connections here, we're going to have to do things the hard way. If you do decide to call them, make sure you use a public phone."

Nick chuckled. "A public phone? Really?"

"I grant you that it's not an easy task finding one these days. You don't see too many phone booths around anymore though there are a few here and there."

Nick furrowed his brow. "I think there's still one at the Mobil station on the corner near our house."

"The point I'm trying to make is that you never, ever use

your cell phone. I personally prefer email, but again, you want to ensure that there's no way to trace the message back to you. A public computer that doesn't require you log in with any traceable credentials is your best bet."

Nick considered this for a moment. "But I'd need to use my email account to send a message. How else could I do it?"

His uncle shook his head. "You create a new email account from the public computer using one of the freebie services like Google or Yahoo Mail, and then you send the message using that account. Of course, you'd use a fake name when creating the account."

"Kinda like a secret identity," said Nick.

"Exactly. And you make sure that never access the account from home. You don't want it to be traceable back to you in any way."

"Did I need to send the message to someone in particular? I don't personally know any policemen."

"Most police department websites include a contact email address," said Mitch. "If you send a message to that address, it should reach someone relevant. I'd hope that they would take evidence in a murder investigation seriously."

"Although it's not technically a murder investigation, given that a heart attack was considered the official cause of death. And you really couldn't call it evidence, because there isn't any. It's more like hearsay."

His uncle smiled. "Good points, Nick. Regardless, your message should hopefully get them to at least ask some more questions, perhaps even open up a new investigation."

Nick studied his uncle for a moment. "Did you do this a lot, anonymously contacting the police?"

"From time to time," his uncle said. "Luckily, most of the ghosts I've worked with were not murdered but some were involved in other dodgy activities that required police involvement. There was the occasional murder victim

though." Mitch's face crumpled. "I remembered one particular case where a teenage boy supposedly passed away by his
own hand. He found me, and I agreed to help him. After a bit
of digging around, we were able to prove that his father had
killed him and had made it look like a suicide. It was truly a
heart-wrenching case. I'm so glad that I was able to help the
young man cross over."

"Sounds sad."

"It was very sad — and such a waste too. This kid's life
ended way too soon. He was a bright, warm-hearted and
likable young man." His uncle locked his gaze onto Nick's
face. "Now that I think about it Nick, he was a lot like you."
His uncle's jaw tightened. "I just hope that his father rots
in jail."

Nick swallowed. "I wouldn't be disappointed if this was
the last murder case I had to deal with."

His uncle smiled. "I hope for your sake that it is too. But
it doesn't matter whether a person died of murder, an accident, a disease, or a slip in the tub. It's never an easy thing to
get involved. Unless you have a heart of stone, you can't help
but feel for the spirits and their families. We never get the
ghosts who have tightened up all of their loose ends. We get
the confused and lost spirits — or the ones who need us to
pass on vital messages to their families. This is not easy work,
by no means."

Nick gave his uncle a weak smile. "Yeah, I'm getting that.
James is certainly a handful." Nick all at once felt that
someone was watching them and he looked up. His father
stood in the doorway looking at the both of them, a stony
expression on his face.

"Hi Dad," Nick said. How long had his father been there
and how much he had heard?

"Nick," his father said. He looked at Mitch. "He's not

keeping you from rest, is he? I know what a chatterbox Nick can sometimes be."

His uncle smiled and looked at Nick. "Not at all. Truth be told, I feel much better after Nick's visits." He then turned his regard back to Nick's father. "I'm glad you came John."

"I'm happy to see that you're doing better," Nick's father said. "Did they set a date yet for the surgery?"

Nick cleared his throat. "I think it's time for me to get going. I got school work to do. I'll come back tomorrow, Uncle."

His uncle gave him a quick wave. "I'm looking forward to it. And be careful Nick."

Nick noticed his father's confused expression. He'd leave it to his uncle to explain it. Nick gave them both a wave and a nod before leaving the hospital room.

As he turned the corner, he nearly collided with a spirit who was shuffling down the hallway. He was a gaunt, youngish man who looked to be in his early 30's and was pushing an IV cart down the hall. A loose tube swung back and forth from the cart. He lingered and stared directly at Nick.

"Have you perchance seen my wife? She's quite beautiful, with long blond hair and blue eyes. She was supposed to come and see me. I don't know where she could be. It's not like her."

"I'm sorry, but I haven't."

The ghost nodded and continued down the hallway. The wheels of the IV cart squeaked as he pushed it and the sound made Nick's heart sink. Nick wondered how long the poor man has been stuck here, looking for his wife. Judging by the man's old-fashioned haircut, it's most likely been awhile.

Nick shook himself and increased the pace of his step. He was off to ask Janet some painfully embarrassing questions.

Chapter Eighteen

Nick sat in his car outside of Janet's house, trying to figure out how to phrase what he needed to ask her so as to minimize the awkwardness. The sun gleamed through the windshield and right into Nick's eyes. He squinted and then blocked his eyes with his arm.

"It's about time you came back," a familiar voice said next to him. Nick jumped so high that he nearly crashed his head into the roof of the car.

"Never do that!" he said, trying to will his heart to slow down. His breath came in short, rapid bursts. "You freakin' scared me half to death. Shit, dude!"

James dismissed him with a wave of his hand. "All I did was talk to you. What would you have me do next time, ring chimes before I appear?"

"I'd be okay with chimes," Nick said. "Chimes would be good. Just don't pop in like that again."

"You'll get used to it eventually," said James.

Nick raised his eyebrows. "What's that supposed to mean?"

James gave an impatient sigh. "If you can see us and we

know that you can see us, then there's bound to be a bit of popping in and out now and then, isn't there?"

Nick made a mental note to ask his uncle how he deals with it. "I'd still prefer a little warning first."

"Chimes it is then," said James. He crossed his arms. "So? What'd you find out? Have you determined who killed me yet?"

Nick noticed a man across the street staring at him. When the man realized that he had caught Nick's attention, he continued walking.

Nick reached down, pulled out his phone and held it to his ear. "I first have a couple of questions for you and Janet."

"What on earth are you doing with that phone?" James asked. "Who are you calling?"

"I'm pretending that I'm talking to someone. That way, people won't think that I'm a big weirdo talking to myself."

"Really Nick?" James said. "I mean *really*?"

Nick put down the phone. His name sounded strange, coming from the ghost's mouth. "It's not you who has to live here and face these people every day. I don't want to become known as the local nutcase."

"How about you put the phone away and just turn to face me. That way, your back will face the sidewalk, and nobody will be able to see your lips move. Nobody will think you're a nutter."

Nick nodded. He stuffed the phone back into the pocket of his jeans.

"What is it that you want to ask me?" James said. His stare made the hairs on Nick's neck stand up.

Nick grabbed hold of the steering wheel and turned his head to face James. "I don't want you to be offended by what I'm going to ask you, but I need to know as much as I can about your and Janet's situation if I'm to help you."

James slowly nodded. "Agreed. Go on."

Nick swallowed. His hands were damp with sweat. All a sudden, he didn't like being trapped in the car with a ghost who had an incredibly short fuse. "Did you have an affair while you were married?"

James raised his eyebrows, and his expression grew cold. "Are you asking me if I ever cheated on my wife?"

"I don't mean to pry, and I know that it's probably none of my business. Believe me, it's not easy asking you this. But I've gotten some strong impressions that there may have been a betrayal of some kind involved with your death."

Nick was surprised when James smiled. "You're a better sleuth than I gave you credit for." He folded his hands in his lap. "And you needn't be afraid to ask me anything. It's the only way we're going to figure out what happened the day I died." The ghost broke his gaze and looked out of the passenger window. "But in this instance, you are asking the wrong person."

"Janet cheated?" Nick asked.

James folded his hands in front of him. "I never knew for certain, but I suspected that she did. I confronted her once but naturally, she denied it. Not that I expected any differently. Put in that situation, I probably would have done the same — lied about it, I mean. Funny, I never did find out for sure if she was cheating on me, and if she did, with whom."

"So what made you think that she was unfaithful?"

James was silent for a moment. He seemed to slowly, almost imperceptibly fade in and out which Nick was beginning to find disconcerting and a bit dizzying.

"It's difficult to pinpoint the exact reason," James said. "There were many little things. Strange smells when she was close to me. Times when she wouldn't answer her cell if I were there in the room with her. I once managed to get a hold of her phone to see if her contact list might give me any clues. So I have a question for you — have you ever heard of anyone using only initials for all of the entries in their address book?"

Nick shook his head. "I don't think so."

"That's what Janet does. People were listed as M, or T, or R, or N. No first or last names. For what reason? Did she do it to cover her tracks?"

The ghost stared intently at Nick as if expecting a response. Nick didn't know how to answer so he shrugged his shoulders but said nothing. James continued.

"That's not all. There were also no entries in her recently received calls list. Now, I know for a fact that she regularly received phone calls, so it was clear that she deleted the list. But again, for what possible reason? This even made me more suspicious."

"Yeah, that's weird, for sure. So you did nothing?"

"What would you have me do, hire a private investigator? Nah, too tacky. No, I simply watched and waited. Then, the strange behavior suddenly stopped. There were no more odd calls, and she seemed to make a deliberate point of making sure that I knew where she was at all times. She was also more loving and more like her old self. I could only assume that either I had been mistaken and she wasn't having an affair after all or that she had stopped seeing him."

"Did you ever give her any reason to suspect that you were cheating on her?"

James shook his head. "Never. I was always a devoted husband." He pursed his lips and frowned. "If anyone was a victim of betrayal, it was me."

"Do you think this gave her the motive to kill you?" Nick asked.

James creased his brow. "What do you mean?"

"Do you think that she was planning on running off with the guy and wanted you out of the way?"

James stared at Nick and blinked a few times. "No, I don't

think so." He let go of a short laugh. "To be truthful, I'd forgotten all about my suspicions until you brought the subject up. It was rather a long time ago — or at least, it seems so now. Funny that it didn't cross my mind." He scratched his head. "I wonder what other things I might be forgetting?"

"So your recent anger towards her was unrelated to the fact that you thought she was cheating?"

"The only thing that I could see over and over in my head was her handing me that damned drink." He paused and rubbed his chin several times. "But now that you mention it, I suppose she could have wanted me out of the way. Maybe she was still seeing the guy and became more adept at covering her tracks."

"Would you come in with me?" Nick asked. "If she is the murderer and tries to hurt me, I'd like to know that there's someone there who can protect me. You could like toss a lamp at her or something."

"No."

"Huh?"

"Can't do that Nick."

"But why not? I know that you can move things. I saw it myself."

"I mean that I can't do it because Janet's not home."

Nick pointed to the house. "She's not there?"

"I'm afraid not. This is her 'Stitch and Bitch' night."

"Her what?" Nick asked.

"Stitch and Bitch. She and a few of her friends get together every Thursday and sew, embroider, crochet, or knit together. It's turned into sort of an informal club that they now call 'Stitch and Bitch.'"

"Do you know what time she gets home?" Nick asked.

The hesitation in his eyes was fleeting, but Nick caught it. "Late," said James. "You'd best try another time."

Nick got the strangest feeling that James wasn't as deter-mined to find out who killed him as he was initially. Nick couldn't detect any anger at all coming from the man. His green eyes only showed what appeared to be sadness. Nick had to get this spirit to cross over and was determined not to fail.

"James, you're not giving up on this, are you?"

"No, of course not. Why do you ask me that?"

"I got a strange feeling from you, that's all."

"You're mistaken. I'm just as resolved as ever. I'm just not sure now whether Janet was the one who killed me."

With that, he was gone. Nick still couldn't shake the feeling that James no longer seemed invested in solving his murder. Something was not quite right with the way James acted. He'd seemed sincere when he told Nick that he hadn't cheated on his wife, but now Nick had to wonder. Why all of a sudden the lack of enthusiasm on James's part? The more Nick thought about it, the more curious it seemed. A few days ago, James was screaming at the poor woman and hurling furniture at her. Now he seemed almost nonchalant about his murder. There was something else going on with the ghost, and what that might be, Nick hadn't a clue.

AFTER SCHOOL, GABE WAS LEANING AGAINST HIS CAR, waiting for him. Nick felt his heart skip a beat in his chest and he couldn't help but smile when seeing his friend. He was afraid that Gabe would never talk to him again.

"Sup," said Nick.

"Got any plans now?" Gabe asked, his face expressionless. His voice sounded odd, cold.

"Not really," said Nick, his feet shuffling. He avoided

meeting Gabe's eyes. "Gonna see my uncle later at the hospital."

"He's the one who's like you, right?"

Nick nodded but said nothing.

"Wanna go for a ride?" Gabe asked.

"Where?" asked Nick.

"I'll tell you when we get there. Won't take too long."

Nick agreed, and they both got in the car. Gabe directed him, and pretty soon it was evident where Gabe was taking him. They were heading toward Forest Lawn Cemetery.

"Gabe, why are you taking us here?" Nick asked.

Gabe was silent and stared straight ahead. Now Gabe was creeping him out.

"Gabe," Nick said. "What are we doing?"

Gabe finally broke the silence. "Park here," he said. When Nick parked the car, Gabe opened the door and hopped out. Nick followed.

"This way," Gabe said, pointing in front of him.

"This has now officially gotten beyond weird," Nick said.

"Casey's buried right over here," Gabe said.

Casey was Gabe's older sister who had died of a drug overdose two years before. Nick heard that her death was a suicide although Gabe had spoken little about the incident. From what Nick had learned, Casey had taken a shitload of Ambien pills along with a huge amount of vodka.

Gabe came to a halt. "Here we are."

Nick stepped up next to him. "Your sister."

Gabe nodded. "We never found out why she did what she did. I don't think my mom and dad ever really recovered from it. I know I haven't. She was in college, got good grades and seemed happy." He indicated to her grave with his hand. "So why this? Why would she kill herself?"

Nick swallowed and said nothing.

Gabe turned his head and met Nick's gaze. "So how does

this work? Do you have to call her? Do I have to call her? Do you need a picture or something that belonged to her? I have a sweater of hers in the car and a picture of her on my phone."

The reason they were there struck Nick like a flying brick. *He wants me to communicate with Casey. He wants to talk to his dead sister.*

"It doesn't work that way, Gabe," Nick said. For Gabe's sake, he wished it did.

Gabe's shoulders tightened, and his eyes grew wide. "This is what y'all do, ain't it? Talk to ghosts? Talk to dead people?"

"Yes and no," said Nick. "I can see them but only the ones who haven't crossed over because of unfinished business."

"Well, I'd reckon that committing suicide without leaving a note constitutes unfinished business, no?" Gabe asked. His voice was cold and distant. "Sounds pretty friggin' unfinished to me."

Gabe's expression was dark, and Nick could hear the anger bursting through in his voice. Nick tensed and took a step back.

"Gabe," Nick said, in as soft a voice as he could. "From what my uncle told me, spirits who haven't crossed over tend to hang around their family in the hopes of getting their attention. The only time they don't leave is if they have some issue with one of their loved ones." Nick reached over touched Gabe's arm. "I haven't seen her Gabe. I've never once seen her around you or your parents."

Gabe jerked his arm away. "Could she be shadowing someone else? A boyfriend maybe? Professor? One of our cousins?"

"Anything's possible I suppose," said Nick. "But from what I understand, they hang around to those closest to them." Nick paused and took a breath. "If she had a message to get to any of you, she probably would have found me by now. According to my Uncle Mitch, spirits always manage to find people like us — those of us who can see them.

Gabe stared at him, and his face fell, all hope dropping from his expression. He sighed and crumpled against a tree, falling into himself. "I don't understand."

Nick sat down next to him. "She must have gone on to the next part of her journey. She went where she was supposed to."

"But how could she leave everything like this, without any of us knowing why she did what she did? It doesn't make any sense!"

"Nobody for sure knows how any of this stuff works Gabe," Nick said. "My uncle said that we learn as we go. Some things might make sense where other things won't." He paused and took a deep breath. "Maybe it was an accident. She might have been drunk and not thinking clearly. But whatever the reason, she apparently was ready to cross over."

Gabe looked up at Nick for a moment and then Gabe's face fell. Tears dribbled out of Gabe's eyes and rolled down his cheeks. Nick reached for him, pulled him close and wrapped his arm around Gabe's shoulders. Gabe pulled in tighter to Nick's chest and sobbed. Nick wanted to say something more, something to make his friend feel better, but he was out of words. Without thinking, he kissed Gabe on the forehead. If it bothered Gabe, he gave no indication. Nick held his friend tightly, inhaling Gabe's scent into his lungs.

A few minutes later, Gabe sat up and met Nick's eyes.

"I'm sorry I was such an ass to you the other day," Gabe said.

"You don't need to apologize," Nick said. "I should never have kept something like that from you. We've always been straight with one another and have never kept secrets. I was wrong to do it."

"I still should have been more understanding. I'm sure this was all super intense for you."

Nick nodded. "It's just that all of this ghost stuff was new to me, and I'll admit it, I was kinda freaked out by it all. I didn't want anyone to know until I decided what to do."

"What to do about what?" Gabe asked.

Nick threw open both hands and pointed at himself with his thumbs. "Me, this freaky thing I have. I was gonna just ignore it. I knew that it'd never go away. But if I pretended that I couldn't see the ghosts, then they wouldn't bother me. I could go on living a normal life."

"You still can," said Gabe. "Pretend you don't see them."

Nick shook his head. "Believe me; I wanted to. But then a couple of people made me see that I was given these abilities for a reason. I'm supposed to help people — at least that's what everyone keeps drilling into my head."

"You mean dead people," Gabe said.

Nick nodded. "And their families as well. But the ghosts — well, they're people too. People without bodies, people who can't be seen by anyone. That's why it's even more important that I help them. Because I can. If not me, then who?"

Gabe stared at him for several long moments. "You're really something else. Just when I think that I know all there is to know about Nick Michelson, you end up surprising me."

"What do you mean?"

"It means that you're even a nicer person than I thought you were."

Nick swallowed, trying not to allow his emotions to get the best of him. "I'm not that nice. Really. I can be kind of a dick sometimes."

They both collapsed in a fit of giggles.

"I'm sorry I couldn't help you with your sister," said Nick. "I wish it worked that way, but it doesn't."

Gabe shrugged. "Hey, it was a long shot, but I figured it was worth a try." He creased his brow. "I didn't mean to put you in such a weird situation. It was kind of shitty of me." Gabe paused, the look on his face becoming more gentle. "That's not the only reason I brought you out here. I also wanted to apologize to you. I didn't think about what you might have been going through. I'm sure that past couple of weeks have been super freaky for you."

Nick laughed. "You have no idea."

"I'd like to," Gabe said. "Have an idea, that is. I want to be a part of this with you, share this with you. No more hiding shit from me, okay?"

Gabe's words struck him as odd, as not something Gabe would typically say. Nick nodded.

"No more hiding," Nick said.

Gabe all at once appeared nervous. "I think it boiled down to Sam."

"Sam? What about him?"

"It was an awesome thing that you did for him, helping him find his dad and helping his mom."

"Sam's mom is one of the reasons that I decided to continue on with this and to help the spirits."

Gabe nodded his head a few times in rapid succession. "But the reason I was so pissed at you the other day was that I was jealous of Sam."

"Jealous of Sam? But why?"

Gabe looked away. "Because you were my best friend and he knew something about you that I didn't. I was pissed off that you shared it with him and not me."

"Believe me, Gabe, his mom didn't give me much of a choice."

Gabe smiled and shook his head. "She always was kinda bossy. Truth be told, I was a little bit afraid of her when she was alive. She could intimidate me like nobody else."

They both laughed. Then Gabe's expression grew serious. "So will you be hanging around Sam now?"

Nick didn't understand the question. "Huh?"

"Will you be spending your free time with Sam, seeing that you shared this special thing together?"

"Gabe, I don't understand where you're going with this. Did you think that I was going to ignore you now that I helped out Sam? That he was going to take your place?"

"I dunno what I thought. I don't know what your relationship with Sam is now."

"There isn't any," said Nick. "And by that I mean it's the same as before. We're not gonna be hanging out or anything like that. Sam's okay, but I don't know him all that well. Besides, he's more your friend than mine."

An uneasy silence settled over them. Gabe drew in a sharp breath.

"I just didn't know how much you liked him." His voice trembled as he spoke.

Then, Nick felt Gabe's hand inside of his. Gabe interlocked his fingers with Nick's. And Nick let him.

Nick's heart started pounding, and he may or may not have gasped. He froze, afraid to turn his head to look at Gabe. He didn't want Gabe to see his expression, see his eyes. What was in Gabe's mind? What was up with this hand holding? Was it just a friendly gesture? Or was it something else? Something more?

At the noise of an approaching car, Gabe abruptly pulled their hands apart. "We probably should be getting back if you're still fixin' to see your uncle tonight."

"Yeah, better," said Nick.

Once in the car, Gabe babbled on in his usual manner, as though nothing out of the ordinary had occurred between them. Maybe nothing had. Maybe Gabe was simply weirded out about his sister and Nick's inability to contact her. Nick would just forget the handholding thing ever happened.

The problem was, could he?

Nick dropped Gabe off at his house. After Gabe had left, Nick noticed that for the first time in like ever, Gabe had not playfully punched him in the shoulder when they parted.

Chapter Nineteen

Nick's hand shook as he brought his mocha latte to his mouth. Luckily, there were only a few people in the cafe with nobody seated close to them. A male college student wearing enormous purple headphones sat two tables away watching a video on his tablet. He glanced up once when Nick had first arrived and then went back to his movie. The roasting machines in the back produced a low rumbling noise that you wouldn't even notice unless you stopped to listen. The sharp roasty smell of fresh coffee hung heavily in the air.

"So you have some news?" Janet asked. "Something that will make James stop tormenting me?"

Nick closed his eyes for a moment and then reopened them. "There's a question that I first need to ask you, and it's not easy."

Janet creased her brow. "What is it? About James?"

Nick nodded and swallowed. "I spoke with James last night. He told me something that might help us figure out what happened to him — though it's kind of a difficult subject for me to bring up with you."

She folded her hands and rested them on the table. "Okay, I'll bite. What did he tell you?"

"He thought that you might have had an affair."

She stiffened and took a sip from her coffee. A line of white foam clung to her lower lip. She placed the cup on the table and dabbed at her lips with her napkin. She looked over her shoulder as it to make sure that nobody was listening.

"Is he here now?" Janet asked. "Can you see James?"

Nick took a look around and shook his head. "I don't see him or feel him."

"What do you mean by feel him?"

"I get a warning signal whenever there's a ghost nearby. I get nauseous, and my skin gets prickly and ultra-sensitive, to the point where even the clothes I'm wearing are uncomfortable against it."

She nodded and let go of a long sigh. "So James knew?"

"He suspected," Nick said, surprised by her revelation. "There were unusual smells and strange phone calls that made him suspect that there was someone else on the side. That and the fact that you had nobody's first or last names in your address book."

"He snooped through my phone?"

Nick shrugged. "Yeah, I guess so."

She let go of a short laugh and stared at the wall as if it were a vanished past. "Yes, there was an affair. It's been an on again and off again type of deal for many years. I've known him since high school." She sighed. "We dated for a short while, but unfortunately, he had a girlfriend at the time. By the time he broke it off with her, I had met James. James and I became serious right way, and I married him." She locked eyes with Nick. "It was a mistake, you see. Marrying James. He was always a bit standoffish, and at first, I found this trait somewhat endearing. But once we got married, he became even more distant. Work was the main focus of his life, so I spent most of my time alone. I know that's no excuse for what I did, but for many years, James was more of a flatmate than a husband. Oh, don't get me wrong. He never mistreated me and was always more than generous. I did love him, and we got along very well — but ours wasn't a passionate marriage."

Nick squirmed in his chair, feeling more than a little bit uncomfortable by the topic of conversation. "James told me that he believed you ended the affair. Did you?"

She chuckled coldly. "He was a lot more observant than I gave him credit for. It's true. I told my friend that we could no longer see each other, that the lies and the deceit were getting to be too much for me. You see, I've never really been a good liar so running around on James was difficult for me. In spite of what you may think of me, I am somewhat old-school. I made the decision to marry James, and it was my duty to see it through. So I broke off the affair."

"How did," Nick paused, "your friend take it?"

"I think he figured that it was a matter of time before I would leave James and run off with him, so he was stunned when I ended it. No, that's not right. Angry. He was angry and bitter." She locked eyes with Nick. "It wasn't as if he was someone that I'd just met. We've known each since I was seventeen. Hell, I think we've loved each other since then as well. Don't get me wrong, I loved James too, but it was different with Matt. There was excitement. There was passion. But I didn't want to be the clichéd cheating wife who asks her husband for a divorce. I needed some time to decide what to do so I stopped seeing Matt."

Nick nodded. "So James was right."

She looked up as if trying to remember something. "James confronted me once, but I denied it. It was then that I knew it was time to end it. The stress was getting to be way too much. Funny though. Once I terminated the affair, I noticed a change in James. He warmed up and became more involved in our marriage. He even began coming home from work earlier, and we would go out together. He became an entirely different person. If he hadn't passed away, I think that we could have made our marriage work. I'd even grown to love him. I mean really love him."

"Funny. He said almost the identical thing about you — that you seemed to change as well."

"He did? I thought he never noticed or cared about anything I did."

"What about the other man?" Nick asked.

Janet looked at Nick soulfully. "What about him?"

"Are you seeing him now?"

She shook her head slowly. "No. I didn't feel that it was right. It's not for his lack of trying. He's been persistent, almost to the point where it's pushed me away. It was as though he expected me to jump into his arms the moment my husband died. He was shocked when I told him that I needed time — time to mourn James properly."

"Have you told him about James haunting you?"

She shook her head. "He came to see me when I was at the hotel for the night." She sucked in a sharp breath. "It was a mistake to call him, I know that now. It turned into a terrible scene." She wrung the napkin in her hands. "I only called him because I was upset, confused and frightened. He mistakenly thought that my call was an invitation back into my life as a lover so when I refused him, it didn't go over very well. I didn't like the vibes that I was getting from him, so I made him leave."

Nick wondered if James had seen the man visit Janet at the hotel.

"What was his name again?" Nick asked.

"Matt," Janet said. "Both of us knew him in high school."

Nick recalled James mentioning someone named Matt.

Then, he got a flash of the Three of Pentacles card that he had pulled at Katrina's office.

"By any chance, did Matt work with James?" Nick asked.

Janet looked at him in surprise and then studied his face for a moment. She finally nodded. "Yes, they worked at the same company. How did you know?"

"James mentioned him in passing," Nick said. "He also came up in a reading."

"You mean like a psychic reading?"

"It's a long story but yeah." He clasped his hands so tight that his knuckles turned white. "Do you think it's possible that Matt could have killed James?"

Her expression darkened with a flash of sudden pain. "Matt and James were incredibly close friends all through high school and college. That was one of the main reasons I broke it off with Matt. He worked too closely with my husband and my husband trusted him. It was too much deception for me to bear."

"So you don't think he could have killed James?"

She was silent for several moments. "I'd like to say no, but truthfully, I don't know," she stammered. She crossed her hands and laid them on the table. "I wouldn't have thought so. But after his display of rage the other day I have to wonder. I saw an entirely different side of him, a darker side that I'd never seen before." She let go a short, harsh laugh. "Now that I think about it, when he came to see me that night, he kept saying that I didn't appreciate all that he had done so we could be together. At the time, I assumed he meant lying and deceiving James." She met Nick's gaze. "Do you think he might have meant something more by that? Something more sinister?"

Nick stared at her, blinking. "I don't know." He was now more certain that Janet did not kill her husband. But if this Matt had done it, how could he prove it?

Nick then realized that his skin was prickly and had been for some time. He looked around. There was only one other couple in the cafe, and they were conversing with each other so they couldn't be spirits. All at once, a breeze blew through the cafe so hard that cups flew to the floor and napkin holders overturned. People screamed in surprise.

Janet gave Nick a deer-in-the-headlights look.

"Uh-oh. I think your friend Matt might be in for a bit of trouble," said Nick.

Chapter Twenty

Nick almost crashed into Gabe as he was leaving the cafe.

"Whoa, dude!" Gabe said. "Where's the fire?"

Nick felt the blood drain from his face. Gabe's blue eyes sparkled like sun on ice and he inwardly sighed. He didn't want to have to explain where he was going to Gabe.

"What a surprise," Nick said. He gave Gabe's shoulder a quick squeeze. "I'd hang out with you, but there's someplace I gotta be," he said simply. "I'll give you a call later."

"Someplace? Like where?" Gabe's hair was wet from a recent shower, and he smelled of fresh strawberries and cinnamon. *Why does he have to always smell so damn good?*

Nick sighed. "Can't get into it right now. There's something that I need to take care of right away."

Gabe crossed his arms, and his expression grew cold. He stepped directly in front of Nick. "What was it that we talked about yesterday? Lemme see. Oh, now I remember. It was about y'all not keeping things from me anymore." Gabe creased his brow and scratched his head. "No, that can't be right — because right now, it seems as though you're hiding something from me."

The sarcasm in Gabe's voice made Nick cringe. He looked around to make sure that nobody was nearby and then gestured for Gabe to move over to the left of the cafe door.

"This is about a you-know-what," Nick said.

Gabe narrowed his eyes. "A ghost? I figured as much, with the weird secrecy act and all. So you're going ghost-hunting?"

Nick twisted away from Gabe's gaze. "No, not exactly hunting. I accidentally let a ghost know the name of the person who I suspect might have killed him and now I'm afraid that this ghost is on his way to hurt the murderer."

"And that's a problem how?" Gabe asked.

"What if the guy's not the killer? I don't know for sure — I was only speculating. I certainly don't want anyone to get hurt because of me, especially if he's innocent. I was just trying to help this ghost find peace so he'd cross over and leave me the hell alone."

"So what are you gonna to do?"

Nick took a deep breath. "I need to warn the guy that James is coming and then make sure that James doesn't hurt him."

"You're going to confront a murderer?"

Nick swallowed. "I don't know for sure that he's a murderer. What if James kills him and it turns out he had nothing to do with James's death? I have to at least try and warn him."

Gabe reached over and squeezed Nick's shoulder. "I'm going with you."

Nick shook his head. "No way Gabe. It's way too dangerous."

"And that's precisely why I ain't letting y'all walk into this by yourself."

"But you don't know anything about ghosts."

"And you do? You told me yourself that you've only been at this for a short time," Gabe said, a stern look on his face. "You don't know that much more about them than I do."

Nick cowered into the side of the building. "Gabe, please. I don't want anything to happen to you. This is my mess and mine alone. The last thing I ever wanted to do was to drag anyone else into it."

"Sorry bud, but that bullshit's not gonna fly with me. I reckon we're in this together from now on."

"Gabe — " Nick started.

"The decision has been made. So are we going or what?"

Nick shuffled his feet and then stuck his hands in his pockets, feeling defeated. He knew how stubborn Gabe could be so convincing him to stay behind was unlikely. "Just don't say I didn't warn you and try to talk you out of it."

"Shall we take my motorcycle?" Gabe asked.

"I think I'd rather take chances with angry ghosts than ride on your motorcycle. We'll take my mom's car. I'll fill you in on all the details when we get there."

"This is it," Nick said as they pulled in front of 2321 Lake Street. The office plaza in front of them was the tallest building on the block, and the brickwork looked brand new.

They got out of the car. Nick was afraid that they'd have to deal with security on the way in and he had no idea what to say if they did. Luckily, there were no gatekeepers in sight. Near the door was a blackboard with white lettering that listed all of the occupants of the building along with their office numbers.

"What's his name?" Gabe asked.

"Matt."

"No last name?"

"Fuck," Nick said. "I don't know his last name."

Nick studied the board and then pointed to a line which read Lenser and Dumond Accounting - 304. "This has to be it. He works for an accounting firm, and this is the only one listed."

"So now what?" Gabe asked.

"We hope that Matt is in the office and we can talk to him — and pray that James hasn't gotten there first."

"On the contrary amigo, we should hope that the ghost is there," Gabe said.

"How do you figure?"

"He might be able to protect us from this guy if he gets violent. You said he could move shit around, right? That might come in handy if the guy does turn out to be the killer and doesn't like the idea of us asking him questions about your ghost friend."

They entered the elevator, and Gabe hit the number three on the button panel. Nick locked eyes with him. "Remember the plan. You remain outside and listen in. If you hear anything go wrong, you call the cops."

Gabe regarded him sharply. "Yeah, I got it. But I don't like it. I just don't feel right about letting you go in there alone to face a ghost and a possible murderer."

"I've communicated with this ghost before, and he's friendly-ish."

"And this Matt fella? What are you gonna say to him exactly?"

"I'm going to tell him that I'm a friend of Janet's and she's being haunted by her dead husband because he thinks that she murdered him."

Before Gabe could reply, the elevator chimed, and the door opened.

"Let the games begin," Nick said.

"You don't think we should call the cops *before* you go in?" Gabe whispered.

"And tell them what? This isn't even a police matter. James Pearce died of a heart attack according to authorities. I can't accuse Matt otherwise without proof."

They stopped just outside the door numbered 304. Nick's heart thumped wildly in his chest. He took a deep breath and leaned toward Gabe's ear.

"Once I go in, don't let the door close all the way. Otherwise, you won't be able to hear what's going on."

Gabe nodded. "*Be careful!* Remember I'll be right here."

Nick walked down the hallway which led to two offices. Janet had told him that James's office used to be the one on the left. Slowly, he approached it. He peeked around the corner so he could see inside. It was empty. Pressed against the wall was a large dark brown table which, according to Janet, was where James had kept his bourbon canister along with glasses. There was no booze container there now. Only a mantel clock. So much for evidence.

Nick felt his heart palpitate in his chest and his mouth grew dry. He shuffled into the office and looked around. A large — no, gigantic — dark oak desk faced the window next to which stood an ornately carved wooden file cabinet. The desk was clear except for a black desk phone and a clear glass pen holder. Plush tan carpeting covered the floor. A couple of picture frames containing what appeared to be diplomas hung on the wall. Nick approached one of them. It was an MBA degree from the University of Michigan that read 'Matthew John Hereon.' So this was Matt's office now.

"Can I help you?" a voice said behind him. He jumped and turned to face a young looking man with short-cropped blond hair and piercing blue eyes. He was wearing a white shirt, black pants and a red and white striped tie.

"I'm looking for Matt Hereon."

"I'm Matt. Did we have an appointment? The secretary is gone for the day, but I was unaware of any client meetings on my calendar."

"No, we didn't. I was just hoping that I could speak with you for a few moments." So which way did the man come from? The hallway? And if so, did he see Gabe? Nick hoped that Gabe still listening because he had a very bad feeling all of a sudden. He felt pressure on his chest and sweat began to form on his forehead. Katrina was always telling him to listen to his gut. Well, right now his gut was telling him to get the hell away from here as quickly as possible.

Matt creased his brow. "And your visit is regarding?"

"I'm a friend of Janet Pearce."

The man drew in a sharp breath. "I see." He gestured to a chair on the opposite side of the desk. "Please sit down."

Nick sunk into the leather chair and glanced around the office. There was no sign of James. Maybe the ghost hadn't overheard them at the cafe after all, which was unfortunate. He now wished that James was here.

Matt studied Nick for a moment. "Do we know each other? You look familiar."

"No, we've never met."

He stared at Nick for another couple of seconds and then nodded. "So you know Janet. Sad thing that, the passing of her husband. I was friends with him since high school." He folded his hands and placed them on the table. It looked as though he were pressing them into the top of the desk. "What can I do for you?"

"This is going to sound strange, but I've been helping Janet out with an unusual situation."

Darkness flashed over Matt's face for just a moment, but Nick caught it. He resumed his tight-lipped smile. "Oh? And what situation might that be?"

Nick cleared his throat. "James."

Matt peered at Nick with steely eyes, his expression unchanged. "Her deceased husband?"

Nick nodded. "He's not really deceased. I mean he is, but he isn't."

Matt's smile slid off his face. "What are you going on about? James is dead. I went to his funeral."

Nick ran his fingers through his hair and let go of the breath he hadn't realized he'd been holding. "I have this weird family thing. Some of the guys in my family can see ghosts and so what we do is to help them cross over to wherever it is spirits go. James is one of the ghosts that I've been seeing around. That's why Janet was staying at the hotel for awhile. James was haunting her, and she was too scared to stay at the house alone."

Matt was glaring now, and Nick could see his chin begin to quiver. "Go on."

"I've spoken with him and discovered the reason why he's still here. I promised him that I'd help him."

"And what is it exactly that you are helping him with?" Matt asked. The tone of his voice bordered on mockery.

Nick held his gaze for a chilly moment. "He thinks someone murdered him. That's why he can't cross over. He can't leave until he finds out who did it."

Matt leapt up. He leaned on the desk and glared. "I think I've heard enough. I won't have you dishonor the memory of James. He was my friend."

"I'm not dishonoring him," Nick said, standing up as well. He was afraid to break his gaze. "I'm helping him."

"So help me if you're upsetting Janet with the garbage —"

"Janet knows it's James." Nick interrupted. "She's the one who asked me to help her."

Matt pointed at Nick. "I don't know who in the hell you are, but you stay far away from Janet, got it? She doesn't need you upsetting her with your crazy notions. I assure you that her husband died of a heart attack and nothing more. So I suggest you leave before I call the police."

"Or before I call the police," said Nick, moving toward an inescapable decision.

Matt raised his eyebrows. "Come again?"

"As I said, James believes that he was murdered. Poisoned, actually. And I think he knows who did it."

Matt's face blanched, then he quickly recomposed himself. "Nonsense. He had heart problems. He passed away from natural causes."

"Not according to him. The last thing he remembers is sipping a drink made from a bottle of bourbon in his office. He's pretty certain that the booze contained poison."

Matt let go of an eerie chortle. He walked around the desk and stood, facing Nick. "So what, you think I poisoned my friend?"

"You appear to have a motive. I know about you and Janet — about the affair."

Nick noticed the first flicker of fear on Matt's face. Matt pursed his lips for a moment and then thrust a powerful blow to Nick's chest. Nick flew backward, his head slamming into the file cabinet. As he slumped to the floor, he saw stars for a moment. He caught his breath and rubbed the back of his head. No blood, but his back hurt like hell.

"Ya know," Matt said, speaking through his teeth, "I'm thinking that you are a bit too much of a fucking know-it-all." He rubbed his chin. "But the question is, what is to be done about it?"

"So you did kill James!" Nick said through his rapid breaths. The tight clench of his chest caused him to steady himself against the cabinet.

Matt hovered over Nick, his face contorting into something menacing. "Sure kid. Had to. Aconite."

"What?" Nick said. He was pressed against the file cabinet, unsure of Matt's next move.

"The poison. It was aconite. It mimics arrhythmic heart dysfunction and is virtually untraceable. Not that I needn't have worried. Janet was more than willing to forgo having an autopsy done."

"You killed him because of Janet," Nick said weakly.

His laugh sounded forced. "That bitch? Hardly. Oh, she would have been a nice prize but she's wasn't playing. After all these years, who would have guessed that she'd get cold feet? We could have been great together." He squinted at Nick. "So no, it wasn't because of her. James just got a little too nosy for his own good, and it turned out to be hazardous to his health." He snickered.

"He figured out that you were sleeping with Janet?"

"This had nothing to do with her. James simply started to butt into business that didn't concern him. Why couldn't he just leave it alone? I didn't want to hurt him. It was the last thing that I wanted. But he finally figured out what I was doing, and the fucking do-gooder threatened to turn me in. I couldn't be having that, now could I?"

Nick looked at Matt for a long moment, first unsure of what he was talking about. Then it hit him.

"You were stealing from the company, and James found out."

With a joyous whoop, Matt clapped his hands. "You certainly are a sharp one, little fella! Yeah, I was hoping to build myself a nice little nest egg and once I had enough, was going to take Janet with me where nobody would find us."

"But I take it she wasn't too keen on your idea?"

"Wrong. Before I could even suggest it to her, she decided that I wasn't good enough for her anymore, that after all this time, she was going to try and work things out with her goody two-shoes of a husband. But no matter. My plans are still in motion. Although now thanks to you, I'll probably have to move things forward a little sooner than I had planned."

Nick glanced toward the door, wondering where in the hell Gabe was. He prayed that he was okay.

"Thinking of running out are you? You know, I don't think that's going to happen. I hate to be a dick about this, but you do know I can't let you leave, right?"

Nick stared at him but said nothing. He butt-scuttled away from the cabinet and leaned his back against the wall.

"But the question is," Matt continued, "what am I to do with you? I wish I didn't have to kill you. You stupid shit. Why did you have to come here?" He took a breath. "You brought this on yourself."

"You don't have to do this," Nick said. He trembled so much that he could barely get the words out and his heart rammed at his chest.

"Unfortunately, I do." He folded his hands under his chin. "But how to do it? "

With his eyes glued to Nick, he walked over to the desk, pulled out a drawer and retrieved a silver letter opener. He glanced at it for a moment, turning his wrist back and forth and then jabbed in the air a couple of times. "I suppose this will have to do. Little messier than I'd have liked, but if all goes well, I'll be long gone before anyone comes in here." He frowned at Nick. "I'd like to tell you that this wasn't going to hurt, but I'd be lying."

Before Nick could say anything, his stomach clenched and flipped. The letter opener that Matt was holding flew out of his hand and landed across the room.

"The fuck?" Matt said, staring at his now empty hand.

James now stood right next to Matt. "*The fuck?*" the ghost mimicked and then laughed.

Nick was about to say something, but James shook his

head and held an index finger to his lips. Matt scowled and walked towards the knife. Just as he was about to reach it, James raised his hands, palms out and pushed on Matt's back. Matt flew into the credenza.

Nick got up off the floor and backed against the desk. Matt, still crumpled into a ball on the floor, glared at him.

"I don't know how in the fuck you did that," Matt said through his teeth. "But the games end now."

Matt started to rise, but James pushed down hard on Matt's shoulders, flinging him back to the floor.

Matt's head swung wildly back and forth, looking for what pushed him.

James looked at Nick and gave him a nod.

"James is here, and boy is he pissed," Nick said, smiling in spite of himself.

"No," he said. "Not possible."

"Very much possible," said James.

James walked over, picked up the letter opener and held it in front of Matt's face. Matt flinched back and gasped.

"It wasn't enough that you screwed my wife and stole from the company we worked for," James said. "But you had to go and murder me too?" James kicked him in the ribs and Matt screamed in pain. "You are one big smelly piece of rotten shit. How could I ever have considered you a friend?"

Matt reached for his pocket and for a moment, Nick gasped, fearing he was going to pull out a gun. Whatever he was going to do, he never got the chance. James grabbed a thick book off of the bookshelf and whacked Matt hard across the head with it. Matt slumped into a heap on the carpet. James dropped the book to the floor. The cover read 'Principles of Accounting.'

Nick slowly stood up on wobbly legs, and his hands shook. He looked at Matt on the floor. "Is he dead?"

"Regretfully, no," said James. "He's only unconscious."

"He was going to kill me," Nick said. "You're right. He's a piece."

"Who's right?" Gabe said as he came around the corner.

"Gabe," Nick stammered. Without thinking, he rushed up to Gabe and pulled him into a tight hug. "I was so worried about you. I was afraid that he caught you." He let Gabe go and took a step back.

"I heard someone coming down the hallway, so I hid. I figured out pretty quickly that it was him. Luckily, I was still able to hear everything. I called the police like you asked."

"But it's our word against his," Nick said. "How are we going to get the cops to believe a couple of high school kids?" He pointed at Matt. "We're in *his* office, and he's been knocked unconscious. It looks like we attacked him."

Gabe reached into his pocket and pulled out his cell phone. "I recorded the entire conversation, including the part where Matt admits to killing James. Although we might have to edit the file before the cops come — remove the part about you telling him about the ghost."

Nick considered this briefly and then shook his head. "No, we leave it in. We'll tell the police that I used that story to bait him, to get a confession out of him. I'll tell them that his wife suspected that he was murdered, so we decided to do a little investigating on our own."

"Do you think they'll buy it? How do we explain our involvement?"

Nick scratched his head. "We're friend's of Janet's and wanted to help. When she told us that Matt threatened her, we decided on our own to come have a chat with him, to try and convince him to leave Janet alone."

"That could work." Gabe gestured at the unconscious figure on the floor with the large book lying next to him. "So the ghost did that?"

Nick nodded. "If James hadn't intervened, we most likely would not be having this conversation right now."

Nick noticed the wetness that shimmered in Gabe's eyes. "I'm glad he did," Gabe said. "I felt so helpless. I was just about to burst in to help you when the office door slammed shut. I couldn't open it."

"James must have done that. After Matt pushed me, I vaguely remember hearing the door slam."

Gabe gestured with his head to Matt. "But what about him? How are we going to explain that he's unconscious on the floor?"

"The recording has me talking to Matt. We'll tell the police that once he threatened to kill me, you snuck in behind him and whacked him with the book."

"That'll have to do," Nick said, listening to the commotion outside the door. "Because the police are here."

Chapter Twenty-One

✿❧✿

Nick sat in Janet's living room. After they had spoken with the police, he dropped off Gabe at his house and then drove to Janet's to tell her all about the evening's events. Luckily, the police seemed to believe their story once they played the recording for them. When Matt regained consciousness, they cuffed him and read him his rights. It was the first time Nick had seen anyone get arrested.

He took a sip from the icy cold Coke that Janet had placed in front of him and then recounted to her the entire evening's events.

"So it wasn't because of me that Matt killed James?"

Nick shook his head. "It was because Matt was siphoning money from the company and James had figured it out. When James threatened to tell their boss, Matt murdered him."

"It's a small consolation knowing that James didn't die because of me," Janet said. She shook her head. "I would never have guessed that Matt was capable of murder. He wasn't at all the person that I thought he was. It looks like he had us all fooled. I know that James thought highly of him too." She sighed. "I'm glad I broke it off with him when I did."

"I would never have guessed it either," James said. "He was my best friend. It's funny that I had forgotten all about that conversation with Matt until he told you about it in the office. Then the memories all came rushing back."

Nick's gaze turned to James, and he nodded. Janet followed Nick's eyes.

"Is it James?" she asked. "Is he here?"

"He is," Nick said. "He said that he wouldn't have guessed that Matt was capable of such an awful thing either."

"Tell her I'm truly sorry for haunting her and frightening her the way I did. But most of all, I'm sorry that I suspected her of killing me. I was confused and couldn't remember much of anything." He paused for a moment, then continued. "I know that I wasn't the easiest person to live with and didn't put in the time or energy into our relationship that I should have. I could have been a much better husband. I don't blame her for seeking love elsewhere."

Nick told Janet what James said and her eyes immediately filled with tears. She looked to where James was standing.

"I apologize too, James. I didn't mean to hurt you and betray you like I did. I was wrong, and for that, I'm eternally sorry. I wish I could somehow make it up to you."

"You can make it up to me by finding someone worthy to love you."

Nick locked eyes with Janet. "He said that you can make it up to him by finding someone to love you, someone worthy of you."

The tears now streamed down her cheeks. She nodded.

"Someday maybe, but not anytime soon," she said. "I'll need some time yet to move past all that's happened. I'm sure that I'll have to testify when Matt's trial comes around."

"Just make sure that bastard goes to prison," said James. He turned his gaze to Nick. "I want to thank you for all that you've done for me. You're quite the young fellow. I'm just thankful that you were around and willing to help. Otherwise, who knows how long I would have just drifted around, angry and alone."

Nick cleared his throat. "I'm glad I was able to help, sir. I appreciate your help too."

"My help?" James asked. "How did I help you?"

"By intervening when Matt was trying to stab me."

James smiled. "Ah yes, that. You needn't have worried. I was there the entire time. I wanted to hear his confession before I butted in. Until that moment, I still had no idea whether he had killed me or not. I didn't want to believe it. The more I thought about it, the more I suspected that maybe I had died of nothing more than a heart attack and that I put you and Janet through all this hell for nothing. That's why I was so hesitant the other day."

"I'm glad it worked out for all of us," Nick said. "I have to admit that I was scared shitless in Matt's office. He's one freakin' screwed up dude." Nick shook his head. "But now I wonder what on earth possessed me to go there and confront him? The only explanation is that I'd temporarily lost my mind."

"It was your need to do what's right," said James. He smiled. "So have you ever thought about being a detective? I'd venture to say that you'd be pretty good at that sort of thing."

Nick shook his head. "I don't think so. I'm not sure yet what I want to do after I graduate but I think I'll have more than enough unpaid detective work with the spirits that show up looking for help."

James laughed. "I suppose you will. I'll make sure to spread the word."

"No, please don't do that," Nick said quickly. "I need

much more practice yet. I still don't have any idea what I'm doing. I've just been winging it."

"Do any of us truly know what we are doing Nick? That's the beauty of life, you know. We stumble through and do the best we can while we're here, learning from our mistakes along the way. You have a knack for dealing with people. I'm sure you'll be fine."

"What's he saying?" Janet asked.

"Sorry about that," Nick said. "I forgot that you can't hear him. He's trying to convince me into becoming a detective."

Janet wiped her face with her sleeve. "Don't you go listening to him Nick. He's always trying to tell people what to do. Still pushy, I see."

"That I am," said James. All at once, he snapped his head and rested his gaze on the far wall. He brought up his arm to shield his eyes.

"What is it?" Nick asked.

"That light," James said, shielding his eyes with his hands. "It just appeared out of nowhere."

"That's your light," Nick said.

James raised his eyebrows. "Mine?"

Nick nodded. "It must be time for you to move on."

James stared at the wall wide-eyed. "I feel so strange all of a sudden as if the light's pulling me toward it like a giant magnet."

"He's leaving?" said Janet. "No, not yet. There's still more I need to say to him."

James looked at her. "It's fine Janet. I forgive you." He turned his gaze to Nick. "And thank your friend for me. Gabe, is it? You two are quite a team." He winked.

Before Nick could answer, James turned to look at the wall again, he took one step forward and disappeared.

"He's gone," Nick said. He realized that his own eyes were damp as well. "He crossed over."

Tears streaked Janet's face. "Funny how you end up appreciating someone only after they're no longer here."

"Before he left, he said that he forgives you and that you'll be fine."

She nodded and dabbed at her eyes with a handkerchief. "Thanks to you, I have a feeling that I will."

~

BOTH OF HIS PARENTS SAT SILENTLY AT THE KITCHEN TABLE, their mouths agape, glaring at Nick. He had just told them the entire story. As much as he didn't want to tell them what happened, he knew that there was no way he could keep it from them. The detective at Matt's office had informed him that he'd have to testify in court when Matt's hearing came up — it was the only way they'd be able to get a conviction. Gabe would need to testify as well, given that he was the one who had recorded the conversation and supposedly had knocked Matt out with a book.

His father finally broke the silence. "I can't believe you would put yourself and your friend in danger like this. What on earth were you thinking Nick? Are you insane? You could have been killed."

"But I wasn't," Nick said. "And James was there the entire time." Nick neglected to tell his parents that in fact, he didn't know that James was there and that his intervention came as a complete surprise to Nick at the time.

"You put your life in the hands of a ghost?" his father asked.

"He's a person, dad. A person just like us. I had to help him."

His father let go of an exasperated sigh. "Okay, so he's a person. That still doesn't excuse what you did. You are *not* a trained police officer and putting yourself at risk like this was sheer recklessness. I don't know what your uncle has been telling you, but this type of behavior is unacceptable."

Nick looked at his mother, but she said nothing, and her eyes did not flinch. He turned his regard back to his father.

"I'm not sorry for what I did Dad. I was able to help these people, and it all turned out fine. I don't understand what you're so pissed about."

His father's demeanor turned frosty. "I'm pissed that you put yourself in a precarious situation with no thought to your or Gabe's safety."

"But James was there."

His father shook his head. "Nick, I don't want you doing this anymore, at least not until you're out of high school. I will not have you running around chasing after spooks while ignoring your school work. You've worked hard to keep up your grades, and I don't want anything jeopardizing your GPA. If you want to do this after you graduate, that's fine. There's not too much I can do about it. But while you're under this roof, I don't want you involved with this sort of thing."

"Oh John," his mother said, "just let it go."

His father's head snapped to meet his mother's eyes. "What?" he choked out.

She sighed. "Forbidding him from doing this thing that he does is only going to alienate him from us. Is that what you want? Look what happened with your brother. Do you want that for Nick as well? Because that's what will happen, you know. If we make him ignore this thing, it'll push him away from us. It didn't work with Mitchell. Why do you think it would work with our son?"

"I don't care what he does when he moves out, but as long as he's here, I don't want him getting involved with any of this...stuff."

Her frustration was evident in her loud sigh. "It won't

work. He'll keep on doing it just like your brother did. Except you know what? We won't know anything about it. We'll have no idea what's going on in his life because he'll be doing it behind our backs. He'll shut us out from his life. We won't know when or if he's putting himself in danger. I'd rather he be honest and upfront with us about what's going on rather than sneaking around — and he *will* sneak, John. Mitchell did."

Nick and his father exchanged surprised looks and then Nick's father stared at his wife wide-eyed. He wrung his hands. "I thought you couldn't stomach the idea of Nick seeing ghosts? Where did this sudden change of heart come from?"

"Whether I like it or not, our son sees them. There's nothing neither of us can do about it. No, I'm not happy about it. But my happiness or unhappiness is not going to change the reality of the situation. The only thing we can do is support him and be there for him as a family. One estranged family member is enough."

Nick shivered, feeling as though he shouldn't be here listening to his parents discuss him, feeling as if he were intruding on a private conversation between them.

"But you said —"

"Never mind what I said," she quickly interrupted him. "Things are different now." She glanced at Nick for a moment and then looked back at Nick's father. "These spirits are going to find him and ask him for assistance — and there's nothing we can do to change that. If he can help people, whether they be dead or living, who are we to expect him to do otherwise? All we can ask of him is to be careful. We can be there for him as an ear when things get challenging. But to forbid him from expressing his nature? We can't do it, John. Not again. It wouldn't be right."

A heavy silence hung in the air for several moments. His

father finally nodded. "Nick, you do understand that your schoolwork comes first? And that you are to tell us if a situation ever gets to the point where it seems dangerous to you? In fact, I prefer you tell us anytime a spirit contacts you."

"I wouldn't hold my breath," his mother said.

"Come again?" said his father.

"He's sixteen. Did you tell your parents everything you did when you were that age?"

"That's different. His secrets could get him killed."

"I'll be careful," Nick said. He was feeling more and more uncomfortable sitting here and wanted this conversation to be over. "And I promise I'll tell you if things get weird or scary."

His father eyed him for a moment. "I suppose we can't ask for much more than that."

Nick breathed a sigh of relief and nodded his thanks. He suddenly remembered his initial reason for telling his parents about the recent events. "I'm going to need you to sign a consent form that allows me to testify at Matt's hearing. They won't let anyone underage testify without the knowledge of their parents."

His father nodded. "But just so you know, your mother and I will be there during the trial."

Nick chuckled. "That's fine, Dad. I expected as much"

"Don't forget about the note for school tomorrow."

Nick raised his eyebrows. "What note?"

"Your uncle is having surgery tomorrow afternoon," his father said. "I assumed you'd want to be there when he wakes up, so we're allowing you to take a half a day off from school. I want you to come home for lunch, and then we'll all drive to the hospital together."

"I didn't know his surgery was tomorrow. I should call him."

"It's too late tonight to call anyone," his mother said. "You can talk to him tomorrow."

Nick nodded in agreement. "I forgot to tell him what happened, with James and all."

"Best wait until after his surgery," his father said. "You don't want to upset him beforehand."

His mother rose. "Enough chit-chat for one night. You gentlemen have dishes to do."

Chapter Twenty-Two

"So how did it go with your parents?" Gabe asked. He was standing next to Nick's orange locker waiting for him. Gabe's hair was different today. Instead of combing it back like he usually does, it was spiked up. Nick liked the new look.

Nick dialed his locker combo and snapped open the lock. "Much better than I expected," he said. "They were both strangely supportive although there weren't too happy that we went to Matt's office to confront him."

Gabe's eyes grew wide. "You told them everything?"

Nick nodded. "Just about." He shut the door of his locker and met his friend's eyes. "How did it go with your folks?"

"Probably better than with yours. I told them the same story that we told the police — that you were talking to Matt and he let it slip that he had killed your friend's husband. I was arriving to meet you when I overheard the conversation. I launched the voice recorder app on my phone and then called the cops."

"And they bought it?"

"I think so. But they still grounded me." He sighed. "I just

241

glad that I didn't have to explain to them that my best friend sees ghosts. At least not yet." He sighed.

Nick raised his eyebrows. "What do you mean not yet?"

Gabe shrugged. "Who knows what the future will bring? We might have to tell them at some point."

"God, I hope not," Nick said. "Too many people know as it is. I'm just grateful that Sam didn't blab it around the school."

"Nah, Sam's cool," said Gabe. "Wanna have lunch together today?"

"Can't. I'm only here for a half a day. My uncle's having surgery today."

"And they made you come to school?"

Nick nodded. "They said that I'd already missed too much school these past few weeks and since he won't be waking up until this afternoon, there's no sense in me wasting a half a day waiting at the hospital."

The bell rang. Gabe scooped up his backpack and swung it over his shoulders. "I'll see you in History. And for goodness sake don't talk to any ghosts today. I think I could use a break."

Nick snickered. "I'll do my best."

HIS DAD'S SUV WAS GONE WHEN NICK ARRIVED HOME, which was strange given that they were all supposed to ride to the hospital together. He looked at the clock on his dashboard and noted that he did arrive home earlier than expected. Eager to get home, he'd decided to blow off Biology. There was no way he could concentrate on anything today so going to that last class would have been a huge waste of time.

He opened the door. "Mom?" he shouted. "You here?"

"In here," a male voice came from the kitchen. It almost sounded like his uncle.

Nick walked into the kitchen. His uncle was sitting, legs crossed, at the kitchen table.

"What are you doing here?" Nick asked. "You're supposed to be having surgery this morning."

His uncle smiled. "At the last minute, the hospital decided that I didn't need the operation right at this time. How about that? I'm off the hook. So I came here, waiting for you."

Nick clapped. "That's a relief! I tried not to think too much about them cutting into you. But where's Mom and Dad?"

"They had an errand to run." He gestured to the empty chair at the table. "Sit, Nick. I want to hear all about your adventures about...what was that ghost's name again?"

"James," said Nick. He couldn't help but wonder if his uncle had completely recovered from the stroke.

"Ah yes. James and Janet. Tell me, did you cross him over?"

Nick nodded and told his uncle the entire story. "And I had no choice but to tell Mom and Dad what happened because Detective Shale, one of the guys who showed up after Gabe called the police, told me that I'd have to testify against Matt."

Mitch uncrossed his legs and rested both feet on the floor. "And how did that go over?"

"They were surprisingly cool about it," Nick said. "They admitted that I was going to keep on seeing ghosts, so there was so sense into trying to make me stop. They just want me to be careful and to tell them if a situation turns dangerous."

His uncle nodded. "I told you they'd come around." His expression then turned more serious. He wagged his index figure at Nick. "And if it's one thing you are going to have to learn my over-zealous nephew, is how to take the advice of others who are more experienced than you."

"What are you talking about?" Nick asked.

"What was it that I told you about the killer?"

Nick scratched his head. "I don't know. We talked about many things."

"Think. What did I tell you about contacting the police."

Nick was about to say he didn't know when all of a sudden he remembered their conversation. "Oh," he said.

"Yes, oh," Mitch said. "You remember now that I told you that you never, ever confront a suspected killer?"

"I don't think you told me that specifically."

"Yes, I'm sure I did. I told you that you are to contact the police through phone or email whenever facing a potentially dangerous situation and hopefully, they'll follow through." He crossed his arms over his chest. "I want you to promise me that you will, under no circumstances, knowingly put yourself in such a precarious position again."

Nick swallowed and nodded. "I promise."

"Good," Mitch said. "Apart from that, you did a fantastic job. This is the second ghost you helped to cross over, right?"

"Yes, Sam's mom and now James."

"And now you understand how doing this work, not only helps the spirits but their loved ones as well. You helped Janet by pulling her out of what could have been a dangerous situation, you helped society by putting a murderer behind bars, and you even helped the accounting firm by uncovering embezzlement."

"Wow," Nick said. "When you put it like that, it sounds impressive."

"It is impressive," said Mitch. "You see how important your abilities are? How you can make a difference?"

"I do. It was scary at first, but now I think I've learned how not to be so afraid of the ghosts."

"You'll do well, of that I little doubt. You're much more powerful than I was. The visions I used to get were random and infrequent, and then usually only bits and pieces of information. It appears that you can almost bring them at will, especially when you're working with Tarot. Who knows what you'll be capable of after a little training? Speaking of Tarot, have you been studying the cards?"

Nick hung his head, avoiding his uncle's eyes. "Not lately. I've been pretty busy with all of this James stuff. I promise I'll get back to it."

"You have an innate talent for the cards Nick. Using them as a tool will make your work that much easier. It's rare to find a medium with such strong psychic abilities as yourself. I know that you're really going to make your mark on the world."

"I'm meeting with Katrina the day after tomorrow. She'll be giving me some more Tarot lessons."

Mitch laughed. "I have a feeling that you'll end up giving her the lessons."

"I don't think I'm at that point yet. I'm just glad that you're both around to teach me."

Before Mitch could respond, Nick's cell began buzzing on the table. Nick reached over for the phone, but his uncle stopped him.

"Don't answer that," his uncle said in a voice so loud that it startled Nick.

"Why?" Nick said. The phone continued to buzz on the table.

"I need to talk to you first."

"About what? And why can't I look at my phone?"

"It's probably your father. He's at the hospital."

Nick creased his brow. "But why's he at the hospital when you're here?"

He uncle stared at him and said nothing. Then, Nick felt it — that familiar flip-flop of his stomach and the prickly sensation on his skin. He'd noticed it when he first came into the house but ignored it. He looked at his phone and glanced back to his uncle. Mitch now had a pained expression on his face. The realization of why his father was calling pitched his senses into an uncontrollable shaking.

"No, no, no, no!" Nick said. His body shook so hard that he could barely stay on the chair. Tears gushed down his cheeks.

"I'm sorry Nick," his uncle said.

Nick shook his head back and forth rapidly. "You can't go! You can't! I need you." The spasms came quicker now, racking his body in agony. Nick could barely see Mitch through his tear-filled eyes. He fought to catch his breath. "You have to teach me, to help me with all of this. Uncle, don't. Please. Not yet. Don't leave me all alone."

"I had no choice in the matter. It was my time. But Nick, you're not alone. You have your family. You have Katrina. They'll help you and will be there for you. There wasn't much more I could teach you — you are already at a level much beyond where I was."

"I wish I had known before," Nick said, barely able to breathe past the lump in his throat. "I wish we had more time."

"Nick, that is one sentence that you're going to hear over and over — 'I wish we had more time.' That's why it's so important to appreciate the people while you have them in your life. It's a lesson you'll undoubtedly pass on to the people you help."

"Can you not go? Can you stay with me?"

His uncle shook his head. "I can't. But don't worry. You will be fine Nick. I know that for a fact."

Before Nick could answer, his phone buzzed again. This time, he grabbed it. It was his father.

"Uncle Mitch is dead," Nick exclaimed into the phone.

"How did you..." his father said and then paused. "Did you see him?"

"He was here when I got home from school," Nick said.

"Will you tell him that I'm deeply sorry for the way this family treated him?"

Nick glanced over at the empty chair across of him. "It's too late Dad. He's already gone."

NICK'S NUMBED GRIEF WAS MIXED WITH DEEP disappointment. He'd hoped that his uncle would show up at the funeral as his grandmother had but he had not made an appearance. At least, not so that Nick noticed. He'd felt his stomach flip a couple of times and had glanced around desperately, but there was no sign of his uncle. Nick ached to see him one last time. He had so many more questions, so much to learn yet and felt lost without him. But mostly, he wanted his uncle back.

The house was so crowded with people that it was hard to maneuver from room to room. The last thing Nick wanted was to be around people, to hear them lie and say what a wonderful man his uncle was. These are the same individuals who wanted little to do with him when he was alive. Once, he had started heading toward the stairs with the intention of hiding out in his room when an icy glare from his mother stopped him.

"I've been looking for you," a voice said behind him.

"Katrina," he said. "I'm so glad you're here. Were you at the service?"

"I was in the back row," she said. She locked eyes with him. "How are you holding up?"

Nick nodded. "Okay, I guess. I just wish I would have known that we'd have so little time left."

"That's one of the cruelest dishes served by life," Katrina said. "We never know how much time we have left with those we love." She rested a hand on his shoulder. "I can see him in you, you know. He wasn't that much older than you when I first met him. Though he was a lot smugger — cocky actually."

They both chuckled. "Thanks for coming," Nick said. "It means a lot that you're here."

"We're still on for next week if you're up for it," she said. "We'll talk more then."

Nick nodded. He caught Gabe's eye across the room and Gabe flashed him a warm smile. All at once goosebumps rose on his skin and Nick felt like someone was staring at him. He turned and for a split second, noticed a young man dressed in a soldier's uniform. The man met Nick's gaze briefly and then was gone. Nick shook himself, not sure if what he had seen was real or imagined.

If the ghost was real, Nick was sure he'd be back — and would no doubt be asking for help.

NICK'S ADVENTURES WILL CONTINUE

Did you like Nick's Awakening?

There's more on the way!

Nick's Awakening is the first book in the Ghost Oracle series, of which there will be at least four other books (I've already written them — but will need some time to polish them up).

If you'd like to be notified when the next book in the series is released, please sign up for my newsletter at http://rogerhyttinen.com/newsletter/

If you enjoyed the book and have a moment to spare, please consider leaving a short review wherever you purchased this book. Your help in spreading the word is gratefully appreciated. Also consider telling your friends, family or even random strangers about it to help me spread the word about my book.

Thank you so much for supporting my work!

Questions? Comments? I'd love to hear from you! Contact me at:

roger@rogerhyttinen.com

Follow Me

Visit the link below for my newsletter, including exclusive stories, bonuses and advance notice about upcoming work.

Subscribe To My Newsletter at
http://rogerhyttinen.com/newsletter/

Connect with me:

Follow Me On Twitter (http://twitter.com/rogerhyttinen)

Like Me On Facebook (http://facebook.com/rogerhyttinen.author)

Visit My Blog (http://rogerhyttinen.com)

Also by Roger Hyttinen

Check out my other books:

A Touch of Cedar

Anaconda